#1 *NEW YORK TIMES* BESTSELLING AUTHOR

DEBBIE MACOMBER

NEW YORK TIMES BESTSELLING AUTHOR

JoAnn Ross
Jennifer Snow

3
GREAT
STORIES

D0034897

Snowflakes
and Starlight

ISBN-13: 978-0-7783-8690-2

DEBBIE MACOMBER

JOANN ROSS
JENNIFER SNOW

Snowflakes and Starlight

mira

mira™

Recycling programs for this product may not exist in your area.

ISBN-13: 978-0-7783-8690-2

Snowflakes and Starlight

Copyright © 2022 by Harlequin Enterprises ULC

Here Comes Trouble
Copyright © 1991 by Debbie Macomber

Once Upon a Wedding
Copyright © 2018 by JoAnn Ross

An Alaskan Christmas Homecoming
Copyright © 2021 by Jennifer Snow

For questions and comments about the quality of this book, please contact us at CustomerService@Harlequin.com.

Mira
22 Adelaide St. West, 41st Floor
Toronto, Ontario M5H 4E3, Canada
www.Harlequin.com

Printed and bound in Barcelona, Spain by CPI Black Print

CONTENTS

HERE COMES TROUBLE

Debbie Macomber

Prologue

"Tomorrow's Christmas Eve, Mom!" nine-year-old Courtney Adams said.

"Mom, you have my list for Santa, don't you?" seven-year-old Bailey asked anxiously. She knelt on her bed, her large brown eyes beseeching.

This, Maryanne Adams recognized, was a blatant attempt to postpone bedtime. Both girls were supposed to turn out their lights ten minutes ago but, as usual, they were looking for any excuse to delay the inevitable. The one thing Maryanne hoped to avoid was yet another discussion about the top item on both their Christmas lists—a puppy.

"What about *my* list?" Courtney asked from her bed. She, at least, had crawled between the covers, but remained in a sitting position.

"Don't worry, I'm sure Santa has both your lists by now," Maryanne reassured her daughters. She stood in the doorway, her hand poised over the light switch. Both her daughters slept in canopy beds their Simpson grandparents had insisted on purchasing for them. It was their prerogative to spoil the grandkids, her father had told her, so she didn't argue too much. The grand-children were the delight of their grandparents' lives and could do no wrong.

"Did you read the list before you gave it to Santa?" Courtney asked.

At nine, Courtney was well aware that Santa was actually her mom and dad, but she was generous enough not to spoil the fantasy for her younger sister.

"You said your prayers?" Maryanne asked, wanting to turn the subject away from a dog.

Bailey nodded. "I prayed for a puppy."

"I did, too," Courtney echoed.

They were certainly persistent. "We'll see what happens," Maryanne said.

Bailey glanced at her older sister. "Is 'we'll see' good news?"

Courtney looked uncertain. "I don't know." She turned pleading eyes to her mother. "Mom, we *have* to know."

"Mom, please, I beg of you," Bailey cried dramatically. "We've just got to have a dog. We've *got* to."

Maryanne sighed. "I hate to disappoint you, but I don't think it's a good idea for our family to get a puppy now."

"Why not?" Courtney demanded, her sweet face filling with disappointment.

Instinctively, Maryanne pressed her hand to her stomach. It was time to tell the girls that there'd be a new family member in six months—past time, really, for them to know. She'd wanted to share the news earlier, but this baby was a complete surprise; she and Nolan had needed time to adjust to the idea first.

Stepping all the way into the room, Maryanne sat on

the edge of Courtney's bed. She'd prefer to tell the girls with Nolan at her side, but her husband was on deadline and had barricaded himself in his home office, coming out once or twice a day. The last fifty pages of a book were always the most difficult for him to write, winding down the plot and tying up all the loose ends. It was never easy, according to Nolan, to part with the characters he'd lived with for the past number of months. They were as real to him as his own flesh and blood, and because she was a writer, too, she understood that.

"We'll discuss this later." Checking her watch, she frowned. "It's past your bedtime as it is."

"Aw, Mom," Bailey moaned.

"Mom, please," Courtney chimed in. "I won't be able to sleep if you don't tell me now."

"Tell them what?" Nolan asked from the doorway.

At the sight of their father both girls squealed with delight. Bailey was out of bed first, flying across the room at breakneck speed. Anyone would think it'd been weeks since she'd last seen their father, when in fact he'd had breakfast with the girls that morning.

"Daddy!" Courtney leaped off the bed, as well.

Bailey was in Nolan's arms, fiercely hugging his neck, and Courtney clasped her skinny arms around his waist.

"Are you finished the book?" Maryanne asked, her gaze connecting with his. She remained seated on the bed, tired out from a long day of Christmas preparations.

"I typed *The End* about five minutes ago," her husband said, smiling down at her.

"What do you think?" she asked. As a wildly popular suspense author, Nolan generally had an excellent feel for his own work.

"I think it's good, but I'll wait for your feedback."

Maryanne loved the way they worked together as husband and wife and as two professional writers. Nolan wrote his novels, and it was the income he generated from the sales of his books that supported their family. Maryanne tackled nonfiction projects. She wrote a weekly column for the *Seattle Review* and contributed articles to various parenting magazines. One day, she might try her hand at fiction, but for the present she was content.

"Mom says now isn't a good time for us to get a puppy," Courtney whined, and it wasn't long before her younger sister added her own disconsolate cries.

"Why can't we, Daddy?" Bailey cried. "Every kid should have a puppy."

"A puppy," Nolan repeated, locking eyes with Maryanne. He sat down on the bed beside her and exhaled slowly. "Well, the truth is, there are other considerations."

"Like what?" Courtney asked. It was inconceivable to her that anything should stand in the way of her heart's desire.

Nolan placed his arm around Maryanne's shoulders, indicating that perhaps now was the time to explain. "Well," he began in thoughtful tones. "When a man and a woman fall in love and marry, they sometimes…" He paused and waited for Maryanne to finish.

"They love each other so much that they…" She hesitated, thinking this might not be the right approach.

"They make babies," Nolan supplied.

"You were a baby once," Maryanne continued, reaching out to tickle Bailey's tummy.

"And you, too," Nolan told Courtney.

The girls sat cross-legged on Bailey's bed, their attention on Nolan and Maryanne. Their long brown hair spilled over their shoulders.

"What has this got to do with a puppy?" Courtney asked, cocking her head to one side, a puzzled frown on her face. How like Nolan she looked just then, Maryanne thought. The Nolan she remembered from the days of their courtship, the newspaper reporter who always seemed to be frowning at her for one reason or another.

"What your mother and I are attempting to explain is that…" He paused and a smile crept across his face.

"You're both going to be big sisters," Maryanne said.

Courtney understood the implications before her little sister did. "Mom's going to have a *baby*?"

Maryanne nodded.

The girls screamed with happiness. As if they'd been practicing the move for a week, they leaped off the bed and immediately started jumping up and down. Soon Nolan was laughing at their antics.

"I want another sister," Bailey insisted.

"No, no, a brother," Courtney said.

"Personally I'll be overjoyed with either," Nolan assured them all. His arm tightened around Maryanne's shoulders, and he buried his face in her neck as she hid a smile. While this baby was certainly unexpected, he was most welcome. Yes, he! Earlier in the day Maryanne had been at the doctor's, had her first ultrasound and received the news. How appropriate for Christmastime… She'd tell Nolan as soon as the kids were asleep.

"Are you excited, Mom?" Courtney asked.

Maryanne nodded and held out her arms to her daughter. "Very much so."

Courtney came into the circle of Maryanne's arms. "A baby is even better than a puppy." She grinned. "But a puppy's good, too!"

"Yeah," Bailey said. She climbed into Nolan's lap, leaning her head against his chest.

"But you girls understand that a baby *and* a puppy at the same time would be too much, don't you?"

"Yes." Both girls nodded.

"Later," Courtney said in a solemn voice. "When the baby's older."

"Yeah," Bailey said again.

"Isn't it bedtime yet?" Nolan asked.

"Not yet," Bailey said. "I can't sleep, I'm too excited."

"I can't either." Courtney gazed up at her mother.

"Tell us a story," Bailey suggested. "A *long* story."

"You should get into bed first," Nolan said, and both girls reluctantly climbed back into their beds, and pulled the covers all the way up to their chins.

"Do you want me to read to you?" Nolan asked.

"Not a book," Courtney said. "Tell us a *real* story."

"About Grandpa and the newspaper business?" Maryanne knew how much her daughters loved to hear about their grandfather Simpson when he'd first started his business.

"No." Courtney shook her head. "Tell us about how you and Daddy met."

"You already know that story," Nolan said.

"We want the unabridged version this time," Bailey piped up.

Unabridged? Only the seven-year-old daughter of a writer would know the meaning of that word.

"What do you think, Annie?" Nolan asked.

Grinning, Maryanne lowered her head. When they'd first met, Nolan had been convinced she was nothing more than a spoiled debutante. From that point on, he'd taken to referring to her as *Deb, Trouble* and, with obvious affection, Annie.

"It was love at first sight," Nolan told his children.

Maryanne smiled again. Despite his sometimes cynical manner, her husband could be a real romantic.

"Your mother was head over heels in love with me the minute we met," he went on.

"I don't remember it quite that way," Maryanne protested.

"You don't?" Nolan feigned surprise.

"No, because you infuriated me no end." She remembered the notorious column he'd written about her—"My Evening with the Debutante."

"Me?" His expression turned to one of exaggerated indignation.

"You thought I was a spoiled rich kid."

"You *were* spoiled."

"I most certainly was not." Although Maryanne could see the gleam in his eye, she wasn't going to let him get away with this. It was true her father owned the newspaper and had arranged for her position, but that didn't mean she didn't deserve the opportunity. She might not have worked her way up through the normal channels, but in time she'd proved herself to the staff at the *Seattle Review*. She'd also proved herself to Nolan— in a rather different way.

Courtney and Bailey exchanged glances.

"Are you fighting?" Bailey asked.

Nolan chuckled. "No, I was just setting your mother straight."

Maryanne raised her eyebrows. "Apparently your father remembers things differently from the way I do."

"Start at the beginning," Bailey urged.

Excitedly clapping her hands, Courtney added, "Don't forget to tell us about the time Daddy embarrassed you in front of the whole city."

Nolan had worked for the *Sun*, the rival paper in town. It wasn't as if Maryanne would ever forget the column he'd written about his evening with her. Even now, after all these years, she bristled at the memory. He'd informed the entire city of Seattle that she was a naive idealist, and worst of all, he'd announced that she was away from home for the first time and lonely.

"I still don't get why that column upset your mother so much," Nolan said, gesturing helplessly toward his daughters. "All I did was thank her for making me dinner."

"Did Daddy kiss you that night?" Bailey asked.

"No, he—"

"Don't tell us," Courtney cried, interrupting Maryanne. "Start at the *very* beginning and don't leave anything out."

Nolan looked at Maryanne. "Why don't you tell them, sweetheart?"

"I'll tell them everything, then."

"Everything?" Nolan repeated.

Courtney rubbed her hands together. "Oh, boy, this is going to be good."

"It all started fifteen years ago…"

One

"Maryanne Simpson of the New York Simpsons, I presume?"

Maryanne glared at the man standing across from her in the reception area of the radio station. She pointedly ignored his sarcasm, keeping her blue eyes as emotionless as possible.

Nolan Adams—Seattle's most popular journalist—looked nothing like the polished professional man in the black-and-white photo that headed his daily column. Instead he resembled a well-known disheveled television detective. He even wore a wrinkled raincoat, one that looked as if he'd slept in it for an entire week.

"Or should I call you Deb?" he taunted.

"Ms. Simpson will suffice," she said in her best finishing-school voice. The rival newspaperman was cocky and arrogant—and the best damn journalist Maryanne had ever read. Maryanne was a good columnist herself, or at least she was desperately striving to become one. Her father, who owned the *Seattle Review* and twelve other daily newspapers nationwide, had seen to it that she was given this once-in-a-lifetime opportunity with the Seattle paper. She was working hard to prove herself. Perhaps too hard. That was when the trouble had begun.

"So how's the heart?" Nolan asked, reaching for a magazine and flipping idly through the dog-eared pages. "Is it still bleeding from all those liberal views of yours?"

Maryanne ignored the question, removed her navy-blue wool coat and neatly folded it over the back of a chair. "My heart's just fine, thank you."

With a sound she could only describe as a snicker, he threw himself down on a nearby chair and indolently brought an ankle up to rest on his knee.

Maryanne sat across from him, stiff and straight in the high-backed chair, and boldly met his eyes. Everything she needed to know about Nolan Adams could be seen in his face. The strong well-defined lines of his jaw told her how stubborn he could be. His eyes were dark, intelligent and intense. And his mouth...well, that was another story altogether. It seemed to wrestle with itself before ever breaking into a smile, as if a gesture of amusement went against his very nature. Nolan wasn't smiling now. And Maryanne wasn't about to let him see how much he intimidated her. But some emotion must have shone in her eyes, because he said abruptly, "You're the one who started this, you know?"

Maryanne was well aware of that. But this rivalry between them had begun unintentionally, at least on her part. The very morning that the competition's paper, the *Seattle Sun*, published Nolan's column on solutions to the city's housing problem, the *Review* had run Maryanne's piece on the same subject. Nolan's article was meant to be satirical, while Maryanne's was deadly serious. Her mistake was in stating that there were those in the city who apparently found the situation amusing, and she blasted anyone who behaved so irresponsibly. This was not a joking matter, she'd pointed out.

It looked as if she'd read Nolan's column and set out to reprimand him personally for his cavalier attitude.

Two days later, Nolan's column poked fun at her, asking what Ms. High Society could possibly know about affordable housing. Clearly a debutante had never had to worry about the roof over her head, he'd snarled. But more than that, he'd made her suggestions to alleviate the growing problem sound both frivolous and impractical.

Her next column came out the same evening and referred to tough pessimistic reporters who took themselves much too seriously. She went so far as to make fun of a fictional Seattle newsman who resembled Nolan Adams to a T.

Nolan retaliated once more, and Maryanne seethed. Obviously she'd have to be the one to put an end to this silliness. She hoped that not responding to Nolan's latest attack would terminate their rivalry, but she should've known better. An hour after her column on community spirit had hit the newsstands, KJBR, a local radio station, called, asking Maryanne to give a guest editorial. She'd immediately agreed, excited and honored at the invitation. It wasn't until later that she learned Nolan Adams would also be speaking. The format was actually a celebrity debate, a fact of which she'd been blithely unaware.

The door opened and a tall dark-haired woman walked into the station's reception area. "I'm Liz Walters," she said, two steps into the room. "I produce the news show. I take it you two know each other?"

"Like family," Nolan muttered with that cocky grin of his.

"We introduced ourselves five minutes ago," Maryanne rebutted stiffly.

"Good," Liz said without glancing up from her clipboard. "If you'll both come this way, we'll get you set up in the control booth."

From her brief conversation with the show's host, Brian Campbell, Maryanne knew that the show taped on Thursday night wouldn't air until Sunday evening.

When they were both seated inside the control booth, Maryanne withdrew two typed pages from her bag. Not to be outdone, Nolan made a show of pulling a small notepad from the huge pocket of his crumpled raincoat.

Brian Campbell began the show with a brief introduction, presenting the evening's subject: the growing popularity of the Seattle area. He then turned the microphone over to Maryanne, who was to speak first.

Forcing herself to relax, she took a deep calming breath, tucked her long auburn hair behind her ears and started speaking. She managed to keep her voice low and as well modulated as her nerves would allow.

"The word's out," she said, quickly checking her notes. "Seattle has been rated one of the top cities in the country for several years running. Is it any wonder Californians are moving up in droves, attracted by the area's economic growth, the lure of pure fresh air and beautiful clean waters? Seattle has appeal, personality and class."

As she warmed to her subject, her voice gained confidence and conviction. She'd fallen in love with Seattle when she'd visited for a two-day stopover before flying to Hawaii. The trip had been a college graduation gift from her parents. She'd returned to New York one week later full of enthusiasm, not for the tourist-cluttered islands, but for the brief glimpse she'd had of the Emerald City.

From the first, she'd intended to return to the Pacific Northwest. Instead she'd taken a job as a nonfiction editor in one of her father's New York publishing houses; she'd been so busy that travelling time was limited. That editorial job lasted almost eighteen months, and although Maryanne had thoroughly enjoyed it, she longed to write herself and put her journalism skills to work.

Samuel Simpson must have sensed her restlessness because he mentioned an opening at the *Seattle Review*, a long-established paper, when they met in Nantucket over Labor Day weekend. Maryanne had plied him with questions, mentioning more than once that she'd fallen in love with Seattle. Her father had grinned, chewing vigorously on the end of his cigar, and looked toward his wife of twenty-seven years before he'd casually reached for the telephone. After a single call lasting less than three minutes, Samuel announced that the job was hers. Within two weeks, Maryanne was packed and on her way west.

"In conclusion I'd like to remind our audience that there's no turning back now," Maryanne said. "Seattle sits as a polished jewel in the beautiful Pacific Northwest. Seattle, the Emerald City, awaits even greater prosperity, even more progress."

She set her papers aside and smiled in the direction of the host, relieved to be finished. She watched in dismay as Nolan scowled at her, then slipped his notepad back inside his pocket. He apparently planned to wing it.

Nolan—who needed, Brian declared, no introduction—leaned toward the microphone. He glanced at Maryanne, frowned once more, and slowly shook his head.

"Give me a break, Ms. Simpson!" he cried. "Doesn't anyone realize it *rains* here? Did you know that until recently, if Seattle went an entire week without rain, we sacrificed a virgin? Unfortunately we were running low on those until you moved to town."

Maryanne barely managed to restrain a gasp.

"Why do you think Seattle has remained so beautiful?" Nolan continued. "Why do you think we aren't suffering from the pollution problems so prevalent in Southern California and elsewhere? You seem to believe Seattle should throw open her arms and invite the world to park on our unspoiled doorstep. My advice to you, and others like you, is to go back where you came from. We don't want you turning Seattle into another L.A.—or New York."

The hair on the back of Maryanne's neck bristled. Although he spoke in general terms, his words seemed to be directed solely at her. He was telling her, in effect, to pack up her suitcase and head home to Mommy and Daddy where she belonged.

When Nolan finished, they were each given two minutes for a rebuttal.

"Some of what you have to say is true," Maryanne admitted through clenched teeth. "But you can't turn back progress. Only a fool," she said pointedly, "would try to keep families from settling in Washington state. You can argue until you've lost your voice, but it won't help. The population in this area is going to explode in the next few years whether you approve or not."

"That's probably true, but it doesn't mean I have to sit still and let it happen. In fact, I intend to do everything I can to put a stop to it," he said. "We in Seattle have a way of life to protect and a duty to future generations. If growth continues in this vein, our schools will soon be overcrowded, our homes so overpriced that no one except those from out of state will be able to afford housing—and that's only if they can find it. If that's what you want, then fine, bask in your ignorance."

"What do you suggest?" Maryanne burst out. "Setting up road blocks?"

"That's a start," Nolan returned sarcastically. "Something's got to be done before this area becomes another urban disaster."

Maryanne rolled her eyes. "Do you honestly think you're going to single-handedly turn back the tide of progress?"

"I'm sure as hell going to try."

"That's ridiculous."

"And that's our Celebrity Debate for this evening," Brian Campbell said quickly, cutting off any further argument. "Join us next week when our guests will be City Council candidates Nick Fraser and Robert Hall."

The microphone was abruptly switched off. "That was excellent," the host said, flashing them a wide enthusiastic smile. "Thank you both."

"You've got your head buried in the sand," Maryanne felt obliged to inform Nolan, although she knew it wouldn't do any good. She dropped her notes back in her bag and snapped it firmly shut, as if to say the subject was now closed.

"You may be right," Nolan said with a grin. "But at least the sand is on a pollution-free beach. If you have your way, it'll soon be cluttered with—"

"If I have my way?" she cried. "You make it sound as though I'm solely responsible for the Puget Sound growth rate."

"You *are* responsible, and those like you."

"Well, excuse me," she muttered sarcastically. She nodded politely to Brian Campbell, then hurried back to the reception room where she'd left her coat. To her annoyance Nolan followed her.

"I don't excuse you, Deb."

"I asked you to use my name," she said furiously, "and it isn't Deb."

Crossing his arms over his chest, Nolan leaned lazily against the doorjamb while she retrieved her wool coat.

Maryanne crammed her arms into the sleeves and nearly tore off the buttons in her rush to leave. The way he stood there studying her did little to cool her temper.

"And another thing…" she muttered.

"You mean there's more?"

"You're darn right there is. That crack about virgins was intolerably rude! I… I expected better of you."

"Hell, it's true."

"How would you know?"

He grinned that insufferable grin of his, infuriating her even more.

"Don't you have anything better to do than follow me around?" she demanded, stalking out of the room.

"Not particularly. Fact is, I've been looking forward to meeting you."

Once she'd recovered from the shock of learning that he'd be her opponent in this radio debate, Maryanne had eagerly anticipated this evening, too. Long before she'd arrived at the radio station, she'd planned to tell Nolan how much she admired his work. This silly rivalry between them was exactly that: silly. She hadn't meant to step on his toes and would've called and cleared the air if he hadn't attacked her in print at the earliest opportunity.

"Sure you wanted to meet me. Hurling insults to my face must be far more fun."

He laughed at that and Maryanne was astonished at how rich and friendly his amusement sounded.

"Come on, Simpson, don't take everything so personally. Admit it. We've been having a good time poking fun at each other."

Maryanne didn't say anything for a moment. Actually he was partially right. She *had* enjoyed their exchanges, although she wouldn't have admitted that earlier. She wasn't entirely sure she wanted to now.

"Admit it," he coaxed, again with a grin.

That uneven smile of his was her undoing. "It hasn't exactly been *fun*," she answered reluctantly, "but it's been…interesting."

"That's what I thought." He thrust his hands into his pockets, looking pleased with himself.

She glanced at him appraisingly. The man's appeal was definitely of the rugged variety: his outrageous charm—Maryanne wasn't sure charm was really the right word—his craggy face and solid compact build. She'd been surprised to discover he wasn't as tall as she'd imagined. In fact, he was probably under six feet.

"Word has it Daddy was the one responsible for landing you this cushy job," he commented, interrupting her assessment.

"Cushy?" she repeated angrily. "You've got to be kidding!" She often put in twelve-hour days, trying to come up with a column that was both relevant and entertaining. In the four weeks since she'd joined the *Seattle Review*, she'd worked damn hard. She had something to prove, not only to herself but to her peers.

"So being a journalist isn't everything it's cracked up to be?"

"I didn't say that," she returned. To be perfectly honest, Maryanne had never tried harder at anything. Her pride and a whole lot more was riding on the outcome of the next few months. Samuel Simpson's daughter or not, she was on probation, after which her performance would be reviewed by the managing editor.

"I wonder if you've ever done anything without Daddy's approval."

"I wonder if you've always been this rude."

He chuckled at that. "Almost always. As I said, don't take it personally."

With her leather purse tucked securely under her arm, she marched to the exit, which Nolan was effectively blocking. "Excuse me, please."

"Always so polite," he murmured before he straightened, allowing her to pass.

Nolan followed her to the elevator, annoying her even more. Maryanne felt his scrutiny, and it flustered her. She knew she was reasonably attractive, but she also knew that no one was going to rush forward with a banner and a tiara. Her mouth was just a little too full, her eyes a little too round. Her hair had been fire-engine red the entire time she was growing up, but it had darkened to a deep auburn in her early twenties, a fact for which she remained truly grateful. Maryanne had always hated her red hair and the wealth of freckles that accompanied it. No one else in her family had been cursed with red hair, let alone freckles. Her mother's hair was a beautiful blonde and her father's a rich chestnut. Even her younger brothers had escaped her fate. If it weren't for the distinctive high Simpson forehead and deep blue eyes, Maryanne might have suspected she'd been adopted. But that wasn't the case. Instead she'd been forced to discover early in life how unfair heredity could be.

The elevator arrived, and both Maryanne and Nolan stepped inside. Nolan leaned against the side—he always seemed to be leaning, Maryanne noticed. Leaning and staring. He was studying her again; she could feel his eyes as profoundly as a caress.

"Would you kindly stop?" she snapped.

"Stop what?"

"Staring at me!"

"I'm curious."

"About what?" She was curious about him, too, but far too civilized to make an issue of it.

"I just wanted to see if all that blue blood showed."

"Oh, honestly!"

"I am being honest," he answered. "You know, you intrigue me, Simpson. Have you eaten?"

Maryanne's heart raced with excitement at the offhand question. He seemed to be leading up to suggesting they dine together. Unfortunately she'd been around Nolan long enough to realize she couldn't trust the man. Anything she said or did would more than likely show up in that column of his.

"I've got an Irish stew simmering in a pot at home,"

she murmured, dismissing the invitation before he could offer it.

"Great! I love stew."

Maryanne opened her mouth to tell him she had no intention of asking him into her home. Not after the things he'd said about her in his column. But when she turned to tell him so, their eyes met. His were a deep, dark brown and almost…she couldn't be sure, but she thought she saw a faint glimmer of admiration. The edge of his mouth quirked upward with an unmistakable hint of challenge. He looked as if he expected her to reject him.

Against her better judgment, and knowing she'd live to regret this, Maryanne found herself smiling.

"My apartment's on Spring Street," she murmured.

"Good. I'll follow you."

She lowered her gaze, feeling chagrined and already regretful about the whole thing. "I didn't drive."

"Is your chauffeur waiting?" he asked, his voice and eyes mocking her in a manner that was practically friendly.

"I took a cab," she said, glancing away from him. "It's a way of life in Manhattan and I'm not accustomed to dealing with a car. So I don't have one." She half expected him to make some derogatory comment and was thankful when he didn't.

"I'll give you a lift, then."

He'd parked his car, a surprisingly stylish sedan, in a lot close to the waterfront. The late-September air was brisk, and Maryanne braced herself against it as Nolan cleared the litter off the passenger seat.

She slipped inside, grateful to be out of the chill. It didn't take her more than a couple of seconds to realize that Nolan treated his car the same way he treated his raincoat. The front and back seat were cluttered with empty paper cups, old newspapers and several paperback novels. Mysteries, she noted. The great Nolan Adams read mysteries. A container filled with loose change was propped inside his ashtray.

While Maryanne searched for the seatbelt, Nolan raced around the front of the car, slid inside and quickly started the engine. "I hope there's a place to park off Spring."

"Oh, don't worry," Maryanne quickly assured him. "I've got valet service."

Nolan murmured something under his breath. Had she made an effort, she might've been able to hear, but she figured she was probably better off not knowing.

He turned up the heater and Maryanne was warmed by a blast of air. "Let me know if that gets too hot for you."

"Thanks, I'm fine."

"Hot" seemed to describe their relationship. From the first, Maryanne had inadvertently got herself into scalding water with Nolan, water that came closer to the boiling point each time a new column appeared. "Hot" also described the way they seemed to ignite sparks off each other. The radio show had proved that much. There was another popular meaning of "hot"—one she refused to think about.

Nevertheless, Maryanne was grateful for the opportunity to bridge their differences, because, despite everything, she genuinely admired Nolan's writing.

They chatted amicably enough until Nolan pulled into the crescent-shaped driveway of The Seattle, the luxury apartment complex where she lived.

Max, the doorman, opened her car door, his stoic face breaking into a smile as he recognized her. When Nolan climbed out of the driver's side, Maryanne watched as Max's smile slowly turned into a frown, as though he wasn't certain Nolan was appropriate company for a respectable young lady.

"Max, this is Mr. Adams from the *Seattle Sun.*"

"Nolan Adams?" Max's expression altered immediately. "You don't look like your picture. I read your work faithfully, Mr. Adams. You gave ol' Larson hell last month. From what I heard, your column was what forced him to resign from City Council."

Nolan had given Maryanne hell, too, but she refrained from mentioning it. She doubted Max had ever read her work or was even aware that Nolan had been referring to her in some of his columns.

"Would you see to Mr. Adams's car?" Maryanne asked.

"Right away, Ms. Simpson."

Burying his hands in his pockets, Nolan and Maryanne walked into the extravagantly decorated foyer with its huge crystal chandelier and bubbling fountain. "My apartment's on the eleventh floor," she said, pushing the elevator button.

"Not the penthouse suite?" he teased.

Maryanne smiled weakly in response. While they rode upward, she concentrated on taking her keys from her bag to hide her sudden nervousness. Her heart was banging against her ribs. Now that Nolan was practically at her door, she wondered how she'd let this happen. After the things he'd called her, the least of which were Ms. High Society, Miss Debutante and Daddy's

Darling, she felt more than a little vulnerable in his company.

"Are you ready to change your mind?" he asked. Apparently, he'd read her thoughts.

"No, of course not," she lied.

She noticed—but sincerely hoped Nolan didn't—that her hand was shaking when she inserted the key.

She turned on the light as she walked into the spacious apartment. Nolan followed her, his brows raised at the sight of the modern white leather-and-chrome furniture. There was even a fireplace.

"Nice place you've got here," he said, glancing around.

She thought she detected sarcasm in his voice, then decided it was what she could expect from him all evening; she might as well get used to it.

"I'll take your raincoat," she said. Considering the fondness with which he wore the thing, he might well choose to eat in it, too.

To Maryanne's surprise, he handed it to her, then walked over to the fireplace and lifted a family photo from the mantel. The picture had been taken several summers earlier, when they'd all been sailing off Martha's Vineyard. Maryanne was facing into the wind and laughing at the antics of her younger brothers. It certainly wasn't her most flattering photo. In fact, she looked as if she was gasping for air after being underwater too long. The wind had caught her red hair, its color even more pronounced against the backdrop of white sails.

"The two young men are my brothers. My mom and dad are at the helm."

Nolan stared at the picture for several seconds and then back at her. "So you're the only redhead."

"How kind of you to mention it."

"Hey, you're in luck. I happen to like redheads." He said this with such a lazy smile that Maryanne couldn't possibly be offended.

"I'll check the stew," she said, after hanging up their coats. She hurried into the kitchen and lifted the lid of the pot. The pungent aroma of stewing lamb, vegetables and basil filled the apartment.

"You weren't kidding, were you?" Nolan asked, sounding mildly surprised.

"Kidding? About what?"

"The Irish stew."

"No. I put it on this morning, before I left for work. I've got one of those all-day cookers." After living on her own for the past couple of years, Maryanne had become a competent cook. When she'd rented her first apartment in New York, she used to stop off at a deli on her way home, but that had soon become monotonous. Over the course of several months, she'd discovered some excellent recipes for simple nutritious meals. Her father wasn't going to publish a cookbook written by her, but she did manage to eat well.

"I thought the stew was an excuse not to have dinner with me," Nolan remarked conversationally. "I didn't know what to expect. You're my first deb."

"Some white wine?" she asked, ignoring his comment.

"Please."

Maryanne got a bottle from the refrigerator and expertly removed the cork. She filled them each a glass, then gave Nolan his and carried the bottle into the living room, where she set it on the glass-topped coffee table. Sitting down on one end of the white leather sofa, she slipped off her shoes and tucked her feet beneath her.

Nolan sat at the other end, resting his ankle on his knee, making himself at home. "Dare I propose a toast?" he asked.

"Please."

"To Seattle," he said, his mischievous gaze meeting hers. "May she forever remain unspoiled." He reached over and touched the rim of her glass with his.

"To Seattle," Maryanne returned. "The most enchanting city on the West Coast."

"But, please, don't let anyone know," he coaxed in a stage whisper.

"I'm not making any promises," she whispered back.

They tasted the wine, which had come highly recommended by a colleague at the paper. Maryanne had only recently learned that wines from Washington state were quickly gaining a world reputation for excellence. Apparently the soil, a rich sandy loam over a volcanic base, was the reason for that.

They talked about the wine for a few minutes, and the conversation flowed naturally after that, as they compared experiences and shared impressions. Maryanne was surprised by how much she was enjoying the company of this man she'd considered a foe. Actually, they did have several things in common. Perhaps she was enjoying his company simply because she was lonely, but she didn't think that was completely true. Still, she'd been too busy with work to do any socializing; she occasionally saw a few people from the paper, but other than that she hadn't had time to establish any friendships.

After a second glass of wine, feeling warm and relaxed, Maryanne was willing to admit exactly how isolated she'd felt since moving to Seattle.

"It's been so long since I went out on a real date," she said.

"There does seem to be a shortage of Ivy League guys in Seattle."

She giggled and nodded. "At least Dad's not sending along a troupe of eligible men for me to meet. I enjoyed living in New York, don't get me wrong, but every time I turned around, a man was introducing himself and telling me my father had given him my phone number. You're the first man I've had dinner with that Dad didn't handpick for me since I moved out on my own."

"I hate to tell you this, sugar, but I have the distinct impression your daddy would take one look at me and have me arrested."

"That's not the least bit true," Maryanne argued. "My dad isn't a snob, only…only if you do meet him take off the raincoat, okay?"

"The raincoat?"

"It looks like you sleep in it. All you need is a hat and a scrap of paper with 'Press' scrawled on it sticking out of the band—you'd look like you worked for the *Planet* in Metropolis."

"I hate to disillusion you, sugar, but I'm not Ivy League and I'm not Superman."

"Oh, darn," she said, snapping her fingers. "And we had such a good thing going." She was feeling too mellow to remind him not to call her sugar.

"So how old are you?" Nolan wanted to know. "Twenty-one?"

"Three," she amended. "And you?"

"A hundred and three in comparison."

Maryanne wasn't sure what he meant, but she let that pass, too. It felt good to have someone to talk to, someone who was her contemporary, or at least close to being her contemporary.

"If you don't want to tell me how old you are, then at least fill in some of the details of your life."

"Trust me, my life isn't nearly as interesting as yours."

"Bore me, then."

"All right," he said, drawing a deep breath. "My family was dirt-poor. Dad disappeared about the time I was ten and Mom took on two jobs to make ends meet. Get the picture?"

"Yes." She hesitated. "What about women?"

"I've had a long and glorious history."

"I'm not kidding, Nolan."

"You think I was?"

"You're not married."

"Not to my knowledge."

"Why not?"

He shrugged as if it was of little consequence. "No time for it. I came close once, but her family didn't consider my writing career noble enough. Her father tried to fix me up with a job in his insurance office."

"What happened?"

"Nothing much. I told her I was going to work for the paper, and she claimed if I really loved her I'd accept her father's generous offer. It didn't take me long to decide. I guess she was right—I didn't love her."

He sounded nonchalant, implying that the episode hadn't cost him a moment's regret, but just looking at him told Maryanne otherwise. Nolan had been deeply hurt. Every sarcastic irreverent word he wrote suggested it.

In retrospect, Maryanne mused one afternoon several days later, she'd thoroughly enjoyed her evening with Nolan. They'd eaten, and he'd raved about her Irish stew until she flushed at his praise. She'd made them cups of café au lait while he built a fire. They'd sat in front of the fireplace and talked for hours. He'd told her more about his own large family, his seven brothers and sisters. How he'd worked his way through two years of college, but was forced to give up his education when he couldn't afford to continue. As it turned out, he'd been grateful because that decision had led to his first newspaper job. And, as they said, the rest was history.

"You certainly seem to be in a good mood," her coworker, Carol Riverside, said as she strolled past Maryanne's desk later that same afternoon. Carol was short, with a pixielike face and friendly manner. Maryanne had liked her from the moment they'd met.

"I'm in a fabulous mood," Maryanne said, smiling. Nolan had promised to pay her back by taking her out to dinner. He hadn't set a definite date, but she half expected to hear from him that evening.

"In that case, I hate to be the bearer of bad tidings, but someone has to tell you, and I was appointed."

"Tell me? What?" Maryanne glanced around the huge open office and noted that several faces were staring in her direction, all wearing sympathetic looks. "What's going on?" she demanded.

Carol moved her arm out from behind her and Maryanne noticed that she was holding a copy of the rival paper's morning edition. "It's Nolan Adams's column," Carol said softly, her eyes wide and compassionate.

"Wh-what did he say this time?"

"Well, let's put it this way. He titled it, 'My Evening with the Debutante.'"

Two

Maryanne was much too furious to stand still. She paced her living room from one end to the other, her mind spitting and churning. A slow painful death was too good for Nolan Adams.

Her phone rang and she went into the kitchen to answer it. She reached for it so fast she nearly ripped it off the wall. Rarely did she allow herself to become this angry, but complicating her fury was a deep and aching sense of betrayal. "Yes," she said forcefully.

"This is Max," her doorman announced. "Mr. Adams is here. Shall I send him up?"

For an instant Maryanne was too stunned to speak. The man had nerve, she'd say that much for him. Raw courage, too, if he knew the state of mind she was in.

"Ms. Simpson?"

It took Maryanne only about a second to decide. "Send him up," she said with deceptive calm.

Arms hugging her waist, Maryanne continued pacing. She was going to tell this man in no uncertain terms what she thought of his duplicity, his treachery. He might have assumed from their evening together that she was a gentle, forgiving soul who'd quietly overlook this. Well, if that was his belief, Maryanne was looking forward to enlightening him.

Her doorbell chimed and she turned to glare at it. Wishing her heart would stop pounding, she gulped in a deep breath, then walked calmly across the living room and opened the door.

"Hello, Maryanne," Nolan said, his eyes immediately meeting hers.

She stood exactly where she was, imitating his tactic of leaning against the door frame and blocking the threshold.

"May I come in?" he asked mildly.

"I haven't decided yet." He was wearing the raincoat again, which looked even more disreputable than before.

"I take it you read my column?" he murmured, one eyebrow raised.

"Read it?" she nearly shouted. "Of course I read it, and so, it seems, did everyone else in Seattle. Did you really think I'd be able to hold my head up after that? Or was that your intention—humiliating me and…and making me a laughingstock?" She stabbed her index finger repeatedly against his solid chest. "And if you think no one'll figure out it was me just because you didn't use my name, think again."

"I take it you're angry?" He raised his eyebrows again, as if to suggest she was overreacting.

"Angry! Angry? That isn't the half of it, buster!" The problem with being raised in a God-fearing, flag-loving family was that the worst thing she could think of to call him out loud was *buster.* Plenty of other names flashed through her mind, but none she dared verbalize. No doubt Nolan would delight in revealing this in his column, too.

Furious, she grabbed his tie and jerked him into the apartment. "You can come inside," she said.

"Thanks. I think I will," Nolan said wryly. He smoothed his tie, which drew her attention to the hard defined muscles of his chest. The last thing Maryanne wanted to do was notice how virile he looked, and she forced her gaze away from him.

Because it was impossible to stand still, she resumed her pacing. With the first rush of anger spent, she had no idea what to say to him, how to make him realize the enormity of what he'd done. Abruptly, she paused at the edge of her living room and pointed an accusing finger at him. "You have your nerve."

"What I said was true," Nolan stated, boldly meeting her glare. "If you'd bothered to read the column all the way through, objectively, you'd have noticed there were several complimentary statements."

"'A naive idealist, an optimist…'" she said, quoting what she remembered, the parts that had offended her the most. "You made me sound like Mary Poppins!"

"Surprisingly unspoiled and gentle," Nolan returned, "and very much a lady."

"You told the entire city I was *lonely*," she cried, mortified to even repeat the words.

"I didn't say you were lonely," Nolan insisted, his voice all too reasonable and controlled. That infuriated her even more. "I said you were away from your family for the first time."

She poked his chest again, punctuating her speech. "But you made it sound like I should be in a day-care center!"

"I didn't imply anything of the kind," he contended. "And I did mention what a good cook you are."

"I'm supposed to be grateful for that? As I recall you said, I was 'surprisingly adept in the kitchen'—as if you were amazed I knew the difference between a goldfish bowl and an oven."

"You're blowing the whole thing out of proportion."

Maryanne barely heard him. "The comment about my being insecure was the worst. You want security, buster, you're looking at security. My feet could be molded in cement, I'm that secure." Defiant angry eyes flashed to him as she pointed at her shoes.

Nolan didn't so much as blink. "You work twice as hard as anyone else at the *Review*, and twice as many hours. You push yourself because you've got something to prove."

A strained silence followed his words. She *did* work hard, she *was* trying to prove herself, and Nolan knew it. Except for high school and college, she'd had no experience working at a newspaper.

"Did you wake up one morning and decide to play Sigmund Freud with my life?" she demanded. "Who, may I ask, gave you that right?"

"What I said is true, Maryanne," he told her again. "I don't expect you to admit it to me, but if you're honest you'll at least admit it to yourself. Your family is your greatest asset and your weakest link. From everything I've read about the Simpsons, they're good people, but they've cheated you out of something important."

"Exactly what do you mean by that?" she snapped, ready to defend her father to the death, if need be. How dared this pompous, arrogant, argumentative man insult her family?

"You'll never know if you're a good enough journalist to get a job like this without your father's help. He handed you this plum position, and at the same time cheated you out of a just reward."

Maryanne opened her mouth, an argument on the tip of her tongue. Instead, she lowered her gaze, since she couldn't deny what he'd just said. From the moment she arrived at the *Seattle Review,* she'd known that Carol Riverside was the one who'd earned the right to be the local-affairs columnist, not her. And yet Carol had been wonderfully supportive and kind.

"It wasn't my intention to insult you or your family," Nolan continued.

"Then why did you write that column?" she asked, her voice quavering. "Did you think I was going to be flattered by it?"

He'd been so quick with the answers that his silence caught her attention more effectively than anything he could've said. She watched as he started pacing. He drew his fingers through his hair and his shoulders rose in a distinct sigh.

"I'm not sure. In retrospect, I believe I wanted to set the record straight. At least that was my original intent. I wrote more than I should have, but the piece was never meant to ridicule you. Whether you know it or not, you impressed the hell out of me the other night."

"Am I supposed to be grateful you chose to thank me publicly?"

"No," he answered sharply. Once more he jerked his fingers roughly through his hair. He didn't wince, but Maryanne did—which was interesting, since only a few minutes earlier she'd been daydreaming about the joy she'd experience watching this man suffer.

"Inviting myself to dinner the other night was an impulse," he admitted grudgingly. "The words slipped out before I realized what I was saying. I don't know who was more surprised, you or me. I tried to act like I knew what I was doing, play it cool, that sort of thing. The fact is, I discovered I like you. Trust me, I wasn't in any frame of mind to talk civilly to you when you got to the radio station. All along I'd assumed you were a spoiled rich kid, but I was wrong. Since I'd published several pieces that suggested as much, I felt it was only fair to set the record straight. Besides, for a deb you aren't half-bad."

"Why is it every time you compliment me I feel a knife between my shoulder blades?"

"We certainly don't have a whole lot in common," Nolan said thoughtfully. "I learned most everything I know on the streets, not in an expensive private school. I doubt there's a single political issue we can agree on. You're standing on one side of the fence and I'm way over on the other. We're about as far apart as any two people could ever be. Socially. Economically. And every other way I could mention. We have no business even speaking to each other, and yet we sat down and shared a meal and talked for hours."

"I felt betrayed by that column today."

"I know. I apologize, although the damage is already done. I guess I wasn't aware it would offend you. Like I said, that wasn't what I intended at all." He released a giant sigh and paused, as though collecting his thoughts. "After I left your place, I felt good. I can't remember a time I've enjoyed myself more. You're a charming, interesting—"

"You might have said *that* in your column!"

"I did, only you were obviously too upset to notice it. When I got home that night, I couldn't sleep. Every time I'd drift off, I'd think of something you'd said, and before I knew it I'd be grinning. Finally I got up and sat at my desk and started writing. The words poured out of me as fast as I could type them. The quality that impressed me the most about you was your honesty. There's no pretense in you, and the more I thought about that, the more I felt you've been cheated."

"And you decided it was your duty to point all this out—for everyone in town to read?"

"No, it wasn't. That's why I'm here. I admit I went further than I should have and came over to apologize."

"If you're telling me this to make me feel better, it isn't working." Her ego was rebounding somewhat, but he still had a lot of apologizing to do.

"To be honest, I didn't give the column a second thought until this afternoon, when someone in the office said I'd really done it now. If I was hoping to make peace with you, I'd failed. This friend said I was likely to get hit by the wrath of a woman scorned and suggested I run for cover."

"Rightly so!"

"Forgive me, Maryanne. It was arrogant in the extreme of me to publish that piece. If it'll make you feel any better, you can blast me to kingdom come in your next column. I solemnly promise I'll never write another word about you."

"Don't be so humble—it doesn't suit you," she muttered, gnawing on her lower lip. "Besides, I won't be able to print a rebuttal."

"Why not?"

"I don't plan on working for the *Review* anymore, or

at least not after tomorrow." The idea seemed to emerge fully formed; until that moment she hadn't known what she was going to say.

The silence following her words was fraught with tension. "What do you mean?"

"Don't act so surprised. I'm quitting the paper."

"What? Why?" Nolan had been standing during their whole conversation, but he suddenly found it necessary to sit. He lowered himself slowly to the sofa, his face pale. "You're overreacting! There's no need to do anything so drastic."

"There's every need. You said so yourself. You told me I've been cheated, that if I'm even half as good a reporter as I think I am I would've got this 'plum position' on my own. I'm just agreeing with you."

He nodded stiffly.

"As painful as this is to admit, especially to you," she went on, "you're right. My family is wonderful, but they've never allowed me to fall on my face. Carol Riverside is the one who deserved the chance to write that column. She's been with the paper for five years— I'd only been there five minutes. But because my name is Simpson, and because my father made a simple phone call, I was given the job. Carol was cheated. She should've been furious. Instead, she was kind and helpful." Maryanne sat down next to Nolan and propped her feet on the coffee table. "And maybe worse than what happened to Carol is what happened to me as a result of being handed this job. What you wrote about me wondering if I had what it takes to make it as a journalist hit too close to home. All my life my father's been there to tell me I can be anything I want to be and then he promptly arranges it."

"Quitting the *Review* isn't going to change that," Nolan argued. "Come on, Maryanne, you're taking this too seriously."

"Nothing you say is going to change my mind," Maryanne informed him primly. "The time has come for me to cut myself loose and sink or swim on my own."

Her mind was galloping ahead, adjusting to the coming changes. For the first time since she'd read Nolan's column that afternoon, she experienced the beginnings of excitement. She glanced around the apartment as another thought struck her. "Naturally I'll have to move out of this place."

"Are you going back to New York?"

"Heavens, no!" she declared, unaccountably thrilled at the reluctance she heard in his voice. "I love Seattle."

"Listen to me, would you? You're leaping into the deep end, you don't know how to swim and the lifeguard's off duty."

Maryanne hardly heard Nolan, mainly because she didn't like what he was saying. How like a man to start a bonfire and then rush to put out the flames. "The first thing I need to worry about is finding another job," she announced. "A temporary one, of course. I'm going to continue writing, but I don't think I'll be able to support myself on that, not at first, anyway."

"If you insist on this folly, you could always freelance for the *Sun*."

Maryanne discounted that suggestion with a shake of her head. "I'd come off looking like a traitor."

"I suppose you're right." His eyebrows drew together as he frowned.

"You know what else I'm going to do?" She shifted

her position, tucking her legs beneath her. "I've got this trust fund that provides a big interest payment every month. That's what I've been using to pay my bills. You and I both know I couldn't afford this place on what I make at the paper. Well, I'm not going to touch those interest payments and I'll live solely on what I earn."

"I...wouldn't do that right away, if I were you."

"Why not?"

"You just said you were quitting your job." Nolan sounded uneasy. "I can see that I've set off an avalanche here, and I'm beginning to feel mildly concerned."

"Where do you live?"

"Capitol Hill. Listen, if you're serious about moving, you need to give some thought as to what kind of neighborhood you're getting into. Seattle's a great town, don't get me wrong, but like any place we have our problem areas." He hesitated. "Annie, I don't feel comfortable with this."

"No one's ever called me Annie before." Her eyes smiled into his. "What do you pay in rent?"

With his hands buried deep in his pants pockets, he mumbled something under his breath, then mentioned a figure that was one-third of what she was currently dishing out every month.

"That's more than reasonable."

Maryanne saw surprise in his eyes, and smiled again. "If you're so concerned about my finding the right neighborhood, then you pick one for me. Anyplace, I don't care. Just remember, you're the one who got me into this."

"Don't remind me." Nolan's frown darkened.

"I may not have appreciated what you said about me

in your column," Maryanne said slowly, "but I'm beginning to think good things might come of it."

"I'm beginning to think I should be dragged to the nearest tree and hanged," Nolan grumbled.

"Hi." Maryanne slipped into the booth opposite Nolan at the greasy spoon called Mom's Place. She smiled, feeling like a child on a grand adventure. Perhaps she *was* going off the deep end, as Nolan had so adamantly claimed the day before. Perhaps, but she doubted it. Everything felt so *right*.

Once the idea of living on her own—on income she earned herself, from a job she'd been hired for on her own merits—had taken hold in her mind, it had fast gained momentum. She could work days and write nights. That would be perfect.

"Did you do it?"

"I handed in my notice this morning," she said, reaching for the menu. Nolan had insisted on meeting her for a late lunch and suggested this greasy spoon with its faded neon sign that flashed Home Cooking. She had the impression he ate there regularly.

"I talked to the managing editor this morning and told him I was leaving."

"I don't imagine he took kindly to that," Nolan muttered, lifting a white ceramic mug half-full of coffee. He'd been wearing a frown from the moment she'd entered the diner. She had the feeling it was the same frown he'd left her apartment with the night before, but it had deepened since she'd last seen him.

"Larry wasn't too upset, but I don't think he appreciated my suggestion that Carol Riverside take over the column, because he said something I'd rather not repeat about how he was the one who'd do the hiring and promoting, not me, no matter what my name was."

Nolan took a sip of coffee and grinned. "I'd bet he'd like my head if it could be arranged, and frankly I don't blame him."

"Don't worry, I didn't mention your name or the fact that your column was what led to my decision."

Maryanne doubted Nolan even heard her. "I'm regretting that column more with each passing minute. Are you sure I can't talk you out of this?"

"I'm sure."

He sighed and shook his head. "How'd the job hunting go?"

The waitress came by, automatically placing a full mug of coffee in front of Maryanne. She fished a pad from the pocket of her pink apron. "Are you ready to order?"

"I'll have a turkey sandwich on rye, no sprouts, a diet soda and a side of potato salad," Maryanne said with a smile, handing her the menu.

"You don't need to worry, we don't serve sprouts here," she said, scribbling down the order.

"I'll have the chili, Barbara," Nolan said. The waitress nodded and strolled away from the booth. "I was asking how your job hunting went," Nolan reminded Maryanne.

"I found one!"

"Where? What will you be doing? And for how much?"

"You're beginning to sound like my father."

"I'm beginning to *feel* like your father. Annie, you're a babe in the woods. You don't have a clue what you're getting involved in. Heaven knows I've tried to talk some sense into you, but you refuse to listen. And, as you so delight in reminding me, I'm the one responsible for all this."

"Stop blaming yourself." Maryanne leaned across the table for her water glass. "I'm grateful, I honestly am—though, trust me, I never thought I'd be saying that. But what you wrote was true. By insulting me, you've given me the initiative to make a name for myself without Dad's help and—"

He closed his eyes. "Just answer the question."

"Oh, about the job. It's for a…service company. It looks like it'll work out great. I didn't think I'd have any chance of getting hired, since I don't have much experience, but they took that into consideration. You see, it's a new company and they can't afford to pay much. Everyone seems friendly and helpful. The only drawback is my salary and the fact that I won't be working a lot of hours at first. In fact, the money is a lot less than I was earning at the paper. But I expect to be able to sell a couple of articles soon. I'll get along all right once I learn to budget."

"How much less than the paper?"

"If I tell you, you'll only get angry." His scowl said he'd be even angrier if she didn't tell him. From the way he was glaring at her, Maryanne knew she'd reached the limits of his patience. She muttered the amount and promptly lowered her gaze.

"You aren't taking the job," Nolan said flatly.

"Yes, I am. It's the best I can do for now. Besides, it's only temporary. It isn't all that easy to find work, you know. I must've talked to fifteen companies today. No one seemed too impressed with my double degree in Early American History and English. I wanted to find employment where I can use my writing skills, but that didn't happen, so I took this job."

"Annie, you won't be able to live on so little."

"I realize that. I've got a list of community news-papers and I'm going to contact them about freelance work. I figure between the writing and my job, I'll do okay."

"Exactly *what* will you be doing?" he demanded.

"Cleaning," she mumbled under her breath.

"What did you say?"

"I'm working for Rent-A-Maid."

"Dear Lord," Nolan groaned. "I hope you're kid-ding."

"Get your mind out of the gutter, Adams. I'm going to work six hours a day cleaning homes and offices and I'll spend the rest of the time doing research for my articles. Oh, and before I forget, I gave your name as a reference."

"You're going to go back and tell whoever hired you that you're terribly sorry, but you won't be able to work there, after all," Nolan said, and the hard set of his mouth told her he brooked no argument.

Maryanne was saved from having to say she had no intention of quitting, because the waitress, bless her heart, appeared with their orders at precisely that mo-ment.

"Now what about an apartment?" Maryanne asked. After his comment about living in a safe neighborhood, she was more than willing to let him locate one for her. "Have you had a chance to check into that for me?"

"I hope you didn't give your notice at The Seattle."

Swallowing a bite of her sandwich, Maryanne nod-ded eagerly. "First thing this morning. I told them I'd be out by the fifteenth, which, in case you were unaware of it, happens to be early next week."

"You shouldn't have done that."

"I can't afford the place! And I won't be able to eat in restaurants every day or take cabs or buy things whenever I want them." She smiled proudly as she said it. Money had never been a problem in her life—it had sometimes been an issue, but never a problem. She felt invigorated just thinking about her new status.

"Will you stop grinning at me like that?" Nolan burst out.

"Sorry, it's sort of a novelty to say I can't afford something, that's all," she explained. "It actually feels kind of good."

"In a couple of weeks it's going to feel like hell." Nolan's face spelled out apprehension and gloom.

"Then I'll learn that for myself." She noticed he hadn't touched his meal. "Go ahead and eat your chili before it gets cold."

"I've lost my appetite." He immediately contradicted himself by grabbing a small bottle of hot sauce and dousing the chili with several hard shakes.

"Now did you or did you not find me a furnished studio apartment to look at this afternoon?" Maryanne pressed.

"I found one. It's nothing like you're used to, so be prepared. I'll take you there once we're finished lunch."

"Tell me about it," Maryanne said eagerly.

"There's one main room, small kitchen, smaller bathroom, tiny closet, no dishwasher." He paused as if he expected her to jump to her feet and tell him the whole thing was off.

"Go on," she said, reaching for her soda.

"The floors are pretty worn but they're hardwood."

"That'll be nice." She didn't know if she'd ever lived in a place that didn't have carpeting, but she'd adjust.

"The furniture's solid enough. It's old and weighs a ton, but I don't know how comfortable it is."

"I'm sure it'll be fine. I'll be working just about every day, so I can't see that there'll be a problem," Maryanne returned absently. As soon as she'd spoken, she realized her mistake.

Nolan stabbed his spoon into the chili. "You seem to have forgotten you're resuming your job hunt. You won't be working for Rent-A-Maid, and that's final."

"You sound like a parent again. I'm old enough to know what I can and can't do, and I'm going to take that job whether you like it or not, and *that's final*."

His eyes narrowed. "We'll see."

"Yes, we will," she retorted. Nolan might be an astute journalist, but there were several things he had yet to learn about her, and one of them was her stubborn streak. The thought produced a small smile as she realized she was thinking of him in a way that suggested a long-term friendship. He was right when he said they stood on opposite sides of the fence on most issues. He was also right when he claimed they had no business being friends. Nevertheless, Nolan Adams was the most intriguing man she'd ever met.

Once they'd finished their meal, Nolan reached for the bill, but Maryanne insisted on splitting it. He clearly wasn't pleased about that but let it pass. Apparently he wasn't going to argue with her, which suited Maryanne just fine. He escorted her to his car, parked outside the diner, and Maryanne slid inside, absurdly pleased that he'd cleaned up the front seat for her.

Nolan hesitated when he joined her, his hands on the steering wheel. "Are you sure you want to go through with this?"

"Positive."

"I was afraid you were going to say that." His mouth twisted. "I can't believe I'm aiding and abetting this nonsense."

"You're my friend, and I'm grateful."

Without another word, he started the engine.

"Where's the apartment?" Maryanne asked as the car progressed up the steep Seattle hills. "I mean, what neighborhood?"

"Capitol Hill."

"Oh, how nice. Isn't that the same part of town you live in?" It wasn't all that far from The Seattle, either, which meant she'd still have the same telephone exchange. Maybe she could even keep her current number.

"Yes," he muttered. He didn't seem to be in the mood for conversation and kept his attention on his driving, instead. He pulled into a parking lot behind an eight-storey post–World War II brick building. "The apartment's on the fourth floor."

"That'll be fine." She climbed out of the car and stared at the old structure. The Dumpster was backed against the wall and full to overflowing. Maryanne had to step around it before entering by a side door. Apparently there was no elevator, and by the time they reached the fourth floor she was so winded she couldn't have found the breath to complain, anyway.

"The manager gave me the key," Nolan explained as he paused in the hallway and unlocked the second door on the right. Nolan wasn't even breathing hard, while

Maryanne was leaning against the wall, dragging deep breaths into her oxygen-starved lungs.

Nolan opened the door and waved her in. "As I said, it's not much."

Maryanne walked inside and was struck by the sparseness of the furnishings. One overstuffed sofa and one end table with a lamp on a dull stained-wood floor. She blinked, squared her shoulders and forced a smile to her lips. "It's perfect."

"You honestly think you can live here after The Seattle?" He sounded incredulous.

"Yes, I do," she said with a determination that would've made generations of Simpsons proud. "How far away is your place?"

Nolan walked over to the window, his back to her. He exhaled sharply before he announced, "I live in the apartment next door."

Three

"I don't need a babysitter," Maryanne protested. She had some trouble maintaining the conviction in her voice. In truth, she was pleased to learn that Nolan's apartment was next door, and her heart did a little jig all its own.

Nolan turned away from the window. His mouth was set in a thin straight line, as if he was going against his better judgment in arranging this. "That night at the radio station," he mumbled softly. "I knew it then."

"Knew what?"

Slowly, he shook his head, apparently lost in his musings. "I took one look at you and deep down inside I heard a small voice cry out, 'Here comes trouble.'"

Despite his fierce expression, Maryanne laughed.

"Like a fool I ignored it, although Lord only knows how I could have."

"You're not blaming me for all this, are you?" Maryanne asked, placing her hands on her hips, prepared to do battle. "In case you've forgotten, you're the one who invited yourself to dinner that night. Then you got me all mellow with wine—"

"You were the one who brought out the bottle. You can't blame me for *that*." He was muttering again and buried his hands deep in the pockets of his raincoat.

"I was only being a good hostess."

"All right, all right, I get the picture," he said through clenched teeth, shaking his head again. "I was the one stupid enough to write that column afterward. I'd give a week's pay to take it all back. No, make that a month's pay. This is the last time," he vowed, "that I'm ever going to set the record straight. Any record." He jerked his hand from his pocket and stared at it.

Maryanne crossed to the large overstuffed sofa covered with faded chintz fabric and ran her hand along the armrest. It was nearly threadbare in places and nothing like the supple white leather of her sofa at The Seattle. "I wish you'd stop worrying about me. I'm not as fragile as I look."

Nolan snickered softly. "A dust ball could bowl you over."

A ready argument sprang to her lips, but she quickly swallowed it. "I'll take the apartment, but I want it understood, right now, that you have no responsibilities toward me. I'm a big girl and I'll manage perfectly well on my own. I have in the past and I'll continue to do so in the future."

Nolan didn't respond. Instead he grumbled something she couldn't hear. He seemed to be doing a lot of that since he'd met her. Maybe it was a long-established habit, but somehow she doubted it.

Nolan drove her back to The Seattle, and the whole way there Maryanne could hardly contain a feeling of delight. For the first time, she was taking control of her own life. Nolan, however, was obviously experiencing no such enthusiasm.

"Do I need to sign anything for the apartment? What about a deposit?"

"You can do that later. You realize this studio apartment is the smallest one in the entire building? My own apartment is three times that size."

"Would you stop worrying?" Maryanne told him. A growing sense of purpose filled her, and a keen exhilaration unlike anything she'd ever felt.

Nolan pulled into the circular driveway at her building. "Do you want to come up for a few minutes?" she asked.

His dark eyes widened as if she'd casually suggested they play a round of Russian roulette. "You've got to be kidding."

She wasn't.

He held up both hands. "No way. Before long, you'll be serving wine and we'll be talking like old friends. Then I'll go home thinking about you, and before I know how it happened—" He stopped abruptly. "No, thanks."

"Goodbye, then," she said, disappointed. "I'll see you later."

"Right. Later." But the way he said it suggested that if he didn't stumble upon her for a decade or two it would be fine with him.

Maryanne climbed out of his car and was about to close the door when she hesitated. "Nolan?"

"Now what?" he barked.

"Thank you," she said softly.

Predictably, he started mumbling and drove off the

instant she closed the door. In spite of his sour mood, Maryanne found herself smiling.

Once inside her apartment, she was immediately struck by the contrast between this apartment at The Seattle and the place Nolan had shown her. One was grey, cramped and dingy, the other polished and spacious and elegant. Her mind's eye went over the dreary apartment on Capitol Hill, and she felt a growing sense of excitement as she thought of different inexpensive ways to bring it color and character. She'd certainly faced challenges before, but never one quite like this. Instinctively she knew there'd be real satisfaction in decorating that place with her newly limited resources.

Turning her new apartment into a home was the least of her worries, however. She had yet to tell her parents that she'd quit her job. Their reaction would be as predictable as Nolan's.

The phone seemed to draw her. Slowly she walked across the room toward it, sighing deeply. Her fingers closed tightly around the receiver. Before she could change her mind, she closed her eyes, punched out the number and waited.

Her mother answered almost immediately.

"I was sitting at my desk," Muriel Simpson explained. She seemed delighted to hear from Maryanne. "How's Seattle? Are you still as fascinated with the Northwest?"

"More than ever," Maryanne answered without a pause; what she didn't say was that part of her fascination was now because of Nolan.

"I'm pleased you like it so well, but I don't mind telling you, sweetie, I miss you terribly."

"I haven't lived at home for years," Maryanne reminded her mother.

"I know, but you were so much closer to home in Manhattan than you are now. I can't join you for lunch the way I did last year."

"Seattle's lovely. I hope you'll visit me soon." But not too soon, she prayed.

"Sometime this spring, I promise," Muriel said. "I was afraid once you settled there all that rain would get you down."

"Mother, honestly, New York City has more annual rainfall than Seattle."

"I know, dear, but in New York the rain all comes in a few days. In Seattle it drizzles for weeks on end, or so I've heard."

"It's not so bad." Maryanne had been far too busy to pay much attention to the weather. Gathering her courage, she forged ahead. "The reason I called is that I've got a bit of exciting news for you."

"You're madly in love and want to get married."

Muriel Simpson was looking forward to grandchildren and had been ever since Maryanne's graduation from college. Both her brothers, Mark and Sean, were several years younger, so Maryanne knew the expectations were all focused on her. For the past couple of years they'd been introducing her to suitable young men.

"It's nothing that dramatic," Maryanne said, then, losing her courage, she crossed her fingers behind her back and blurted out, "I've got a special assignment… for the—uh—paper." The lie nearly stuck in her throat.

"A special assignment?"

All right, she was stretching the truth about as far

as it would go, and she hated doing it. But she had no choice. Nolan's reaction would look tame compared to her parents' if they ever found out she was working as a janitor. Rent-A-Maid gave it a fancy name, but basically she'd been hired to clean. It wasn't a glamorous job, nor was it profitable, but it was honest work and she needed something to tide her over until she made a name for herself in her chosen field.

"What kind of special assignment?"

"It's a research project. I can't really talk about it yet." Maryanne decided it was best to let her family assume the "assignment" was with the newspaper. She wasn't happy about this; in fact, she felt downright depressed to be misleading her mother this way, but she dared not hint at what she'd actually be doing. The only comfort she derived was from the prospect of showing them her published work in a few months.

"It's not anything dangerous, is it?"

"Oh, heavens, no," Maryanne said, forcing a light laugh. "But I'm going to be involved in it for several weeks, so I won't be mailing you any of my columns, at least not for a while. I didn't want you to wonder when you didn't hear from me."

"Will you be travelling?"

"A little." Only a few city blocks, as a matter of fact, but she couldn't very well say so. "Once everything's completed, I'll get in touch with you."

"You won't even be able to phone?" Her mother's voice carried a hint of concern.

Not often, at least not on her budget, Maryanne realized regretfully.

"Of course I'll phone," she hurried to assure her mother. She didn't often partake in subterfuge, and being new to the game, she was making everything up as she went along. She hoped her mother would be trusting enough to take her at her word.

"Speaking of your columns, dear, tell me what happened with that dreadful reporter who was harassing you earlier in the month."

"Dreadful reporter?" Maryanne repeated uncertainly. "Oh," she said with a flash of insight. "You mean Nolan Adams."

"That's his name?" Her mother's voice rose indignantly. "I hope he's stopped using that column of his to irritate you."

"It was all in good fun, Mother." All right, he *had* irritated her, but Maryanne was willing to forget their earlier pettiness. "We're friends now. As it happens, I like him quite a lot."

"Friends," her mother echoed softly. Slowly. "Your newfound friend isn't married, is he? You know your father and I started our own relationship at odds with each other, don't you?"

"Mother, honestly. Stop matchmaking."

"Just answer me one thing. Is he married or not?"

"Not. He's in his early thirties and he's handsome." A noticeable pause followed the description. "Mother?"

"You're attracted to him, aren't you?"

Maryanne wasn't sure she should admit it, but on the other hand she'd already given herself away. "Yes," she said stiffly, "I am…a little. There's a lot to like about him, even though we don't always agree. He's very talented. I've never read a column of his that didn't make me smile—and think. He's got this—er—interesting sense of humor."

"So it seems. Has he asked you out?"

"Not yet." *But he will*, her heart told her.

"Give him time." Muriel Simpson's voice had lowered a notch or two. "Now, sweetie, before we hang up, I want you to tell me some more about this special assignment of yours."

They talked for a few minutes longer, and Maryanne was astonished at her own ability to lie by omission—and avoid answering her mother's questions. She hated this subterfuge, and she hated the guilt she felt afterward. She tried to reason it away by reminding herself that her motives were good. If her parents knew what she was planning, they'd be sick with worry. But she couldn't remain their little girl forever. She had something to prove, and for the first time she was going to compete like a real contender—without her father standing on the sidelines, bribing the judges.

Maryanne didn't hear from Nolan for the next three days, and she was getting anxious. At the end of the week, she'd be finished at the *Review;* the following Monday she'd be starting at Rent-A-Maid. To her delight, Carol Riverside was appointed as her replacement. The look the managing editor tossed Maryanne's way suggested he'd given Carol the job not because of her recommendation, but despite it.

"I'm still not convinced you're doing the right thing," Carol told her over lunch on Maryanne's last day at the paper.

"But *I'm* convinced, and that's what's important," Maryanne returned. "Why is everyone so afraid I'm going to fall flat on my face?"

"It's not that, exactly."

"Then what is it?" she pressed. "I don't think Nolan

stopped grumbling from the moment I announced I was quitting the paper, finding a job and moving out on my own."

"And well he should grumble!" Carol declared righteously. "He's the one who started this whole thing. You're such a nice girl. I can't see you getting mixed up with the likes of him."

Maryanne had a sneaking suspicion her friend wasn't saying this out of loyalty to the newspaper. "Mixed up with the likes of him? Is there something I don't know about Seattle's favorite journalist?"

"Nolan Adams may be the most popular newspaper writer in town, but he's got a biting edge to him. Oh, he's witty and talented, I'll give him that, but he has this scornful attitude that makes me want to shake him till he rattles."

"I know he's a bit cynical."

"He's a good deal more than cynical. The problem is, he's so darn entertaining that his attitude is easy to overlook. I'd like two minutes alone with that man just so I could set him straight. He had no business saying what he did about you in that 'My Evening with the Debutante' piece. Look where it's led!"

For that matter, Maryanne wouldn't mind spending two minutes alone with Nolan, either, but for an entirely different reason. The speed with which the thought entered her mind surprised her enough to produce a soft smile.

"Only this time his words came back to bite him," Carol continued.

"Everything he wrote was true," Maryanne felt obliged to remind her friend. She hadn't been all that thrilled when he'd decided to share those truths with the entire western half of Washington state, but she couldn't fault his perceptions.

"Needless to say, I'm not as concerned about Nolan as I am about you," Carol said, gazing down at her sandwich. "I've seen that little spark in your eye when you talk about him, and frankly it worries me."

Maryanne immediately lowered her betraying eyes. "I'm sure you're mistaken. Nolan and I are friends, but that's the extent of it." She wasn't sure Nolan would even want to claim her as a friend; she rather suspected he thought of her as a nuisance.

"Perhaps it's friendship on his part, but it's a lot more on yours. I'm afraid you're going to fall in love with that scoundrel."

"That's crazy," Maryanne countered swiftly. "I've only just met him." Carol's gaze narrowed on her like a diamond drill bit and Maryanne sighed. "He intrigues me," she admitted, "but that's a long way from becoming emotionally involved with him."

"I can't help worrying about you. And, Maryanne, if you're falling in love with Nolan, that worries me more than the idea of you being a Rent-a-Maid or finding yourself an apartment on Capitol Hill."

Maryanne swallowed tightly. "Nolan's a talented, respected journalist. If I was going to fall in love with him, which I don't plan to do in the near future, but if I *did* fall for him, why would it be so tragic?"

"Because you're sweet and caring and he's so…" Carol paused and stared into space. "Because he's so scornful."

"True, but underneath that gruff exterior is a heart of gold. At least I think there is," Maryanne joked.

"Maybe, but I doubt it," Carol went on. "Don't get

me wrong—I respect Nolan's talent. It's his devil-may-care attitude that troubles me."

But it didn't trouble Maryanne. Not in the least. Perhaps that was what she found most appealing about him. Yet everything Carol said about Nolan was true. He did tend to be cynical and a bit sardonic, but he was also intuitive, reflective and, despite Carol's impression to the contrary, considerate.

Since it was her last day at the paper, Maryanne spent a few extra minutes saying goodbye to her co-workers. Most were sorry to see her go. There'd been a fair amount of resentment directed at her when she arrived, but her hard work seemed to have won over all but the most skeptical doubters.

On impulse, Maryanne stopped at the diner where Nolan had met her earlier in the week, hoping he'd be there. Her heart flew into her throat when she saw him sitting in a booth by the window, a book propped open in front of him. He didn't look up when she walked in.

Nor did he notice her when she approached his booth. Without waiting for an invitation, she slid in across from him.

"Hi," she murmured, keeping her voice low and secretive. "Here comes trouble to plague you once more."

Slowly, with obvious reluctance, Nolan dragged his gaze from the novel. Another mystery, Maryanne noted. "What are you doing here, Trouble?"

"Looking for you."

"Why? Have you thought up any other ways to test my patience? How about walking a tightrope between two skyscrapers? That sounds right up your alley."

"I hadn't heard from you in the past few days." She paused, hoping he'd pick up the conversation. "I thought there was something I should do about the apartment. Sign a lease, give the manager a deposit, that sort of thing."

"Annie—"

"I hope you realize I don't even know the address. I only saw it that one time."

"I told you not to worry about it."

"But I don't want anyone else to rent it."

"They won't." He laid the book aside just as the waitress appeared carrying a glass of water and a menu. Maryanne recognized her from the other day. "Hello, Barbara," she said, reading the woman's name tag. "What's the special for the day? Mr. Adams owes me a meal and I think I'll collect it while I've got the chance." She waited for him to ask her what she was talking about, but apparently he remembered his promise of dinner to pay her back for the Irish stew he'd eaten at her house the first evening they'd met.

"Cabbage rolls, with soup or salad," Barbara said, pulling out her pad and pencil while Maryanne quickly scanned the menu.

"I'll have a cheeseburger and a chocolate shake," Maryanne decided.

Barbara grinned. "I'll make sure it comes up with Mr. Adams's order."

"Thanks," she said, handing her back the menu. Barbara sauntered off toward the kitchen, scribbling on her order pad as she walked.

"It was my last day at the paper," Maryanne said.

"I'll ask you one more time—are you *sure* you want to go through with this?" Nolan demanded. "Hell, I never thought for a moment you'd want that apartment. Damn it all, you're a stubborn woman."

"Of course I'm taking the apartment."

"That's what I thought." He closed his eyes briefly. "What did the Rent-A-Maid agency say when you told them you wouldn't be taking the job?"

Maryanne stared purposely out the window. "Nothing."

He cocked an eyebrow. "Nothing?"

"What could they say?" she asked, trying to ignore the doubt reflected in his eyes. Maybe she was getting good at this lie-telling business, which wasn't a comforting thought. The way she'd misled her mother still bothered her.

Nolan drew one hand across his face. "You didn't tell them, did you? Apparently you intend to play the Cinderella role to the hilt."

"And you intend to play the role of my wicked stepmother to perfection."

He didn't say anything for a long moment. "Is there a part in that fairy tale where Cinderella gets locked in a closet for her own good?"

"Why?" she couldn't resist asking. "Is that what you're going to do?"

"Don't tempt me."

"I wish you had more faith in me."

"I do have faith in you. I have faith that you're going to make my life hell for the next few months while you go about proving yourself. Heaven knows what possessed me to write that stupid column, but, trust me, there hasn't been a minute since it hit the streets that I haven't regretted it. Not a single minute."

"But—"

"Now you insist on moving into the apartment next to mine. That's just great. Wonderful. Whatever peace

I have in my life will be completely and utterly destroyed."

"That's not true!" Maryanne cried. "Besides, I'd like to remind you, you're the one who found that apartment, not me. I have no intention of pestering you."

"Like I said, I figured just seeing the apartment would be enough to put you off. Now I won't have a minute to myself. I know it, and you know it." His eyes were darker and more brooding than she'd ever seen them. "I wasn't kidding when I said you were trouble."

"All right," Maryanne said, doing her best to disguise her crushing sense of defeat. "It's obvious you never expected me to take the place. I suppose you arranged it to look as bleak as you could. Don't worry, I'll find somewhere else to live. Another apartment as far away from you as I can possibly get." She was out of the booth so fast, so intent on escaping, that she nearly collided with Barbara.

"What about your cheeseburger?" the waitress asked.

Maryanne glanced at Nolan. "Wrap it up and give it to Mr. Adams. I've lost my appetite."

The tears that blurred her eyes only angered her more. Furious with herself for allowing his words to wound her, she hurried down the street, headed in the direction of the Seattle waterfront. It was growing dark, but she didn't care; she needed to vent some of her anger, and a brisk hike would serve that purpose nicely.

She wasn't concerned when she heard hard quick footsteps behind her. As the wind whipped at her, she shivered and drew her coat closer, tucking her hands in her pockets and hunching her shoulders forward.

Carol and Nolan both seemed to believe she needed

a keeper! They apparently considered her incompetent, and their doubts cut deeply into her pride.

Her head bowed against the force of the wind, she noticed a pair of male legs matching steps with her own. She looked up and discovered Nolan had joined her.

For the longest time, he said nothing. They were halfway down a deserted pier before he spoke. "I don't want you to find another apartment."

"I think it would be for the best if I did." He'd already told her she was nothing but trouble, and if that wasn't bad enough, he'd implied she was going to be a constant nuisance in his life. She had no intention of bothering him. As far as she was concerned, they could live on opposite sides of town. That was what he wanted and that was what he was going to get.

"It isn't for the best," he argued.

"It is. We obviously rub each other the wrong way."

Nolan turned and gripped her by the shoulders. "The apartment's been cleaned. It's ready for you to move into anytime you want. The rent is reasonable and the neighborhood's a good one. As I recall, this whole ridiculous business between us started over an article about the lack of affordable housing. You're not going to find anyplace else, not with what you intend to live on."

"But you live next door!"

"I'm well aware of that."

Maryanne bristled. "I won't live beside a man who considers me a pest. And furthermore, you still owe me dinner."

"I said you were trouble," he pointed out, ignoring her claim. "I didn't say you were a pest."

"You did so."

"I said you were going to destroy my peace—"

"Exactly."

"—of mind," he went on. He closed his eyes briefly and expelled a sharp frustrated sigh, then repeated, "You're going to destroy my peace of mind."

Maryanne wasn't sure she understood. She stared up at him, intrigued by the emotion she saw in his intense brown eyes.

"Why the hell should it matter if you live next door to me or in The Seattle?" he exclaimed. "My serenity was shot the minute I laid eyes on you."

"I don't understand," she said, surprised when her voice came out a raspy whisper. She continued to look up at him, trying to read his expression.

"You don't have a clue, do you?" he whispered. His fingers found their way into her hair as he lowered his mouth with heart-stopping slowness toward hers. "Heaven keep me from redheaded innocents."

But heaven apparently didn't receive the message, because even as he whispered the words Nolan's arms were pulling her toward him. With a sigh of regret—or was it pleasure?—his mouth settled over hers. His kiss was light and undemanding, and despite her anger, despite his words, Maryanne felt herself melting.

With a soft sigh, she flattened her hands on his chest and slid them up to link behind his neck. She leaned against him, letting his strength support her, letting his warmth comfort her.

He pulled her even closer, wrapped his arms around her waist and half lifted her from the pier. Maryanne heard a low hungry moan; she wasn't sure if it came from Nolan or from her.

It didn't matter. Nothing mattered except this wonderful feeling of being cherished and loved and protected.

Over the years, Maryanne had been kissed by her share of men. She'd found the experience pleasant, but no one had ever set her on fire the way Nolan did now.

"See what I mean," he whispered unsteadily. "We're in trouble here. Big trouble."

Four

Maryanne stood in the doorway of her new apartment, the key held tightly in her hand. She was embarking on her grand adventure, but now that she'd actually moved out of The Seattle her confidence was a bit shaky.

Carol joined her, huffing and puffing as she staggered the last few steps down the narrow hallway. She sagged against the wall, panting to catch her breath.

"This place doesn't have an elevator?" she demanded, when she could speak.

"It's being repaired."

"That's what they always say."

Maryanne nodded, barely hearing her friend. Her heart in her throat, she inserted the key and turned the lock. The door stuck, so she used the force of one hip to dislodge it. The apartment was just as she remembered: worn hardwood floors, the bulky faded furniture, the kitchen appliances that would soon be valuable antiques. But Maryanne saw none of that.

This was her new life.

She walked directly to the window and gazed out. "I've got a great view of Volunteer Park," she an-

nounced to her friend. She hadn't noticed it the day
Nolan had shown her the apartment. "I had no idea the
park was so close." She turned toward Carol, who was
still standing in the threshold, her expression one of
shock and dismay. "What's wrong?"

"Good heavens," Carol whispered. "You don't really
intend to live here, do you?"

"It isn't so bad," Maryanne said with a smile, glancing around to be sure she hadn't missed anything. "I've
got lots of ideas on how to decorate the place." She
leaned back against the windowsill, where much of the
dingy beige paint was chipped away to reveal an even
dingier grey-green. "What it needs is a fresh coat of
paint, something light and cheerful."

"It's not even half the size of your other place."

"There was a lot of wasted space at my apartment."
That might be true, Maryanne thought privately, but
she wouldn't have minded bringing some of it with her.

"What about your neighbor?" Carol asked in a
grudging voice. "He's the one who started this. The
least he could do is offer a little help."

Straightening, Maryanne brushed the dust from her
palms and looked away. "I didn't ask him to. I don't
think he even knows when I was planning to move in."

Nolan was a subject Maryanne wanted to avoid.
She hadn't talked to him since the night he'd followed
her to the waterfront…the night he'd kissed her. He'd
stopped off at The Seattle to leave the apartment key
and a rental agreement with the doorman. Max had
promptly delivered both. The implication was obvious;
Nolan didn't want to see her and was, in fact, doing his
best to avoid her.

Clearly he disapproved of the way things had developed on the pier that night. She supposed he didn't like kissing her. Then again, perhaps he did. Perhaps he liked it too much for his oft-lamented "peace of mind."

Maryanne knew how *she* felt about it. She couldn't sleep for two nights afterward. Every time she closed her eyes, the image of Nolan holding her in his arms danced through her mind like a waltzing couple from a 1940s movie. She remembered the way he'd scowled down at her when he'd broken off the kiss and how he'd struggled to make light of the incident. And she remembered his eyes, so warm and gentle, telling her another story.

"Hey, lady, is this the place where I'm supposed to bring the boxes?" A lanky boy of about fourteen stood in the doorway, carrying a large cardboard box.

"Y-yes," Maryanne said, recognizing the container as one of her own. "How'd you know to bring it up here?"

"Mr. Adams. He promised a bunch of us guys he'd play basketball with us if we'd help unload the truck."

"Oh. How nice. I'm Maryanne Simpson," she said, her heart warming at Nolan's unexpected thoughtfulness.

"Nice to meet you, lady. Now where do you want me to put this?"

Maryanne pointed to the kitchen. "Just put it in the corner over there." Before she finished, a second and third boy appeared, each hauling boxes.

Maryanne slipped past them and ran down the stairs to the parking area behind the building. Nolan was standing in the back of Carol's husband's pickup, noisily distributing cardboard boxes and dire warnings. He didn't see her until she moved closer. When he did, he fell silent, a frown on his face.

"Hi," she said, feeling a little shy. "I came to thank you."

"You shouldn't have gone up and left the truck unattended," he barked, still frowning. "Anyone could've walked off with this stuff."

"We just arrived."

"We?"

"Carol Riverside and me. She's upstairs trying to regain her breath. How long will it be before the elevator's fixed?"

"Not soon."

She nodded. Well, if he'd hoped to discourage her, she wasn't going to let him. So what if she had to walk up four flights of stairs every day! It was wonderful aerobic exercise. In the past she'd paid good money to attend a health club for the same purpose.

Nolan returned to his task, lifting boxes and handing them to a long line of teenage boys. "I'm surprised you didn't have a moving company manage this for you."

"Are you kidding?" she joked. "Only rich people use moving companies."

"Is this all of it, or do you need to make a second trip?"

"This is it. Carol and I put everything else in storage earlier this morning. It's only costing me a few dollars a month. I have to be careful about money now, you know."

He scowled again. "When do you start with the cleaning company?"

"Monday morning."

Nolan placed his hands on his hips and glared down at her. "If you're really intending to take that job—"

"Of course I am!"

"Then the first thing you'll need to do is ask for a raise."

"Oh, honestly, Nolan," she protested, walking backward. "I can't do that!"

"What you can't do is live on that amount of money, no matter how well you budget," he muttered. He leapt off the back of the truck as agilely as a cat. "Will you listen to me for once?"

"I am listening," she said. "It just so happens I don't agree. Quit worrying about me, would you? I'm going to be perfectly all right, especially once I start selling articles."

"I'm not a knight in shining armor, understand?" he shouted after her. "If you think I'll be racing to your rescue every time you're in trouble, then you need to think again."

"You're insulting me by even suggesting I'd accept your help." She tried to be angry with him but found it impossible. He might insist she was entirely on her own, but all the while he was lecturing her he was doling out her boxes so she wouldn't have to haul them up the stairs herself. Nolan might claim not to be a knight riding to her rescue, but he was behaving suspiciously like one.

Two hours later, Maryanne was alone in her new apartment for the first time. Standing in the middle of her living room, she surveyed her kingdom. As she'd told Carol, it wasn't so bad. Boxes filled every bit of available space, but it wouldn't take her long to unpack and set everything in order.

She was grateful for the help Carol, Nolan and the neighborhood teenagers had given her, but now it was up to her. And she had lots of plans—she'd paint the

walls and put up her pictures and buy some plants—
to make this place cheerful and attractive. To turn it
into a home.

It was dark before she'd finished unpacking, and by
that time she was both exhausted and hungry. Actually
famished more adequately described her condition. Her
hunger and exhaustion warred with each other: she was
too tired to go out and buy herself something to eat, but
too hungry to go to bed without eating. Making the decision about which she should do created a dilemma of
startling proportions.

She'd just decided to make do with a bowl of corn-
flakes, without milk, when there was a loud knock at
her door. She jerked it open to find Nolan there, wearing grey sweatpants and a sweat-soaked T-shirt. He held
a basketball under one arm and clutched a large white
paper sack in his free hand.

"Never open the door without knowing who's on
the other side," he warned, walking directly into the
apartment. He dropped the basketball on the sofa and
placed his sack—obviously from a fast-food restaurant—on the coffee table. "That security chain's there
for a reason. Use it."

Maryanne was still standing at the door, inhaling
the aroma of french fries and hamburgers. "Yes, your
majesty."

"Don't get testy with me, either. I've just lost two
years of my life on a basketball court. I'm too old for
this, but luckily what I lack in youth I make up for in
smarts."

"I see," she said, closing the door. For good mea-
sure she clipped the chain in place and turned the lock.

"A little show of appreciation would go a long way

toward soothing my injuries," he told her, sinking on to the sofa. He rested his head against the cushion, eyes drifting shut.

"You can't be that smart, otherwise you'd have managed to get out of playing with boys twenty years younger than you," she said lightly. She had trouble keeping her eyes off the white sack on the scratched mahogany coffee table.

Nolan straightened, wincing as he did so. "I thought you might be hungry." He reached for the bag and removed a wrapped hamburger, which he tossed to her before taking a second for himself. Next he set out two cardboard cartons full of hot french fries and two cans of soda.

Maryanne sat down beside him, her hand pressed against her stomach to keep it from growling. "You'd better be careful," she said. "You're beginning to look suspiciously like that knight in shining armor."

"Don't kid yourself."

Maryanne was too hungry to waste time arguing. She devoured the hamburger and fries within minutes. Then she relaxed against the back of the sofa and sighed, content.

"I came to set some ground rules," Nolan explained. "I think you and I need to get a few things straight."

"Sure," she agreed, although she was fairly certain she knew what he wanted to talk about. "I've already promised not to pester you."

"Good. I intend to stay out of your way, too."

"Perfect." It didn't really sound all that wonderful, but it seemed to be what he wanted, so she didn't have much choice. "Anything else?"

Nolan hesitated. Then he leaned forward, resting

his forearms on his knees. "Yes, one other thing." He turned to her with a frown. "I don't think we should… you know, kiss again."

A short silence followed his words. At first Maryanne wasn't sure she'd heard him correctly.

"I realize talking about this may be embarrassing," Nolan continued, sounding as detached as if he'd introduced the subject of football scores. "I want you to know I'm suggesting this for your own good."

"I'm pleased to hear that." It was an effort not to mock him by rolling her eyes.

He nodded and cleared his throat, and Maryanne could see he wasn't nearly as indifferent as he wanted her to believe.

"There appears to be a certain amount of physical chemistry between us," he said, avoiding even a glance in her direction. "I feel that the sooner we settle this, the less likelihood there'll be for misunderstandings later on. The last thing I need is for you to fall in love with me."

"That's it!" she cried, throwing up her arms. The ridiculousness of his comment revived her enough to indulge in some good-natured teasing. "If I can't have your heart and soul, then I'm leaving right now!"

"Damn it, Annie, this is nothing to joke about."

"Who's joking?" she asked. She made her voice absurdly melodramatic. "I knew the minute I walked into the radio station for the Celebrity Debate that if I couldn't taste your lips there was nothing left to live for."

"If you're going to make a joke out of this, then you can forget the whole discussion." He vaulted to his feet and stuffed the wrappers from their burgers and fries into the empty sack. "I was hoping we could have a mature talk, one adult to another, but that's obviously beyond you."

"Don't get so bent out of shape," she said, trying not to smile. "Sit down before you do something silly, like leave in a huff. We both know you'll regret it." She didn't know anything of the sort, but it sounded good.

He complied grudgingly, but he stared past her, training his eyes on the darkened window.

Maryanne got stiffly to her feet, every muscle and joint protesting. "It seems to me that you're presuming a great deal with this hands-off decree," she said with all the dignity she could muster. "What makes you think I'd even *want* you to kiss me again?"

A slow cocky grin raised the corners of his mouth. "A man can tell. My biggest fear is that you're going to start thinking things I never meant you to think. Eventually you'd end up getting hurt. I intend to make damn sure nothing romantic develops between us. Understand?"

"You're saying my head's in the clouds when it comes to you?"

"That's right. You're a sweet kid, stubborn and idealistic, but nonetheless naive. One kiss told me you've got a romantic soul, and frankly I don't want you fluttering those pretty blue eyes at me and dreaming of babies and a white picket fence. You and I are about as different as two people can get."

"Different?" To Maryanne's way of thinking, she had more in common with Nolan Adams than with any other man she'd ever dated.

"That's right. You come from this rich upstanding family—"

"Stop!" she cried. "Don't say another word about our economic differences. They're irrelevant. If you're looking for excuses, find something else."

"I don't need excuses. It'd never work between us and I want to make sure neither of us is ever tempted to try. If you want someone to teach you about being a woman, go elsewhere."

His words were like a slap in the face. "Naturally a man of your vast romantic experience gets plenty of requests." She turned away, so angry she couldn't keep still. "As for being afraid I might fall in love with you, let me assure you right now that there's absolutely no chance of it. In fact, I think you should be more concerned about falling for me!" Her voice was gaining strength and conviction with every word. The man had such colossal nerve. At one time she might have found herself attracted to him, but that possibility had disappeared the minute he walked in her door and opened his mouth.

"Don't kid yourself," he argued. "You're halfway in love with me already. I can see it in your eyes."

Carol had said something about her eyes revealing what she felt for Nolan, too.

Maryanne whirled around, intent on composing a suitably sarcastic retort, away from his searching gaze. But before any mocking words could pass her lips, a sharp pain shot through her neck, an ache so intense it brought immediate tears to her eyes. She must have moved too quickly, too carelessly.

Her hands flew to the back of her neck.

Nolan was instantly on his feet. "What's wrong?"

"Nothing," she mumbled, easing her way back to the sofa. She sat down, hand still pressed to her neck, waiting a moment before slowly rotating her head, wanting to test the extent of her injury. Quickly, she realized her mistake.

"Annie," Nolan demanded, kneeling in front of her, "what is it?"

"I…don't know. I moved wrong, I guess."

His hands replaced hers. "You've got a crick in your neck?"

"If I do, it's all your fault. You say the most ridiculous things."

"I know." His voice was as gentle as his hands. He began to knead softly, his fingers tenderly massaging the tight muscles.

"I'm all right."

"Of course you are," he whispered. "Just close your eyes and relax."

"I can't." How could he possibly expect her to do that when he was so close, so warm and sensual? He was fast making a lie of all her protestations.

"Yes, you can," he said, his voice low and seductive. He leaned over her, his face, his lips, scant inches from hers. His hands were working the tightness from her neck and shoulders and at the same time creating a dizzying heated sensation that extended to the tips of her fingers and the soles of her feet.

She sighed and clasped his wrist with both hands, wanting to stop him before she made a fool of herself by swaying toward him or doing something equally suggestive. "I think you should stop. Let me rephrase that. I *know* you should stop."

"I know I should, too," he admitted quietly. "Remember what I said earlier?"

"You mean the hands-off policy?"

"Yes." She could hardly hear him. "Let's delay it for a day—what do you think?"

At that moment, clear organized thought was something of a problem. "Wh-whatever you feel is best."

"Oh, I know what's best," he whispered. "Unfortunately that doesn't seem to make a damn bit of difference right now."

She wasn't sure exactly when it happened, but her hands seemed to have left his wrists and were splayed across the front of his T-shirt. His chest felt rigid and muscular; his heart beneath her palms pounded hard and fast. She wondered if her own pulse was keeping time with his.

With infinite slowness, Nolan lowered his mouth to hers. Maryanne's eyes drifted closed of their own accord and she moaned, holding back a small cry of welcome. His touch was even more compelling than she remembered. Nolan must have felt something similar, because his groan followed, an echo of hers.

He kissed her again and again. Maryanne wanted more, but he resisted giving in to her desires—or his own. It was as if he'd decided a few kisses were of little consequence and wouldn't seriously affect either one of them.

Wrong. Maryanne wanted to shout it at him, but couldn't.

His mouth left hers and blazed a fiery trail of kisses across her sensitized skin. His lips brushed her throat, under her chin to the vulnerable hollow. Only minutes earlier, moving her neck without pain had been impossible; now she did so freely, turning it, arching, asking—no, demanding—that he kiss her again the way he had that night at the waterfront.

Nolan complied, and he seemed to do it willingly,

surrendering the battle. He groaned anew and the sound came from deep in his throat. His fingers tangled in the thick strands of her hair as his mouth rushed back to hers.

Maryanne was experiencing a renewal of her own. She felt as if she had lain dormant and was bursting to life, like a flower struggling out of winter snows into the light and warmth of spring.

All too soon, Nolan pulled away from her. His eyes met and held hers. She knew her eyes were filled with questions, but his gave her no answers.

He got abruptly to his feet.

"Nolan," she said, shocked that he would leave her like this.

He looked back at her and she saw it then. The regret. A regret tinged with compassion. "You're so exhausted you can barely sit up. Go to bed and we'll both forget this ever happened. Understand?"

Too stunned to reply, she nodded. Maybe Nolan could forget it, but she knew she wouldn't.

"Lock the door after me. And next time don't be so eager to find out who's knocking. There isn't any doorman here."

Once more she nodded. She got up and followed him to the door, holding it open.

"Damn it, Annie, don't look at me like that."

"Like what?"

"Like that," he accused, then slowly shook his head as if to clear his thoughts. He rubbed his face and sighed, then pressed his knuckle under her chin. "The two of us are starting over first thing tomorrow. There won't be any more of this." But even as he was speaking, he was leaning forward to gently brush her mouth with his.

* * *

It was the sound of Nolan pounding furiously away on his electric typewriter—a heavy, outdated office model—that woke Maryanne the next morning. She yawned loudly, stretching her arms high above her head, arching her back. Her first night in her new apartment, and she'd slept like a rock. The sofa, which opened into a queen-size sleeper, was lumpy and soft, nearly swallowing her up, but she'd been too exhausted to care.

Nolan's fierce typing continued most of the day. Maryanne hadn't expected to see him, so she wasn't disappointed when she didn't. He seemed determined to avoid her and managed it successfully for most of the week.

Since she'd promised not to make a nuisance of herself, Maryanne kept out of his way, too. She started work at the cleaning company and wrote three articles in five days, often staying up late into the night.

The work for Rent-A-Maid was backbreaking and arduous. She spent three afternoons a week picking up after professional men who were nothing less than slobs. Maryanne had to resist the urge to write them each a note demanding that they put their dirty dishes in the sink and their soiled clothes in the laundry basket.

Rent-A-Maid had made housekeeping sound glamorous. It wasn't. In fact, it was the hardest, most physically exhausting job she'd ever undertaken.

By the end of the week, her nails were broken and chipped and her hands were red and chapped.

It was by chance rather than design that Maryanne bumped into Nolan late Friday afternoon. She was carrying a bag of groceries up the stairs when he bounded past her, taking the steps two at a time.

"Annie." He paused on the landing, waiting for her to catch up. "How's it going?"

Maryanne didn't know what to say. She couldn't very well inform him that the highlight of her week was scraping a crusty patch off the bottom of an oven at one of the apartments she cleaned. She'd had such lofty expectations, such dreams. Nor could she casually announce that the stockbroker she cleaned for had spilled wine on his carpet and she'd spent an hour trying to get the stain out and broken two nails in the process.

"Fine," she lied. "Everything's just wonderful."

"Here, let me take that for you."

"Thanks." She handed him the single bag, her week's allotment of groceries. Unfortunately it was all she could afford. Everything had seemed so exciting when she started out; her plans had been so promising. The reality was proving to be something else again.

"Well, how do you like cleaning?"

"It's great, really great." It was shocking how easily the lie came. "I'm finding it...a challenge."

Nolan smiled absently. "I'm glad to hear it. Have you got your first paycheck yet?"

"I cashed it this afternoon." She used to spend more each week at the dry cleaners than she'd received in her first paycheck from Rent-A-Maid. The entire amount had gone for food and transportation, and there were only a few dollars left. Her budget was tight, but she'd make it. She'd have to.

Nolan paused in front of her door and waited while she scrabbled through her bag, searching for the key. "I hear you typing at night," she said. "Are you working on anything special?"

"No."

She eyed him curiously. "How fast do you type? Eighty words a minute? A hundred? And for heaven's sake, why don't you use a computer like everyone else?"

"Sixty words a minute on a good day. And for your information, I happen to like my electric. It may be old, but it does the job."

She finally retrieved her key, conscious of his gaze on her hands.

Suddenly he grasped her fingers. "All right," he demanded. "What happened to you?"

Five

"Nothing's happened to me," Maryanne insisted hotly, pulling her hand free of Nolan's.

"Look at your nails," he said. "There isn't one that's not broken."

"You make it sound like I should be dragged before a firing squad at dawn. So I chipped a few nails this week. I'll survive." Although she was making light of it, each broken fingernail was like a small loss. She took pride in her perfect nails, or at least she once had.

His eyes narrowed as he scrutinized her. "There's something you're not telling me."

"I didn't realize you'd appointed yourself my father confessor."

Anger flashed in his dark eyes as he took the key from her unresisting fingers. He opened the door and, with one hand at her shoulder, urged her inside. "We need to talk."

"No, we don't." Maryanne marched into the apartment, plunked her bag of groceries on the kitchen counter and spun around to confront her neighbor. "Listen here, buster, you've made it perfectly clear that you don't want anything to do with me. That's your choice, and I'm certainly not going to bore you with the sorry details of my life."

He ignored her words and started pacing the small living area, pausing in front of the window. His presence filled the apartment, making it seem smaller than usual. He pivoted sharply, pointing an accusatory finger in her direction. "These broken nails came from swinging a dust mop around, didn't they? What the hell are you doing?"

Maryanne didn't answer him right away. She was angry, and his sudden concern for her welfare made her even angrier. "I told you before, I don't need a guardian."

"Against my advice, you took that stupid job. Anyone with half a brain would know it wasn't going to—"

"Will you stop acting like you're responsible for me?" Maryanne snapped.

"I can't help it. I *am* responsible for you. You wouldn't be here if I hadn't written that damn column. I don't want to intrude on your life any more than you want me to, but let's face it, there's no one else to look out for you. Sooner or later someone's going to take advantage of you."

That did it. Maryanne stalked over to him and jabbed her index finger into his chest with enough force to bend what remained of her nail. "In case you need reminding, I'm my own woman. I make my own decisions. I'll work any place I damn well please. Furthermore, I can take care of myself." She whirled around and opened her front door. "Now kindly leave!"

"No."

"No?" she repeated.

"No," he said again, returning to the window. He crossed his arms over his chest and sighed impatiently. "You haven't eaten, have you? I can tell, because you get testy when you're hungry."

"If you'd leave my apartment the way I asked, that wouldn't be a problem."

"How about having dinner with me?"

The invitation took Maryanne by surprise. Her first impulse was to throw it back in his face. After an entire week of pretending she didn't exist, he had a lot of nerve even asking.

"Well?" he prompted.

"Where?" As if that made a difference. Maryanne was famished, and the thought of sharing her meal with Nolan was more tempting than she wanted to admit, even to herself.

"The diner."

"Are you going to order chili?"

"Are you going to ask them to remove the nonexistent bean sprouts from your sandwich?"

Maryanne hesitated. She felt confused by all her contradictory emotions. She was strongly attracted to Nolan and every time they were together she caught herself hoping they could become friends—more than friends. But, equally often, he infuriated her or left her feeling depressed. He made the most outlandish remarks to her. He seemed to have appointed himself her guardian. When he wasn't issuing decrees, he neglected her as if she were nothing more than a nuisance. And to provide a finishing touch, she was lying to her parents because of him! Well, maybe that wasn't quite fair, but...

"I'll throw in dessert," he coaxed with a smile.

That smile was her Waterloo, yet she still struggled. "A la mode?"

His grin widened. "You drive a hard bargain."

Maryanne's eyes met his and although Nolan could make her angrier than anyone she'd ever known, a smile trembled on her own lips.

They agreed to meet a half hour later. That gave Maryanne time to unpack her groceries, change clothes and freshen her makeup. She found herself humming as she applied lip gloss, wondering if she was reading too much into this impromptu dinner date.

When Nolan came to her door to pick her up, Maryanne noted that he'd changed into jeans and a fisherman's sweater. It was the first time she'd seen him without the raincoat, other than the day he'd played basketball with the neighborhood boys. He looked good. All right, she admitted grudgingly, he looked fantastic.

"You dressed up," she said before she could stop herself, grateful she'd understated her attraction to him.

"So did you. You look nice."

"Thanks."

"Before I forget to tell you, word has it the elevator's going to be fixed Monday morning."

"Really? That's the best news I've heard all week." Goodness, could she take all these glad tidings at once? First Nolan had actually invited her out on a date, and now she wouldn't have to hike up four flights of stairs every afternoon. Life was indeed treating her well.

They were several blocks from the apartment building before Maryanne realized Nolan was driving in the opposite direction of the diner. She said as much.

"Do you like Chinese food?" he asked.

"I love it."

"The diner's short-staffed—one of the waitresses quit. I thought Chinese food might be interesting, and I promise we won't have to wait for a table."

It sounded heavenly to Maryanne. She didn't know how significant Nolan's decision to take her to a different restaurant might be. Perhaps it was foolish, but Maryanne hoped it meant she was becoming special to him. As if he could read her mind, Nolan was unusually quiet on the drive into Seattle's International District.

So much for romance. Maryanne could almost hear his thoughts. If she were a betting woman, she'd place odds on the way their dinner conversation would go. First Nolan would try to find out exactly what tasks had been assigned to her by Rent-A-Maid. Then he'd try to convince her to quit.

Only she wasn't going to let him. She was her own woman, and she'd said it often enough to convince herself. If this newsman thought he could sway her with a fancy dinner and a few well-spoken words, then he was about to learn a valuable lesson.

The restaurant proved to be a Chinese version of the greasy spoon where Nolan ate regularly. The minute they walked into the small room, Maryanne was greeted by a wide variety of tantalizing scents. Pungent spices and oils wafted through the air, and the smells were so appealing it was all she could do not to follow them into the kitchen. She knew before sampling a single bite that the food would be some of the best Asian cuisine she'd ever tasted.

An elderly Chinese gentleman greeted Nolan as if he were a long-lost relative. The two shared a brief exchange in Chinese before the man escorted them to a table. He shouted into the kitchen, and a brightly painted ceramic pot of tea was quickly delivered to their table.

Nolan and Maryanne were never given menus. Almost from the moment they were seated, food began appearing on their table. An appetizer plate came first, with several items Maryanne couldn't readily identify. But she was too hungry to care. Everything was delicious and she happily devoured one after another.

"You seem well acquainted with the waiter," Maryanne commented, once the appetizer plate was empty. She barely had time to catch her breath before a bowl of thick spicy soup was brought to them by the same elderly gentleman. He paused and smiled proudly at Nolan, then glanced at Maryanne, before nodding in a profound way.

"Wong Su's the owner. I went to school with his son."

"Is that where you picked up Chinese?"

"Yes. I only know a few words, just enough to get the gist of what he's saying," he answered brusquely, reaching for his spoon.

"What was it he said when we first came in? I noticed you seemed quick to disagree with him."

Nolan dipped his spoon into the soup, ignoring her question.

"Nolan?"

"He said you're too thin."

Maryanne shook her head, immediately aware that he was lying. "If he really thought that, you'd have agreed with him."

"All right, all right," Nolan muttered, looking severely displeased. "I should've known better than to bring a woman to Wong Su's place. He assumed there was something romantic between us. He said you'd give me many fine sons."

"How sweet."

Nolan reacted instantly to her words. He dropped his spoon beside the bowl with a clatter, planted his elbows on the table and glared at her heatedly. "Now don't go all sentimental on me. There's nothing between us and there never will be."

Maryanne promptly saluted. "Aye, aye, Captain," she mocked.

"Good. Well, now that's settled, tell me about your week."

"Tell me about yours," she countered, unwilling to change the subject to herself quite so easily. "You seemed a whole lot busier than I was."

"I went to work, came home…"

"…worked some more," she finished for him. Another plate, heaped high with sizzling hot chicken and crisp vegetables, was brought by Wong Su, who offered Maryanne a grin.

Nolan frowned at his friend and said something in Chinese that caused the older man to laugh outright. When Nolan returned his attention to Maryanne, he was scowling again. "For heaven's sake, don't encourage him."

"What did I do?" To the best of her knowledge she was innocent of any wrongdoing.

Nolan thought it over for a moment. "Never mind, no point in telling you."

Other steaming dishes arrived—prawns with cashew nuts, then ginger beef and barbecued pork, each accompanied by small bowls of rice until virtually every inch of the small table was covered.

"You were telling me about your week," Maryanne reminded him, reaching for the dish in the center of the crowded table.

"No, I wasn't," Nolan retorted.

With a scornful sigh, Maryanne passed him the chicken. "All right, have it your way."

"You're going to needle me to death until you find out what I'm working on in my spare time, aren't you?"

"Of course not." If he didn't want her to know, then fine, she had no intention of asking again. Acting as nonchalant as possible, she helped herself to a thick slice of the pork. She dipped it into a small dish of hot mustard, which proved to be a bit more potent than she'd expected; her eyes started to water.

Mumbling under his breath, Nolan handed her his napkin. "Here."

"I'm all right." She wiped the moisture from her eyes and blinked a couple of times before picking up her water glass. Once she'd composed herself, she resumed their previous discussion. "On the contrary, Mr. Adams, whatever project so intensely occupies your time is your own concern."

"Spoken like a true aristocrat."

"Obviously you don't care to share it with me."

He gave an exaggerated sigh. "It's a novel," he said. "There now, are you satisfied?"

"A novel," she repeated coolly. "Really. And all along, I thought you were taking in typing jobs on the side."

He glared at her, but the edges of his mouth turned up in a reluctant grin. "I don't want to talk about the plot, all right? I'm afraid that would water it down."

"I understand perfectly."

"Damn it all, Annie, would you stop looking at me with those big blue eyes of yours? I already feel guilty as hell without you smiling serenely at me and trying to act so blasé."

"Guilty about what?"

He expelled his breath sharply. "Listen," he said in a low voice, leaning toward her. "As much as I hate to admit this, you're right. It's none of my business where you work or how many nails you break or how much you're paid. But damn it all, I'm worried about you."

She raised her chopsticks in an effort to stop him. "It seems to me I've heard this argument before. Actually, it's getting downright boring."

Nolan dropped his voice even lower. "You've been sheltered all your life. I know you don't want me to feel responsible for what you're doing—or for you. And I wish I didn't. Unfortunately I can't help it. Believe me, I've tried. It doesn't work. Every night I lie awake wondering what trouble you're going to get into next. I don't know what's going to happen first—you working yourself to death, or me getting an ulcer."

Maryanne's gaze fell to her hands, and the uneven length of her once perfectly uniform fingernails. "They are rather pitiful, aren't they?"

Nolan glanced at them and grimaced. "As a personal favor to me would you consider giving up the job at Rent-A-Maid?" He ran his fingers through his hair, sighing heavily. "It doesn't come easy to ask you this, Annie. If for no other reason, do it because you owe me a favor for finding you the apartment. But for heaven's sake, quit that job."

She didn't answer him right away. She wanted to do as he asked, because she was falling in love with him.

Because she craved his approval. Yet she wanted to reject his entreaties, flout his demands. Because he made her feel confused and contrary and full of unpredictable emotions.

"If it'll do any good, I'll promise not to interfere again," he said, his voice so quiet it was almost a whisper. "If you'll quit Rent-a-Maid."

"As a personal favor to you," she repeated, nodding slowly. So much for refusing to be swayed by dinner and a few well-chosen words.

Their eyes met and held for a long moment. Deliberately, as though it went against his will, Nolan reached out and brushed an auburn curl from her cheek. His touch was light yet strangely intimate, as intimate as a kiss. His fingers lingered on her cheek and it was all Maryanne could do not to cover his hand with her own and close her eyes to savor the wealth of sensations that settled around her.

Nolan's dark eyes narrowed, and she could tell he was struggling. She could read it in every line, every feature of his handsome face. But struggling against what? She could only speculate. He didn't want to be attracted to her; that much was obvious.

As if he needed to break contact with her eyes, he lowered his gaze to her mouth. Whether it was intentional or not, Maryanne didn't know, but his thumb inched closer to her lips, easing toward the corner. Then, with an abrupt movement, he pulled his hand away and returned to his meal, eating quickly and methodically.

Maryanne tried to eat, but her own appetite was gone. Wong Su refused payment although Nolan tried to insist. Instead the elderly man said something in Chinese that sent every eye in the place straight to Maryanne. She smiled benignly, wondering what he could possibly have said that would make the great Nolan Adams blush.

The drive back to the apartment was even more silent than the one to the restaurant had been. Maryanne considered asking Nolan exactly what Wong Su had said just before they'd left, but she thought better of it.

They took their time walking up the four flights of stairs. "Will you come in for coffee?" Maryanne asked when they arrived at her door.

"I can't tonight," Nolan said after several all-too-quiet moments.

"I don't bite, you know." His eyes didn't waver from hers. The attraction was there—she could feel it as surely as she had his touch at dinner.

"I'd like to finish my chapter."

So he was going to close her out once again. "Don't work too hard," she said, opening the apartment door. Her disappointment was keen, but she managed to disguise it behind a shrug. "Thank you for dinner. It was delicious."

Nolan thrust his hands into his pockets. It might have been her imagination, but she thought he did it to keep from reaching for her. The idea comforted her ego and she smiled up at him warmly.

She was about to close the door when he stopped her. "Yes?" she asked.

His eyes were as piercing and dark as she'd ever seen them. "My typing. Does it keep you awake nights?"

"No," she told him and shook her head for emphasis. "The book must be going well."

He nodded, then sighed. "Listen, would it be possible…" He paused and started again. "Are you busy tomorrow night? I've got two tickets to the Seattle Repertory Theatre and I was wondering..."

"I'd love to go," she said eagerly, before he'd even finished the question.

Judging by the expression on his face, the invitation seemed to be as much a surprise to him as it was to her. "I'll see you tomorrow, then."

"Right," she answered brightly. "Tomorrow."

The afternoon was glorious, with just the right mixture of wind and sunshine. Hands clasped behind her back, Maryanne strolled across the grass of Volunteer Park, kicking up leaves as she went. She'd spent the morning researching an article she hoped to sell to a local magazine and she was taking a break.

The basketball court was occupied by several teenage boys, a couple of whom she recognized from the day she'd moved. With time on her hands and an afternoon to enjoy, Maryanne paused to watch the hotly contested game. Sitting on a picnic table, she swung her legs, content to laze away the sunny afternoon. Everything was going so well. With hardly any difficulty she'd found another job. Nolan probably wasn't going to approve of this one, either, but that was just too bad.

"Hi." A girl of about thirteen, wearing a jean jacket and tight black stretch leggings, strolled up to the picnic table. "You're with Mr. Adams, aren't you?"

Maryanne would've liked to think so, but she didn't feel she could describe it quite that way. "What makes you ask that?"

"You moved in with him, didn't you?"

"Not exactly. I live in the apartment next door."

"I didn't believe Eddie when he said Mr. Adams had

a woman. He's never had anyone live with him before. He's just not the type, if you know what I mean."

Maryanne did know. She was learning not to take his attitude toward her personally. The better acquainted she became with Nolan, the more clearly she realized that he considered all women a nuisance. The first night they met, he'd mentioned that he'd been in love once, but his tone had been so casual it implied this romance was merely a long-ago mistake. He'd talked about the experience as if it meant little or nothing to him. Maryanne wasn't sure she believed that.

"Mr. Adams is a really neat guy. All the kids like him a lot." The girl smiled, suggesting she was one of his legion of admirers. "I'm Gloria Masterson."

Maryanne held out her hand. "Maryanne Simpson."

Gloria smiled shyly. "If you don't live with him, are you his girlfriend?"

"Not really. We're just friends."

"That's what he said when I asked him about you."

"Oh." It wasn't as though she could expect him to admit anything more.

"Mr. Adams comes around every now and then and talks to us kids in the park. I think he's checking up on us and making sure no one's into drugs or gangs."

Maryanne smiled. That sounded exactly like the kind of thing Nolan would do.

"Only a few kids around here are that stupid, but you know, I think a couple of the boys might've been tempted to try something if it wasn't for Mr. Adams."

"Hey, Gloria," a lanky boy from the basketball court called out. "Come here, woman."

Gloria sighed loudly, then shouted. "Just a minute."

She turned back to Maryanne. "I'm really not Eddie's woman. He just likes to think so."

Maryanne smiled. She wished she could say the same thing about her and Nolan. "It was nice to meet you, Gloria. Maybe I'll see you around."

"That'd be great."

"Gloria," Eddie shouted, "are you coming or not?"

The teenage girl shook her head. "I don't know why I put up with him."

Maryanne left the park soon afterward. The first thing she noticed when she got home was an envelope taped to her door.

She waited until she was inside the apartment to open it, and as she did a single ticket and a note slipped out. "I'm going to be stuck at the office," the note read. "The curtain goes up at eight—don't be late. N."

Maryanne was mildly disappointed that Nolan wouldn't be driving her to the play, but she decided to splurge and take a taxi. By seven-thirty, when the cab arrived, she was dressed and ready. She wore her best evening attire, a long black velvet skirt and matching blazer with a cream-colored silk blouse. She'd even put on her pearl earrings and cameo necklace.

The theatre was one of the nicest in town, and Maryanne's heart sang with excitement as the usher escorted her to her seat. Nolan hadn't arrived yet and she looked around expectantly.

The curtain was about to go up when a man she mentally categorized as wealthy and a bit of a charmer settled in the vacant seat next to hers.

"Excuse me," he said, leaning toward her, smiling warmly. "I'm Griff Bradley. Nolan Adams sent me."

It didn't take Maryanne two seconds to figure out

what Nolan had done. The low-down rat had matched her up with someone he considered more appropriate. Someone he assumed she had more in common with. Someone wealthy and slick. Someone her father would approve of.

"Where's Nolan?" Maryanne demanded. She bolted to her feet and grabbed her bag, jerking it so hard the gold chain strap threatened to break.

Griff looked taken aback by her sharp question. "You mean he didn't discuss this with you?"

"He invited me to this play. I assumed… I believed the two of us would be attending it together. He didn't say a word about you. I'm sorry, but I can't agree to this arrangement." She started to edge her way out of the row just as the curtain rose.

To her dismay, Griff followed her into the aisle. "I'm sure there's been some misunderstanding."

"You bet there has," Maryanne said, loudly enough to attract the angry glares of several patrons sitting in the aisle seats. She rushed toward the exit with Griff in hot pursuit.

"If you'll give me a moment to explain—"

"It won't be necessary."

"You are Maryanne Simpson of the New York Simpsons?"

"Yes," she said, walking directly outside. Moving to the curb, she raised her hand and shouted, "Taxi!"

Griff raced around to stand in front of her. "There isn't any need to rush off like this. Nolan was just doing me a good turn."

"And me a rotten one. Listen, Mr. Bradley, you look like a very nice gentleman, and under any other circumstances I would've been more than happy to make your acquaintance, but there's been a mistake."

"But—"

"I'm sorry, I really am." A cab raced toward her and squealed to a halt.

Griff opened the back door for her, looking more charming and debonair than ever. "I'm not sure my heart will recover. You're very lovely, you know."

Maryanne sighed. The man was overdoing it, but he certainly didn't deserve the treatment she was giving him. She smiled and apologized again, then swiftly turned to the driver and recited her address.

Maryanne fumed during the entire ride back to her apartment. Rarely had she been more furious. If Nolan Adams thought he could play matchmaker with her, he was about to learn that everything he'd ever heard about redheads was true.

"Hey, lady, you all right?" the cabbie asked.

"I'm fine," she said stiffly.

"That guy you were with back at the theatre didn't try anything, did he?"

"No, some other man did, only he's not going to get away with it." The driver pulled into her street. "That's the building there," Maryanne told him. She reached into her bag for her wallet and pulled out some of her precious cash, including a generous tip. Then she ran into the apartment building, heedless of her clothes or her high-heeled shoes.

For the first time since moving in, Maryanne didn't pause to rest on the third-floor landing. Her anger carried her all the way to Nolan's apartment door. She could hear him typing inside, and the sound only heightened her temper. Dragging breath through her lungs, she slammed her fist against the door.

"Hold on a minute," she heard him grumble.

His shocked look as he threw open the door would have been comical in different circumstances. "Maryanne, what are you doing here?"

"That was a rotten underhanded thing to do, you deceiving, conniving, low-down…rat!"

Nolan did an admirable job of composing himself. He buried his hands in his pockets and smiled nonchalantly. "I take it you and Griff Bradley didn't hit it off?"

Six

Maryanne was so furious she couldn't find the words to express her outrage. She opened and closed her mouth twice before she collected herself enough to proceed.

"I told you before that I don't want you interfering in my life, and I meant it."

"I was doing you a favor," Nolan countered, clearly unmoved by her angry display. In fact, he yawned loudly, covering his mouth with the back of his hand. "Griff's a stockbroker friend of mine and one hell of a nice guy. If you'd given him half a chance, you might have found that out yourself. I could see the two of you becoming good friends. Why don't you give it a try? You might hit it off, after all."

"The only thing I'd consider hitting is *you*." To her horror, tears of rage flooded her eyes. "Don't ever try that again. Do you understand?" Not waiting for his reply, she turned abruptly, stalked down the hall to her apartment and unlocked the door. She flung it shut with sufficient force to rattle the windows on three floors.

She paced back and forth several times, blew her nose once and decided she hadn't told him nearly enough. Throwing open her door, she rushed down the hall to Nolan's apartment again. She banged twice as hard as she had originally.

Nolan opened the door, wearing a martyr's expression. He cocked one eyebrow expressively. "What is it this time?"

"And furthermore you're the biggest coward I've ever met. If I still worked for the newspaper, I'd write a column so all of Seattle would know exactly what kind of man you are." Her voice wobbled just a little, but that didn't diminish the strength of her indignation.

She stomped back to her own apartment and she hadn't been there two seconds before there was a pounding on her door. It didn't surprise her to find Nolan Adams on the other side. He might have appeared calm, but his eyes sparked with an angry fire. They narrowed slightly as he glowered at her.

"What did you just say?" he asked.

"You heard me. You're nothing but a coward. Coward, coward, coward!" With that she slammed her door so hard that a framed family photo hanging on the wall crashed to the floor. Luckily the glass didn't break.

Her chest heaving, Maryanne picked up the photo, wiped it off and carefully replaced it. But for all her outward composure, her hands were trembling. No sooner had she completed the task than Nolan beat on her door a second time.

"Now what?" she demanded, whipping open the door. "I would have thought you got my message."

"I got it all right. I just don't happen to like it."

"Tough." She would have slammed the door again, but before she could act, a loud banging came from the

direction of the floor. Not knowing what it was, Maryanne instinctively jumped back.

Nolan drew a deep breath, and Maryanne could tell
he was making an effort to compose himself. "All right,
Mrs. McBride," Nolan shouted at the floor, "we'll hold
it down."

"Who's Mrs. McBride?"

"The lady who lives in the apartment below you."

"Oh." Maryanne had been too infuriated to realize
she was shouting so loudly half the apartment building
could hear. She felt ashamed at her loss of control and
guilty for disturbing her neighbors—but she was still
furious with Nolan.

The man in question glared at her. "Do you think it's
possible to discuss this situation without involving any
more doors?" he asked sharply. "Or would you rather
wait until someone phones the police and we're both
arrested for disturbing the peace?"

She glared back at him defiantly. "Very funny," she
said, turning around and walking into her apartment.
As she knew he would, Nolan followed her inside.

Maryanne moved into the kitchen. Preparing a pot
of coffee gave her a few extra minutes to gather her
dignity, which had been as abused as her apartment
door. Mixed with the anger was a chilling pain that cut
straight through her heart. Nolan's thinking so little of
her that he could casually pass her on to another man
was mortifying enough. But knowing he considered it
a favor only heaped on the humiliation.

"Annie, please listen—"

"Did it ever occur to you that arranging this date
with Griff might offend me?" she cried.

Nolan seemed reluctant to answer. "Yes," he finally

said, "it did. I tried to catch you earlier this afternoon, but you weren't in. This wasn't the kind of situation I felt comfortable explaining in a note, so I took the easy way out and left Griff to introduce himself. I didn't realize you'd take it so personally."

"How else was I supposed to take it?"

Nolan glanced away uncomfortably. "Let's just say I was hoping you'd meet him and the two of you would spend the evening getting to know each other. Griff comes from a well-established family and—"

"That's supposed to impress me?"

"He's the type of man your father would arrange for you to meet," Nolan said, his voice sandpaper-gruff.

"How many times do I have to tell you I don't need a second father?" His mention of her family reminded her of the way she was deceiving them, which brought a powerful sense of remorse.

He muttered tersely under his breath, then shook his head. "Obviously I blew it. Would it help if I apologized?"

An apology, even a sincere one, wouldn't dissolve the hurt. She looked up, about to tell him exactly that, when her eyes locked with his.

He stood a safe distance from her, his expression so tender that her battered heart rolled defencelessly to her feet. She knew she ought to throw him out of her home and refuse to ever speak to him again. No one would blame her. She tried to rally her anger, but something she couldn't explain or understand stopped her.

All the emotion must have sharpened her perceptions. Never had she been more aware of Nolan as a man. The space separating them seemed to close, drawing them toward each other. She could smell the clean scent of the soap he used and hear the music of the rain as it danced against her window. She hadn't even realized, until this moment, that it was raining.

"I am sorry," he said quietly.

Maryanne nodded and wiped the moisture from her eyes. She wasn't a woman who cried easily, and the tears were a surprise.

"What you said about my being a coward is true," Nolan admitted. He sighed heavily. "You frighten me, Annie."

"You mean my temper?"

"No, I deserved that." He grinned that lazy insolent grin of his.

"What is it about me you find so unappealing?" She had to know what was driving him away, no matter how much the truth damaged her pride.

"Unappealing?" His abrupt laugh was filled with irony. "I wish I could find something, *anything*, unappealing about you, but I can't." Dropping his gaze, he stepped back and cleared his throat. When he spoke again, his words were brusque, impatient. "I was a lot more comfortable with you before we met."

"You thought of me as a debutante."

"I assumed you were a pampered immature…girl. Not a woman. I expected to find you ambitious and selfish, so eager to impress your father with what you could do that it didn't matter how many people you stepped on. Then we did the Celebrity Debate, and I discovered that none of the things I wanted to believe about you were true."

"Then why—"

"What you've got to understand," Nolan added forcefully, "is that I don't *want* to become involved with you."

"That message has come through loud and clear." She moistened her lips and cast her gaze toward the floor, afraid he'd see how vulnerable he made her feel.

Suddenly he was standing directly in front of her, so close his breath warmed her face. With one gentle finger, he lifted her chin, raising her eyes to his.

"All evening I was telling myself how noble I was," he said. "Griff Bradley is far better suited to you than I'll ever be."

"Stop saying that!"

He wrapped his arms around her waist and pulled her against him. "There can't ever be any kind of relationship between us," he said, his voice rough. "I learned my lesson years ago, and I'm not going to repeat that mistake." But contrary to everything he was saying, his mouth lowered to hers until their lips touched. The kiss was slow and familiar. Their bottom lips clung as Nolan eased away from her.

"That wasn't supposed to happen," he murmured.

"I won't tell anyone if you won't," she whispered.

"Just remember what I said," he whispered back. "I don't do well with rich girls. I already found that out. The hard way."

"I'll remember," she said softly, looking up at him.

"Good." And then he kissed her again.

It was three days before Maryanne saw Nolan. She didn't need anyone to tell her he was avoiding her. Maybe he thought falling in love would wreak havoc with his comfortable well-ordered life. If he'd given her a chance, Maryanne would've told him she didn't expect him to fill her days. She had her new job, and she was fixing up her apartment. Most importantly, she had her writing, which kept her busy the rest of the time. She'd recently queried a magazine about doing a humorous article on her experiences working for Rent-A-Maid.

"Here's Nolan now," Barbara whispered as she hurried past Maryanne, balancing three plates.

Automatically Maryanne reached for a water glass and a menu and followed Nolan to the booth. He was halfway into his seat when he saw her. He froze and his narrowed gaze flew across the room to the middle-aged waitress.

Barbara didn't appear in the least intimidated. "Hey, what did you expect?" she called out. "We were one girl short, and when Maryanne applied for the job she gave you as a reference. Besides, she's a good worker."

Nolan didn't bother to look at the menu. Standing beside the table, Maryanne took her green order pad out of her apron pocket.

"I'll have the chili," he said gruffly.

"With or without cheese?"

"Without," he bellowed, then quickly lowered his voice. "How long have you been working here?"

"Since Monday morning. Don't look so angry. You were the one who told me about the job. Remember?"

"I don't want you working here!"

"Why not? It's a respectable establishment. Honestly, Nolan, what did you expect me to do? I had to find another job, and fast. I can't expect to sell any articles for at least a month, if then. I've got to have some way of paying the bills."

"You could've done a hell of a lot better than Mom's Place if you wanted to be a waitress."

"Are we going to argue? Again?" she asked with an impatient sigh.

"No," he answered, grabbing his napkin just in time to catch a violent sneeze.

Now that she had a chance to study him, she saw his nose was red and his eyes rheumy. In fact he looked downright miserable. "You've got a cold."

"Are you always this brilliant?"

"I try to be. And I'll try to ignore your rudeness. Would you like a glass of orange juice or a couple of aspirin?"

"No, Florence Nightingale, all I want is my usual bowl of chili, *without* the cheese. Have you got that?"

"Yes, of course," she said, writing it down. Nolan certainly seemed to be in a rotten mood, but that was nothing new. Maryanne seemed to bring out the worst in him.

Barbara met her at the counter. "From the looks your boyfriend's been sending me, he'd gladly cut off my head. What's with him, anyway?"

"I don't think he's feeling well," Maryanne answered in a low worried voice.

"Men, especially sick ones, are the biggest babies on earth," Barbara said wryly. "They get a little virus and think someone should rush in to make a documentary about their life-threatening condition. My advice to you is let him wallow in his misery all by himself."

"But he looks like he might have a fever," Maryanne whispered.

"And he isn't old enough to take an aspirin all on his own?" The older woman glanced behind her. "His order's up. You want me to take it to him?"

"No…"

"Don't worry, if he gets smart with me I'll just whack

him upside the head. Someone needs to put that man in his place."

Maryanne picked up the large bowl of chili. "I'll do it."

"Yes," Barbara said, grinning broadly. "I have a feeling you will."

Maryanne got home several hours later. Her feet hurt and her back ached, but she felt a pleasant glow of satisfaction. After three days of waitressing, she was beginning to get the knack of keeping orders straight and remembering everything she needed to do. It wasn't the job of her dreams, but she was making a living wage, certainly better money than she'd been getting from Rent-A-Maid. Not only that, the tips were good. Maryanne didn't dare imagine what her family would say if they found out, though. She suffered a stab of remorse every time she thought about the way she was deceiving them. In fact, it was simpler not to think about it at all.

After his initial reaction, Nolan hadn't so much as mentioned her working at Mom's Place. He clearly wasn't thrilled, but that didn't surprise her. Little, if anything, she'd done from the moment she'd met him had gained his approval.

Maryanne had grown accustomed to falling asleep most nights to the sound of Nolan's typing. She found herself listening for it when she climbed into bed. But she didn't hear it that night or the two nights that followed.

"How's Nolan?" Barbara asked her on Friday afternoon.

"I don't know." Maryanne hadn't seen him in days, but then, she rarely did.

"He must have got a really bad bug."

Maryanne hated the way her heart lurched. She'd tried not to think about him. Not that she'd been successful...

"His column hasn't been in the paper all week. The *Sun*'s been running some of his old ones—Nolan's Classics. Did you read the one last night?" Barbara asked, laughing. "It was about how old-fashioned friendly service has disappeared from restaurants today." She grinned. "He said there were a few exceptions, and you know who he was talking about."

As a matter of fact, Maryanne had read the piece and been highly amused—and flattered, even though the column had been written long before she'd even come to Seattle, let alone worked at Mom's Place. As always she'd been impressed with Nolan's dry wit. They often disagreed—Nolan was too much of a pessimist to suit her—but she couldn't help admiring his skill with words.

Since the afternoon he'd found her at Mom's, Nolan hadn't eaten there again. Maryanne didn't consider that so strange. He went to great lengths to ensure that they didn't run into each other. She did feel mildly guilty that he'd decided to stay away from his favorite diner, but it *was* his choice, after all.

During the rest of her shift, Maryanne had to struggle to keep Nolan out of her mind. His apartment had been unusually quiet for the past few days, but she hadn't been concerned about it. Now she was.

"Do you think he's all right?" she asked Barbara some time later.

"He's a big boy," the older woman was quick to remind her. "He can take care of himself."

Maryanne wasn't so sure. After work, she hurried home, convinced she'd find Nolan hovering near death, too ill to call for help. She didn't even stop at her own apartment, but went directly to his.

She knocked politely, anticipating all kinds of disasters when there was no response.

"Nolan?" She pounded on his door and yelled his name, battling down a rising sense of panic. She envisioned him lying on his bed, suffering—or worse. "Nolan, please answer the door," she pleaded, wondering if there was someone in the building with a passkey.

She'd waited hours, it seemed, before he yanked open the door.

"Are you all right?" she demanded, so relieved to see him she could hardly keep from hurling herself into his arms. Relieved, that was, until she got a good look at him.

"I was feeling just great," he told her gruffly, "until I had to get out of bed to answer the stupid door. Which, incidentally, woke me up."

Maryanne pressed her fingers over her mouth to hide her hysterical laughter. If Nolan felt anywhere near as bad as he looked, then she should seriously consider phoning for an ambulance. He wore grey sweatpants and a faded plaid robe, one she would guess had been moth fodder for years. His choice of clothes was the least of her concerns, however. He resembled someone who'd just surfaced from a four-day drunk. His eyes were red and his face ashen. He scowled at her and it was clear the moment he spoke that his disposition was as cheery as his appearance.

"I take it there's a reason for this uninvited visit?" he growled, then sneezed fiercely.

"Yes…" Maryanne hedged, not knowing exactly what to do now. "I just wanted to make sure you're all right."

"Okay, you've seen me. I'm going to live, so you can leave in good conscience." He would have closed the door, but Maryanne stepped forward and boldly forced her way into his apartment.

In the weeks they'd lived next door to each other, she'd never seen his home. The muted earth colors, the rich leather furniture and polished wood floors appealed to her immediately. Despite her worry about his condition, she smiled; this room reminded her of Nolan, with papers and books littering every available space. His apartment seemed at least twice the size of hers. He'd once mentioned that it was larger, but after becoming accustomed to her own small rooms, she found the spaciousness of his a pleasant shock.

"In case you haven't noticed, I'm in no mood for company," he informed her in a surly voice.

"Have you been to a doctor?"

"No."

"Do you need anything?"

"Peace and quiet," he muttered.

"You could have bronchitis or pneumonia or something."

"I'm perfectly fine. At least, I was until you arrived." He walked across the carpet—a dark green-and-gold Persian, Maryanne noted automatically—and slumped onto an overstuffed sofa piled with blankets and pillows. The television was on, its volume turned very low.

"Then why haven't you been at work?"

"I'm on vacation."

"Personally, I would've chosen a tropical island over

a sofa in my own apartment." She advanced purpose-
fully into his kitchen and stopped short when she caught
sight of the dirty dishes stacked a foot high in the stainless-steel sink. She was amazed he could cram so much
into such a tight space.

"This place is a mess!" she declared, hands on her
hips.

"Go ahead and call the health department if you're
so concerned."

"I probably should." Instead, she walked straight to
the sink, rolled up her sleeves and started stacking the
dishes on the counter.

"What are you doing now?" Nolan shouted from the
living room.

"Cleaning up."

He muttered something she couldn't hear, which was
probably for the best.

"Go lie down, Nolan," she instructed. "When I'm
done here, I'll heat you some soup. You've got to get
your strength back in order to suffer properly."

At first he let that comment pass. Then, as if she was
taxing him to the limit of his endurance, he called out,
"The way you care is truly touching."

"I was hoping you'd notice." For someone who'd been
outraged at the sight of her dishpan hands a week earlier,
he seemed oddly unconcerned that she was washing his
dirty dishes. Not that Maryanne minded. It made her
feel good to be doing something for him.

She soon found herself humming as she rinsed the
dishes and set them in his dishwasher.

Fifteen minutes passed without their exchanging a
word. When Maryanne had finished, she looked in the
living room and wasn't surprised to find him sound

asleep on the sofa. A curious feeling tugged at her heart as she gazed down at him. He lay on his back with his left hand flung across his forehead. His features were relaxed, but there was nothing remotely angelic about him. Not about the way his thick dark lashes brushed the arch of his cheek—or about the slow hoarse breaths that whispered through his half-open mouth.

Maryanne felt a strong urge to brush the hair from his forehead, to touch him, but she resisted. She was afraid he'd wake up. And she was even more afraid she wouldn't want to stop touching him.

Moving about the living room, she turned off the television, picked up things here and there and straightened a few piles of magazines. She should leave now; she knew that. Nolan wouldn't welcome her staying. She eyed the door regretfully, looking for an excuse to linger. She closed her eyes and listened to the sound of Nolan's raspy breathing.

More by chance than design, Maryanne found herself standing next to his typewriter. Feeling brave, and more than a little foolish, she looked down at the stack of paper resting beside it. Glancing over her shoulder to make sure he was still asleep, Maryanne carefully turned over the top page and quickly read the last couple of paragraphs on page 212. The story wasn't finished, but she could tell he'd stopped during a cliff-hanger scene.

Nolan had been so secretive about his project that she dared not invade his privacy any more than she already had. She turned the single sheet back over, taking care to place it exactly as she'd found it.

Once again, she reminded herself that she should go back to her own apartment, but she felt strangely reluctant to end these moments with Nolan. Even a sleeping Nolan who would certainly be cranky when he woke up.

Seeking some way to occupy herself, she moved down the hall and into the bathroom, picking up several soiled towels on the way. His bed was unmade. She would've been surprised to find it in any other condition. The sheets and blankets were sagging onto the floor, and two or three sets of clothing were scattered all about.

Without questioning the wisdom of her actions, she bundled up the dirty laundry to take to the coin-operated machine in the basement. She loaded it into a large garbage bag, then set about vigorously cleaning the apartment. Scrubbing, scouring and sweeping were skills she'd perfected in her Rent-A-Maid days. If nothing else, she'd had lots of practice cleaning up after messy bachelors.

Studying the contents of his refrigerator, more than an hour later, proved to be a humorous adventure. She found an unopened bottle of wine, a carton of broken eggshells and one limp strand of celery. Concocting anything edible from that would be impossible, so she searched the apartment until she found his keys. Then, with his garbage bag full of laundry in her arms, she let herself out the door, closing it softly.

She returned a half hour later, clutching two bags of groceries bought with her tip money. Then she went down to put his laundry in the dryer. To her relief, Nolan was still asleep. She smiled down at him indulgently before she began preparing his dinner. After another forty-five minutes she retrieved his clean clothes and put them neatly away.

She was in the kitchen peeling potatoes when she

heard Nolan get up. She continued her task, knowing he'd discover she was there soon enough. He stopped cold when he did.

"What are you doing here?"

"Making your dinner."

"I'm not hungry," he snapped with no evidence of appreciation for her efforts.

His eyes widened as he glanced around. "What happened here? Oh, you've cleaned the place up."

"I didn't think you'd notice," she answered sweetly, popping a small piece of raw potato in her mouth. "I'll get soup to the boiling stage before I leave you to your... peace of mind. It should only take another ten or fifteen minutes. Can you endure me that much longer?"

He made another of his typical grumbling replies before disappearing. No more than two seconds had passed before he let out a bellow loud enough to shake the roof tiles.

"What did you do to my bed?" he demanded as he stormed into the kitchen.

"I made it."

"What else have you been up to? Damn it, a man isn't safe in his own home with you around."

"Don't look so put out, Nolan. All I did was straighten up the place a bit. It was a mess."

"I happen to like messes. I thrive in messes. The last thing I want or need is some neat-freak invading my home, organizing my life."

"Don't exaggerate," Maryanne said serenely, as she added a pile of diced carrots to the simmering broth. "All I did was pick up a few things here and there and run a load of laundry."

"You did my laundry, too?" he exploded, jerking

both hands through his hair. Heaven only knew, she thought, what would happen if he learned she'd read a single word of his precious manuscript.

"Everything's been folded and put away, so you needn't worry."

Nolan abruptly left the kitchen, only to return a couple of moments later. He circled the table slowly and precisely, then took several deep breaths.

"Listen, Annie," he began carefully, "it isn't that I don't appreciate what you've done, but I don't need a nurse. Or a housekeeper."

She looked up, meeting his eyes, her own large and guileless. "I quite agree," she answered.

"You do?" Some of the stiffness left his shoulders. "Then you aren't going to take offence?"

"No, why should I?"

"No reason," he answered, eyeing her suspiciously.

"I was thinking that what you really need," she said, smiling at him gently, "is a wife."

Seven

"A wife," Nolan echoed. His dark eyes widened in undisguised horror. It was as if Maryanne had suggested he climb to the roof of the apartment building and leap off.

"Don't get so excited. I wasn't volunteering for the position."

With his index finger pointing at her like the barrel of a shotgun, Nolan walked around the kitchen table again, his journey made in shuffling impatient steps. He circled the table twice before he spoke.

"You cleaned my home, washed my clothes and now you're cooking my dinner." Each word came at her like an accusation.

"Yes?"

"You can't possibly look at me with those baby-blues of yours and expect me to believe—"

"Believe what?"

"That you're not applying for the job. From the moment we met, you've been doing all these…these sweet *girlie* things to entice me."

"Sweet girlie things?" Maryanne repeated, struggling to contain her amusement. "I don't think I understand."

"I don't expect you to admit it."

"I haven't the foggiest idea what you're talking about."

"You know," he accused her with an angry shrug.

"Obviously I don't. What could I possibly have done to make you think I'm trying to *entice* you?"

"Sweet girlie things," he said again, but without the same conviction. He chewed on his bottom lip for a moment while he mulled the matter over. "All right, I'll give you an example—that perfume you're always wearing."

"Windchime? It's a light fragrance."

"I don't know the name of it. But it hangs around for an hour or so after you've left the room. You know that, and yet you wear it every time we're together."

"I've worn Windchime for years."

"That's not all," he continued quickly. "It's the way I catch you looking at me sometimes."

"*Looking* at you?" She folded her arms at her waist and rolled her eyes toward the ceiling.

"Yes," he said, sounding even more peevish. He pressed his hand to his hip, cocked his chin at a regal angle and fluttered his eyelashes like fans.

Despite her effort to hold in her amusement, Maryanne laughed. "I can only assume that you're joking."

Nolan dropped his hand from his hip. "I'm not. You get this innocent look and your lips pout just so… Why, a man—any man—couldn't keep from wanting to kiss you."

"That's preposterous." But Maryanne instinctively pinched her lips together and closed her eyes.

Nolan's arm shot out. "That's another thing."

"What now?"

"The way you get this helpless flustered look and it's all a simpleminded male can do not to rush in and offer to take care of whatever's bothering you."

"By this time you should know I'm perfectly capable of taking care of myself," Maryanne felt obliged to remind him.

"You're a lamb among wolves," Nolan said. "I don't know how long you intend to play out this silly charade, but personally I think you've overdone it. This isn't your world, and the sooner you go back where you belong, the better."

"Better for whom?"

"Me!" he cried vehemently. "And for you," he added with less fervor, as though it was an afterthought. He coughed a couple of times and reached for a package of cough drops in the pocket of his plaid robe. Shaking one out, he popped it in his mouth with barely a pause.

"I don't think it's doing you any good to get so excited," Maryanne said with unruffled patience. "I was merely making an observation and it still stands. I believe you need a wife."

"Go observe someone else's life," he suggested, sucking madly on the cough drop.

"Aha!" she cried, waving her index finger at him. "How does it feel to have someone interfering in *your* life?"

Nolan frowned and Maryanne turned back to the stove. She lifted the lid from the soup to stir it briskly. Then she lowered the burner. When she was through, she saw with a glimmer of fun that Nolan was standing as far away from her as humanly possible, while still remaining in the same room.

"That's something else!" he cried. "You give the impression that you're in total agreement with whatever I'm saying and then you go about doing exactly as you damn well please. I've never met a more frustrating woman in my entire life."

"That's not true," Maryanne argued. "I quit my job at Rent-A-Maid because you insisted." It had worked out for the best, since she had more time for her writing now, but this wasn't the moment to mention that.

"Oh, right, bring *that* up. It's the only thing you've ever done that I wanted. I practically had to get down on my knees and beg you to leave that crazy job before you injured yourself."

"You didn't!"

"Trust me, it was a humbling experience and not one I intend to repeat. I've known you how long? A month?" He paused to gaze at the ceiling. "It seems like an eternity."

"You're trying to make me feel guilty. It isn't going to work."

"Why should you feel anything of the sort? Just because living next door to you is enough to drive a man to drink."

"You're the one who found me this place. If you don't like living next door to me, then I'm not the one to blame!"

"Don't remind me," he muttered.

The comment about Nolan finding himself a wife had been made in jest, but he'd certainly taken it seriously. In fact, he seemed to have strong feelings about the entire issue. Realizing her welcome had worn extremely thin, Maryanne headed for his apartment door. "Everything's under control here."

"Does that mean you're leaving?"

She hated the enthusiastic lift in his voice, as if he couldn't wait to be rid of her. Although he wasn't admitting it, she'd done him a good turn. Fair exchange, she supposed; Nolan had been generous enough to her over the past month.

"Yes, I'm leaving."

"Good." He didn't bother to disguise his delight.

"But I still think you'd do well to consider what I said." Maryanne had the irresistible urge to heap coals on the fires of his indignation. "A wife could be a great help to you."

Nolan frowned heavily, drawing his eyebrows into a deep V. "I think the modern woman would find your suggestion downright insulting."

"What? That you marry?"

"Exactly. Haven't you heard? A woman's place isn't in the home anymore. It's out there in the world, forging a career for herself. Living a fuller life, and all that. It's not doing the mundane tasks you're talking about."

"I wasn't suggesting you marry for the convenience of gaining a live-in housekeeper."

His brown eyes narrowed. "Then what *were* you saying?"

"That you're a capable talented man," she explained. She glanced surreptitiously at his manuscript, still tidily stacked by the typewriter. "But unfortunately, that doesn't mean a whole lot if you don't have someone close—a friend, a companion, a...wife—to share it with."

"Don't you worry about me, Little Miss Muffet. I've

lived my own life from the time I was thirteen. You may think I need someone, but let me assure you, I don't."

"You're probably right," she said reluctantly. She opened his door, then hesitated. "You'll call if you want anything?"

"No."

She released a short sigh of frustration. "That's what I thought. The soup should be done in about thirty minutes."

He nodded, then, looking a bit chagrined, added, "I suppose I should thank you."

"I suppose you should, too, but it isn't necessary."

"What about the money you spent on groceries? You can't afford acts of charity, you know. Wait a minute and I'll—"

"Forget it," she snapped. "I can spend my money on whatever I damn well please. I'm my own person, remember? You can just owe me. Buy me dinner sometime." She left before he could say anything else.

Maryanne's own apartment felt bleak and lonely after Nolan's. The first thing she did was walk around turning on all the lights. No sooner had she finished when there was a loud knock at her door. She opened it to find Nolan standing there in his disreputable motheaten robe, glaring.

"Yes?" she inquired sweetly.

"You read my manuscript, didn't you?" he boomed in a voice that echoed like thunder off the apartment walls.

"I most certainly did not," she denied vehemently. She straightened her back as if to suggest she found the very question insulting.

Without waiting for an invitation, Nolan stalked

into her living room, then whirled around to face her. "Admit it!"

Making each word as clear and distinct as possible, Maryanne said, "I did not read your precious manuscript. How could I possibly have cleaned up, done the laundry, prepared a big kettle of homemade soup, and still had time to read 212 pages of manuscript?"

"How did you know it was 212 pages?" Sparks of reproach shot from his eyes.

"Ah—" she swallowed uncomfortably "—it was a guess, and from the looks of it, a good one."

"It wasn't any guess."

He marched toward her and for every step he took, she retreated two. "All right," she admitted guiltily, "I did look at it, but I swear I didn't read more than a few lines. I was straightening up the living room and… it was there, so I turned over the last page and read a couple of paragraphs."

"Aha! Finally, the truth!" Nolan pointed directly at her. "You did read it!"

"Just a few lines," she repeated in a tiny voice, feeling completely wretched.

"And?" His eyes softened.

"And what?"

"What did you think?" He looked at her expectantly, then frowned. "Never mind, I shouldn't have asked."

Rubbing her palms together, Maryanne took one step forward. "Nolan, it was wonderful. Witty and terribly suspenseful and… I would have given anything to read more. But I knew I didn't dare because, well, because I was invading your privacy…which I didn't want to do, but I did and I really didn't want…that."

"It is good, isn't it?" he asked almost smugly, then his expression sobered as quickly as it had before.

She grinned, nodding enthusiastically. "Tell me about it."

He seemed undecided, then launched excitedly into his idea. "It's about a Seattle newspaperman, Leo, who stumbles on a murder case. Actually, I'm developing a series with him as the main character. This one's not quite finished yet—as I'm sure you know."

"Is there a woman in Leo's life?"

"You're kidding, aren't you?"

Maryanne wasn't. The few paragraphs she'd read had mentioned a Maddie who was apparently in danger. Leo had been frantic to save her.

"You had no business going anywhere near that manuscript," Nolan reminded her.

"I know, but the temptation was so strong. I shouldn't have peeked, I realize that, but I couldn't help myself. Nolan, I'm not lying when I say how good the writing was. Do you have a publisher in mind? Because if you don't, I have several New York editor friends I could recommend and I know—"

"I'm not using you or any influence you may have in New York. I don't want anything to do with your father's publishing company. Understand?"

"Of course, but you're overreacting." He seemed to be doing a lot of that lately. "My father wouldn't stay in business long if he ordered the editors to purchase my friends' manuscripts, would he? Believe me, it would all be on the up and up, and if you've got an idea for a series using Leo—"

"I said no."

"But—"

"I mean it, Annie. This is my book and I'll submit it myself without any help from you."

"If that's what you want," she concurred meekly.

"That's the way it's going to be." The stern unyielding look slipped back into place. "Now if you don't mind, I'll quietly go back to my messy little world, sans wife and countless interruptions from a certain neighbor."

"I'll try not to bother you again," Maryanne said sarcastically, since he was the one who'd invaded *her* home this time.

"It would be appreciated," he said, apparently ignoring her tone.

"Your apartment is yours and mine is mine, and I'll uphold your privacy with the utmost respect," she continued, her voice still faintly mocking. She buried her hands in her pockets and her fingers closed around something cold and metallic.

"Good." Nolan was nodding. "Privacy, that's what we need."

"Um, Nolan…" She paused. "This is somewhat embarrassing, but it seems I have…" She hesitated again, then resolutely squared her shoulders. "I suppose you'd appreciate it if I returned your keys, right?"

"My keys?" Nolan exploded.

"I just found them. They were in my pocket. You see, all you had in your refrigerator was one limp strand of celery and I couldn't very well make soup out of that, so I had to go to the store and I didn't want to leave your door unlocked and—"

"You have my keys?"

"Yes."

He held out his palm, casting his eyes toward the

ceiling. Feeling like a pickpocket caught in the act, Maryanne dropped the keys into his hand and stepped quickly back, almost afraid he was going to grab her by the shoulders and shake her. Which, of course, was ludicrous.

Nolan left immediately and Maryanne followed him to the door, staring out into the hallway as he walked back to his own apartment.

The next Thursday, Maryanne was hurrying to get ready for work when the phone rang. She frowned and stared at it, wondering if she dared take the time to answer. It might be Nolan, but every instinct she possessed told her otherwise. They hadn't spoken all week. Every afternoon, like clockwork, he'd arrived at Mom's Diner. More often than not, he ordered chili. Maryanne waited on him most of the time, but she might have been a robot for all the attention he paid her. His complete lack of interest dented her pride; still, his attitude shouldn't have come as any surprise.

"Hello," she said hesitantly, picking up the receiver.

"Maryanne," her mother responded, her voice rising with pleasure. "I can't believe I finally got hold of you. I've been trying for the past three days."

Maryanne immediately felt swamped by guilt. "You didn't leave a message on my machine."

"You know how I hate those things."

Maryanne did know that. She also knew she should have phoned her parents herself, but she wasn't sure how long she could continue with this farce. "Is everything all right?"

"Yes, of course. Your father's working too hard, but that's nothing new. The boys are busy with soccer and growing like weeds." Her mother's voice fell slightly. "How's the job?"

"The job?"

"Your special assignment."

"Oh, that." Maryanne had rarely been able to fool her mother, and she could only wonder how well she was succeeding now. "It's going…well. I'm learning so much."

"I think you'll make a terrific investigative reporter, sweetie, and the secrecy behind this assignment makes it all the more intriguing. When are your father and I going to learn exactly what you've been doing? I wish we'd never promised not to check up on your progress at the paper. We're both so curious."

"I'll be finished with it soon." Maryanne glanced at her watch and was about to close the conversation when her mother asked, "How's Nolan?"

"Nolan?" Maryanne's heart zoomed straight into her throat. She hadn't remembered mentioning him, and just hearing his name sent a feverish heat through her body.

"You seemed quite enthralled with him the last time we spoke, remember?"

"I was?"

"Yes, sweetie, you were. You claimed he was very talented, and although you were tight-lipped about it I got the impression you were strongly attracted to this young man."

"Nolan's a friend. But we argue more than anything."

Her mother chuckled. "Good."

"How could that possibly be good?"

"It means you're comfortable enough with each other to be yourselves, and that's a positive sign. Why, your father and I bickered like old fishwives when we first met. I swear there wasn't a single issue we could agree on." She sighed softly. "Then one day we looked at each other, and I knew then and there I was going to love this man for the rest of my life. And I have."

"Mom, it isn't like that with Nolan and me. I... I don't even think he likes me."

"Nolan doesn't like you?" her mother repeated. "Why, sweetie, that would be impossible."

Maryanne started to laugh then, because her mother was so obviously biased, yet sounded completely objective and matter-of-fact. It felt good to laugh again, good to find something amusing. She hadn't realized how melancholy she'd become since her last encounter with Nolan. He was still making such an effort to keep her at arm's length for fear... She didn't know exactly *what* he feared. Perhaps he was falling in love with her, but she'd noticed precious little evidence pointing to that conclusion. If anything, Nolan considered her an irritant in his life.

Maryanne spoke to her mother for a few more minutes, then rushed out the door, hoping she wouldn't be late for her shift at Mom's Place. Some investigative reporter she was!

At the diner, she slipped the apron around her waist and hurried out to help with the luncheon crowd. Waiting tables, she was learning quite a lot about character types. This could be helpful for a writer, she figured. Some of her customers were pretty eccentric. She observed them carefully, wondering if Nolan did the same thing. But she wasn't going to think about Nolan....

Halfway through her shift, she began to feel light-headed and sick to her stomach.

"Are you feeling all right?" Barbara asked as she slipped past, carrying an order.

"I—I don't know."

"When was the last time you ate?"

"This morning. No," she corrected, "last night. I didn't have much of an appetite this morning."

"That's what I thought." Barbara set the hamburger and fries on the counter in front of her customer and walked back to Maryanne. "Now that I've got a good look at you, you do seem a bit peaked."

"I'm all right."

Hands on her hips, Barbara continued to study Maryanne as if memorizing every feature. "Are you sure?"

"I'm fine." She had the beginnings of a headache, but nothing she could really complain about. It probably hadn't been a good idea to skip breakfast and lunch, but she'd make up for it when she took her dinner break.

"I'm not sure I believe you," Barbara muttered, dragging out a well-used phone book. She flipped through the pages until she apparently found the number she wanted, then reached for the phone.

"Who are you calling?"

She held the receiver against her shoulder. "Nolan Adams, who else? Seems to me it's his turn to play nursemaid."

"Barbara, no!" She might not be feeling a hundred per cent, but she wasn't all that sick, either. And the last person she wanted running to her rescue was Nolan. He'd only use it against her, as proof that she should go back to the cosy comfortable world of her parents. She'd almost proved she could live entirely on her own, without relying on interest from her trust fund.

"Nolan's not at the office," Barbara said a moment

later, replacing the receiver. "I'll talk to him when he comes in."

"No, you won't! Barbara, I swear to you I'll personally give your phone number to every trucker who comes into this place if you so much as say a single word to Nolan."

"Honey," the other waitress said, raising her eyebrows, "you'd be doing me a favor!"

Grumbling, Maryanne returned to her customers.

By closing time, however, she was feeling slightly worse. Not exactly sick, but not exactly herself, either. Barbara was watching Maryanne closely, regularly feeling her cheeks and forehead and muttering about her temperature. If there was one thing to be grateful for, it was the fact that Nolan hadn't shown up. Barbara insisted Maryanne leave a few minutes early and shooed her out the door. Had she been feeling better, Maryanne would have argued.

By the time she arrived back at her apartment, she knew beyond a doubt that she was coming down with some kind of virus. Part of her would've liked to blame Nolan, but she was the one who'd let herself into his apartment. She was the one who'd lingered there, straightening up the place and staying far longer than necessary.

After a long hot shower, she put on her flannel pyjamas and unfolded her bed, climbing quickly beneath the covers. She'd turned the television on for company and prepared herself a mug of soup. As she took her first sip, she heard someone knock at her door.

"Who is it?" she called out.

"Nolan."

"I'm in bed," she shouted.

"You've seen me in my robe. It's only fair I see you in yours," he yelled back.

Maryanne tossed aside her covers and sat up. "Go away."

A sharp pounding noise came from the floor, followed by an equally loud roar that proclaimed it time for "Jeopardy." Apparently Maryanne's shouting match with Nolan was disrupting Mrs. McBride's favorite television show.

"Sorry." Maryanne cupped her hands over her mouth and yelled at the hardwood floor.

"Are you going to let me in, or do I have to get the passkey?" Nolan demanded.

Groaning, Maryanne shuffled across the floor in her giant fuzzy slippers and turned the lock. "Yes?" she asked with exaggerated patience.

For the longest moment, Nolan said nothing. He shoved his hands deep into the pockets of his beige raincoat. "How are you?"

Maryanne glared at him with all the indignation she could muster, which at the moment was considerable. "Do you mean to say you practically pounded down my door to ask me that?"

He didn't bother to answer, but walked into her apartment as though he had every right to do so. "Barbara phoned me."

"Oh, brother! And what exactly did she say?" She continued to hold open the door, hoping he'd get the hint and leave.

"That you caught my bug." His voice was rough with ill-disguised worry.

"Wrong. I felt a bit under the weather earlier, but I'm fine now." The last thing she wanted Nolan motivated by was guilt. He'd succeeded in keeping his distance up to now; if he decided to see her, she wanted to be sure his visit wasn't prompted by an overactive sense of responsibility.

"You look…"

"Yes?" she prompted.

His gaze skimmed her, from slightly damp hair to large fuzzy feet. "Fine," he answered softly.

"As you can see I'm really not sick, so you needn't concern yourself."

Her words were followed by a lengthy silence. Nolan turned as though to leave. Maryanne should have felt relieved to see him go; instead, she experienced the strangest sensation of loss. She longed to reach out a hand, ask him to stay, but she didn't have the courage.

She brushed the hair from her face and smiled, even though it was difficult to put on a carefree facade.

"I'll stop by in the morning and see how you're doing," Nolan said, hovering by the threshold.

"That won't be necessary."

He frowned. "When did you get so prickly?"

"When did you get so caring?" The words nearly caught in her throat and escaped on a whisper.

"I *do* care about you," he said.

"Oh, sure, the same way you'd care about an annoying younger sister. Believe me, Nolan, your message came through loud and clear. I'm not your type. Fine, I can accept that, because you're not my type, either." She didn't really think she had a type, but it sounded philosophical and went a long way toward salving her badly bruised ego. Nolan couldn't have made his views toward her any plainer had he rented a billboard. He'd even said he'd taken one look at her and immediately thought, "Here comes trouble."

She'd never been more attracted to a man in her life, and here she was, standing in front of him lying through her teeth rather than admit how she truly felt.

"So I'm not your type, either?" he asked, almost in a whisper.

Maryanne's heartbeat quickened. He studied her as intently as she studied him. He gazed at her mouth, then slipped his hand behind her neck and slowly, so very slowly, lowered his lips to hers.

He paused, their mouths a scant inch apart. He seemed to be waiting for her to pull away, withdraw from him. Everything inside her told her to do exactly that. He was only trying to humiliate her, wasn't he? Trying to prove how powerful her attraction to him was, how easily he could bend her will to his own.

And she was letting him.

Her heart was beating so furiously her body seemed to rock with the sheer force of it. Every throb seemed to drive her directly into his arms, right where she longed to be. She placed her palms against his chest and sighed as his mouth met hers. The touch of his lips felt warm and soft. And right.

His hand cradled her neck while his lips continued to move over hers in the gentlest explorations, as though he feared she was too delicate to kiss the way he wanted.

Gradually his hands slipped to her shoulders. He drew a ragged breath, then put his head back as he stared up at the ceiling. He exhaled slowly, deliberately.

It took all the restraint Maryanne possessed not to ask him why he was stopping. She wanted these incredible sensations to continue. She longed to explore the feelings his kiss produced and the complex responses she experienced deep within her body. Her pulse hammered erratically as she tried to control her breathing.

"Okay, now we've got that settled, I'll leave." He backed away from her.

"Got what settled?" she asked swiftly, then realized she was only making a bigger fool of herself. Naturally he was talking about the reason for this impromptu visit, which had been her health. Hadn't it? "Oh, I see."

"I don't think you do," Nolan said enigmatically. He turned and walked away.

Eight

"Whose turn next?" Maryanne asked. She and her two friends were sitting in the middle of her living room floor, having a "pity party."

"I will," Carol Riverside volunteered eagerly. She ceremonially plucked a tissue from the box that rested in the center of their small circle, next to the lit candle. Their second large bottle of cheap wine was nearly empty, and the three of them were feeling no pain.

"For years I've wanted to write a newspaper column of my own," Carol said, squaring her shoulders and hauling in a huge breath. "But it's not what I thought it'd be like. I ran out of ideas for things to write about after the first week."

"Ah," Maryanne sighed sympathetically.

"Ah," Barbara echoed.

"That's not all," Carol said sadly. "I never knew the world was so full of critics. No one seems to agree with me. I—I didn't know Seattle had so many cantankerous readers. I try, but it's impossible to make everyone happy. What happens is that some of the people like me some of the time and all the rest hate everything

I write." She glanced up. "Except the two of you, of course."

Maryanne nodded her head so hard she nearly toppled over. She spread her hands out at either side in an effort to maintain her balance. The wine made her yawn loudly.

Apparently in real distress, Carol dabbed at her eyes. "Being a columnist is hard work and nothing like I'd always dreamed." The edges of her mouth turned downward. "I don't even like writing anymore," she sobbed.

"Isn't that a pity!" Maryanne cried, ritually tossing her tissue into the center of the circle. Barbara followed suit, and then they both patted Carol gently on the back.

Carol brightened once she'd finished. "I don't know what I'd do without the two of you. You and Betty are my very best friends in the whole world," she announced.

"Barbara," Maryanne corrected. "Your very best friend's name is Barbara."

The three of them looked at each other and burst into gales of laughter. Maryanne hushed them by waving her hands. "Stop! We can't allow ourselves to become giddy. A pity party doesn't work if all we do is laugh. We've got to remember this is sad and serious business."

"Sad and serious," Barbara agreed, sobering. She grabbed a fresh tissue and clutched it in her hand, waiting for the others to share their sorrows and give her a reason to cry.

"Whose idea was the wine?" Maryanne wanted to know, taking a quick sip.

Carol blushed. "I thought it would be less fattening than the chocolate ice-cream bars you planned to serve."

"Hey," Barbara said, narrowing her eyes at Maryanne. "You haven't said anything about your problem."

Maryanne suddenly found it necessary to remove lint from her jeans. Sharing what disturbed her most was a little more complicated than being disappointed in her job or complaining about fingernails that cracked all too easily, as Barbara had done. She hadn't sold a single article since she'd quit the paper, or even received a positive response to one of her queries. But worst of all she was falling in love with Nolan. He felt something for her, too—she knew that—but he was fighting her every step of the way. Fighting her and fighting himself.

He was attracted to her, he couldn't deny it, although he'd tried to, more than once. When they were alone together, the tension seemed to throb between them.

He was battling the attraction so hard he'd gone as far as arranging a date for her with another man. Since the evening they'd met, Nolan had insulted her, harangued her and lectured her. He'd made it plain that he didn't want her around. And yet there were times he sought out her company. He argued with her at every opportunity, took it upon himself to be her guardian, and yet...

"Maryanne?" Carol said, studying her with concern. "What's wrong?"

"Nolan Adams," she whispered. Lifting her wineglass, she took a small swallow, hoping that would give her the courage to continue.

"I should have guessed," Carol muttered, frowning. "From the moment you moved in here, next door to that madman, I just knew he'd cause you nothing but problems."

Her friend's opinion of Nolan had never been high and Maryanne had to bite back the urge to defend him.

"Tell us everything," Barbara said, drawing up her knees and leaning against the sofa.

"There isn't much to tell."

"He's the one who got you into this craziness in the first place, remember?" Carol pointed out righteously—as if Maryanne needed reminding. Carol then turned to Barbara and began to explain to the older woman how it had all started. "Nolan wrote a derogatory piece about Maryanne in his column a while back, implying she was a spoiled debutante, and she took it to heart and decided to prove him wrong."

"He didn't mean it. In fact, he's regretted every word of that article." This time Maryanne did feel obliged to defend him. As far as she was concerned, all of that was old business, already resolved. It was the unfinished business, the things happening between them now, that bothered her the most.

The denial. The refusal on both their parts to accept the feelings they shared. Only a few days earlier, Maryanne had tried to convince Nolan he wasn't her type, that nothing about them was compatible. He'd been only too eager to agree.

But they'd been drawn together, virtually against their wills, by an attraction so overwhelming, so inevitable, they were powerless against it. Their sensual and emotional awareness of each other seemed more intense every time they met. This feeling couldn't be anything except love.

"You're among friends, so tell us everything," Barbara pressed, handing Maryanne the entire box of tissues. "Remember, I've known Nolan for years, so nothing you say is going to shock me."

"For one thing, he's impossible," Maryanne whispered, finding it difficult to express her thoughts.

"He deserves to be hanged from the closest tree," Carol said scornfully.

"And at the same time he's wonderful," Maryanne concluded, ignoring Carol's comment.

"You're not…" Carol paused, her face tightening as if she was having trouble forming the words. "You don't mean to suggest you're falling in—" she swallowed "—*love* with him, are you?"

"I don't know." Maryanne crumpled the soggy tissue. "But I think I might be."

"Oh, no," Carol cried, covering her mouth with both hands, "you've got to do something quick. A man like Nolan Adams eats little girls like you for breakfast. He's cynical and sarcastic and—"

"Talented and generous," Maryanne finished for her.

"You're not thinking clearly. It probably has something to do with that fever you had. You've got to remember the facts. Nolan insulted you in print, seriously insulted you, and then tried to make up for it. You're mistaking that small attack of conscience for something more—which could be dangerous." Awkwardly, Carol rose to her feet and started pacing.

"He's probably one of the most talented writers I've ever read," Maryanne continued, undaunted by her friend's concerns. "Every time I read his work, I can't help being awed."

"All right," Carol said, "I'll concede he does possess a certain amount of creative talent, but that doesn't change who or what he is. Nolan Adams is a bad-tempered egotistical self-centered…grouch."

"I hate to say this," Barbara said softly, shaking her

head, "but Carol's right. Nolan's been eating at Mom's Place for as long as I've worked there, and that's three years. I feel I know him better than you do, and he's everything Carol says. But," she said thoughtfully, "underneath it all, there's more to him. Oh, he'd like everyone to believe he's this macho guy. He plays that role to the hilt, but after you've been around him awhile, you can tell it's all a game to him."

"I told you he's wonderful!" Maryanne exclaimed.

"The man's a constant," Carol insisted. "Constantly in a bad mood, constantly making trouble, constantly getting involved in matters that are none of his business. Maryanne here is the perfect example. He should never have written that column about her." Carol plopped back down and jerked half a dozen tissues from the box in quick succession. She handed them to Maryanne. "You've got blinders on where he's concerned. Take it from me, a woman can't allow herself to become emotionally involved with a man she plans to change."

"I don't want to change Nolan."

"You don't?" Carol echoed, her voice low and disbelieving. "You mean to say you like him as he is?"

"You just don't know him the way I do," Maryanne said. "Nolan's truly generous. Did either of you know he's become sort of a father figure to the teenagers in this neighborhood? He's their friend in the very best sense. He keeps tabs on them and makes sure no one gets involved in drugs or is lured into gang activities. The kids around here idolize him."

"Nolan Adams does that?" Carol sounded skeptical. She arched her brows as though she couldn't completely trust Maryanne's observations.

"When Barbara told him I was coming down with a virus, he came over to check on me and—"

"As well he should!" Barbara declared. "He was the one who gave you that germ in the first place."

"I'm not entirely sure I caught it from him."

Carol and Barbara exchanged a look. Slowly each shook her head, and then all three shared a warm smile.

"I think we might be too late," Barbara said theatrically, speaking from the side of her mouth.

"She's showing all the signs," Carol agreed solemnly.

"You're right, I fear," Barbara responded in kind. "She's already in love with him."

"Good grief, no," Carol wailed, pressing her hands to her mouth. "Say it isn't so. She's too young and vulnerable."

"It's a pity, such a pity."

"I can't help but agree. Maryanne is much too sweet for Nolan Adams. I just hope he appreciates her."

"He won't," Carol muttered, reverting to her normal voice, "but then no man ever fully appreciates a woman."

"It's such a pity men act the way they do," Barbara said in a sad voice.

"Some men," Maryanne added.

Carol and Barbara dabbed their eyes and solemnly tossed the used tissues into the growing heap in the middle of their circle.

The plan had been to gather all the used tissues and ceremonially dump them in the toilet, flush their "pity pot," and then celebrate all the good things in their lives.

The idea for this little party had been an impromptu one of Maryanne's on a lonely Friday night. She'd been feeling blue and friendless and decided to look for a little innocent fun. She'd phoned Carol and learned she was a weekend widow; her husband had gone fishing with some cronies. Barbara had thought the idea was a good one herself, since she'd just broken her longest fingernail and was in the mood for a shoulder to cry on.

A pity party seemed just the thing to help three lonely women make it through a bleak Friday night.

Maryanne awoke Saturday morning with a humdinger of a headache. Wine and the ice cream they'd had at the end of the evening definitely didn't mix.

If her head hadn't been throbbing so painfully, she might have recognized sooner that her apartment had no heat. Her cantankerous radiator was acting up again. It did that some mornings, but she'd always managed to coax it back to life with a few well-placed whacks. The past few days had been unusually cold for early November—well below freezing at night.

She reached for her robe and slippers, bundling herself up like a December baby out in her first snowstorm. Cupping her hands over her mouth, she blew until a frosty mist formed.

A quickly produced cup of coffee with two extra-strength aspirin took the edge off her headache. Maryanne shivered while she slipped into jeans, sweatshirt and a thick winter coat. She suspected she resembled someone preparing to join an Arctic expedition.

She fiddled with the radiator, twisting the knobs and slamming her hand against the side, but the only results were a couple of rattles and a hollow clanking.

Not knowing what else to try, she got out her heavy cast-iron skillet and banged it against the top of the rad in hopes of reviving the ageing pipes.

The noise was deafening, vibrating through the room like a jet aircraft crashing through the sound barrier. If that wasn't enough, Maryanne's entire body began to quiver, starting at her arm and spreading outward in a rippling effect that caused her arms and legs to tremble.

"What the hell's going on over there?" Nolan shouted from the other side of the wall. He didn't wait for her to answer and a couple of seconds later came barreling through her front door, wild-eyed and dishevelled.

"What... Where?" He was carrying a baseball bat, and stalked to the middle of her apartment, scanning the interior for what Maryanne could only assume were invaders.

"I don't have any heat," she announced, tucking the thin scarf more tightly around her ears.

Nolan blinked. She'd apparently woken him from a sound sleep. He was barefoot and dressed in pyjama bottoms, and although he wore a shirt, it was unbuttoned, revealing a broad muscular chest dusted with curly black hair.

"What's with you? Are you going to a costume party?"

"Believe me, this is no party. I'm simply trying to keep warm."

His gaze lowered to the heavy skillet in her hand. "Do you plan to cook on that radiator?"

"I might if I could get it to work. In case you hadn't noticed, there isn't any heat in this place."

Nolan set the baseball bat aside and moved to the far wall to look at the radiator. "What's wrong with it?"

How like a man to ask stupid questions! If Maryanne had *known* what was wrong with it, she wouldn't be standing there shivering, with a scarf swaddling her face like an old-time remedy for toothache.

"How in heaven's name am I supposed to know?" she answered testily.

"What went on here last night, anyway? A wake?"

She glanced at the mound of tissues and shrugged. He was scanning the area as if it were a crime scene and he should take caution not to stumble over a dead body.

Walking across the living room, he picked up the two empty wine bottles and held them aloft for her inspection, pretending to be shocked.

"Very funny." She put the skillet down and removed the bottles from his hands, to be deposited promptly in the garbage.

"So you had a party and I wasn't invited." He made it sound as though he'd missed the social event of the year.

Maryanne sighed loudly. "If you must know, Carol, Barbara and I had a pity party."

"A what? You're kidding, right?" He didn't bother to hide his mocking grin.

"Never mind." She should've realized he'd only poke fun at her. "Can you figure out how to get this thing working before the next ice age?"

"Here, give me a shot at it." He gently patted the top of the radiator as he knelt in front of it. "Okay, ol' Betsy, we're trusting you to be good." He began fiddling with knobs, still murmuring ridiculous endearments—like a cowboy talking to his horse.

"It doesn't do any good to talk to an inanimate object," she advised primly, standing behind him.

"You want to do this?"

"No," she muttered. Having Nolan in her home, dressed in his nightclothes, did something odd to her, sent her pulse skittering erratically. She deliberately allowed her attention to wander to the scene outside her window. The still-green lawns of Volunteer Park showed in the distance and she pretended to be absorbed in their beauty.

"I thought I told you to keep that door chain in place," he said casually as he worked. "This isn't The Seattle."

"Do you honestly think you need to remind me of that now?" She rubbed her hands together, hoping to generate some warmth before her fingers went numb.

"There," he said, sounding satisfied. "All she needed was a little loving care."

"Thanks," Maryanne said with relief.

"No problem, only the next time something like this happens don't try to fix it yourself."

"Translated, that means I shouldn't try to fix the radiator again while *you're* trying to sleep."

"Right."

She smiled up at him, her eyes alive with appreciation. He really had been good to her from the day she'd moved in—before then, too. Discounting what he'd written about her in his column, of course. And even that had ended up having a positive effect.

It'd been a week since she'd seen him. A long week. A lonely week. Until now, she'd hardly been able to admit, even to herself, how much she'd missed him. Standing there as he was, Maryanne was struck by just how attractive she found him. If only he'd taken the time to button his shirt! She reveled in his lean strength and his aura of unquestionable authority—and that chest of his was driving her to distraction.

She wasn't the only one enthralled. Nolan was staring at her, too. The silence lingered between them, lengthening moment by moment as they gazed into each other's eyes.

"I have to go," he finally said, breaking eye contact by glancing past her, out the window.

"Right. I—I understand," she stammered, stepping back. Her hands swung at her sides as she followed him to the door. "I really do appreciate this." Already she could feel the warmth spilling into her apartment. And none too soon, either.

"Just remember to keep the door locked."

She grinned and mockingly saluted him. "Aye, aye, sir."

He left then. Maryanne hated to see him go, hated to see him walk away from her, and yet it seemed he was always doing exactly that.

Later that same afternoon, after she'd finished her errands, Maryanne was strolling through the park when a soft feminine voice spoke from behind her.

Maryanne turned around and waved when she discovered Gloria, the teenager she'd met here earlier. But this time Gloria wasn't alone.

"This is my little sister, Katie, the pest," Gloria explained. "She's three."

"Hello, Katie," Maryanne said, smiling.

"Why am I a pest?" Katie asked, gazing at Gloria, but apparently not offended that her older sister referred to her that way.

"Because." Looking annoyed, the teenager shrugged in the same vague manner Maryanne had so often seen in her younger brothers. "Katie's three and every other word is 'why.' Why this? Why that? It's enough to drive a person straight to the loony bin."

"I have brothers, so I know what you mean."

"You do?"

"They're several years younger than I am. So trust me, I understand what you're talking about."

"Did your brothers want to go every place you did? And did your mother make you take them even if it was a terrible inconvenience?"

Maryanne tried to disguise a smile. "Sometimes."

"Eddie asked me to come and watch him play basketball this afternoon with Mr. Adams, and I had to drag Katie along because she wanted to come to the park, too. My mom pressured me into bringing her. I didn't even get a chance to say no." Gloria made it sound as if she were being forced to swim across Puget Sound with the three-year-old clinging to her back.

"I'm not a pest," Katie insisted now, flipping her braid over one shoulder in a show of defiance. Looking up at Maryanne, the little girl carefully manipulated her fingers and proudly exclaimed, "I'm three."

"Three?" Maryanne repeated, raising her eyebrows, feigning surprise. "Really? I would've thought you were four or five."

Katie grinned delightedly. "I'm nearly four, you know."

"Mr. Adams is already here," Gloria said, brightening. She frowned as she glanced down at her little sister and jerked the small arm in an effort to hurry her along. "Come on, Katie, we have to go. Eddie wants me to watch him play ball."

"Why?"

Gloria groaned. "See what I mean?"

"You go on," Maryanne said, offering Katie her hand. The youngster obediently slipped her small hand into Maryanne's much larger one, willingly abandoning her cranky older sister. "Katie and I will follow behind."

Gloria looked surprised by the offer. "You mean you don't mind? I mean, Katie's my responsibility and it wouldn't be fair to palm her off on you. You're not going to kidnap her or anything, are you? I mean, I know you're not—you're Mr. Adams's friend. I wouldn't let her go with just anyone, you know. But if anything happened to her, my mother would kill me."

"I promise to take the very best care of her."

Gloria grinned, looking sheepish for having suggested anything else. "You're sure you don't mind?"

"I don't mind in the least. I don't think Katie does, either. Is that right, Katie?"

"Why?"

"Are you *really* sure? Okay, then…" Once she'd made a token protest Gloria raced off to join her friends.

Katie was content to skip and hop at Maryanne's side until they reached a huge pile of leaves under a chestnut tree, not far from the basketball court. Almost before Maryanne realized it, Katie raced toward the leaves, bunching as many as she could in her small arms and carrying them back to Maryanne as though presenting her with the rarest of jewels.

"Look," she cried happily. "Leafs."

"Leaves," Maryanne corrected, bending over and grabbing an armful herself. She tossed them in the air and grinned as Katie leapt up to catch as many as she could and in the process dropped the armload she was holding.

Laughing, Maryanne clasped the child by the waist and swung her around, while Katie shrieked with delight. Dizzy, Maryanne leaned against the tree in an effort to regain her equilibrium and her breath.

It was then that she saw Nolan had stopped playing and was standing in the middle of the basketball court, staring at her. The game was going on all around him, boys scattering in one direction and then another, racing to one end of the court and back again. Nolan seemed oblivious to them and to the game—to everything but her.

A tall boy bumped into him from behind and Nolan stumbled. Maryanne gasped, fearing he might fall, but he caught himself in time. Without a pause, he rejoined the game, racing down the court at breakneck speed. He stole the ball and made a slam dunk, coming down hard on the pavement.

Gloria ran back toward Maryanne and Katie. "I thought you said you and Mr. Adams were just friends?" she teased. She was grinning in a way that suggested she wasn't about to be fooled again. "He nearly got creamed because he couldn't take his eyes off you."

With Katie on her lap, Maryanne sat beside the teenage girls watching the game. Together she and the three-year-old became Nolan's personal cheering squad, but whether or not he appreciated their efforts she didn't know. He didn't give a single indication that he heard them.

When the game was finished, Nolan walked breathlessly off the court. His grey sweatshirt was stained with perspiration, and his face was red and damp from the sheer physical exhaustion of keeping up with kids half his age.

For an anxious moment, Maryanne assumed he was planning to ignore her and simply walk away. But after he'd stopped at the water fountain, he came over to the bench where she and Katie were sitting.

He slumped down beside her, dishevelled and still breathing hard. "What are you doing here?" he grumbled.

"I happened to be in the park," she answered, feeling self-conscious now and unsure. "You don't need to worry, Nolan. I didn't follow you."

"I didn't think you had."

"You look nice in blue," he said hoarsely, then cleared his throat as if he hadn't meant to say that, as if he wanted to withdraw the words.

"Thanks." The blue sweater was one of her favorites. She'd worn her long wool coat and was surprised he'd even noticed the periwinkle-blue sweater beneath.

"Hello, Katie."

Katie beamed, stretching out both arms for Nolan to lift her up, which he did. The little girl hugged him quickly, then leapt off the bench and ran to her sister, who stood talking to her boyfriend.

"You're good with children," Nolan said. His voice fell slightly, as though the fact surprised him.

"I do have a knack with them. I always have." She'd been much-sought as a babysitter by her parents' friends and for a time had considered becoming a teacher. If she'd pursued that field of study she would have preferred to teach kindergarten. She found five-year-olds, with their eagerness to learn about the world, delightful. A couple of articles she'd written the week before were geared toward children's magazines. If only she'd hear something soon. It seemed to take so long.

"How many years of your life did you lose this time?" Maryanne asked teasingly.

"Another two or three, at least."

He smiled at her and it was that rare special smile he granted her only in those brief moments when his guard was lowered. His resistance to the attraction he felt to her was at its weakest point, and they both knew it.

Maryanne went still, almost afraid to move or speak for fear of ruining the moment. His eyes, so warm and gentle, continued to hold hers. When she tried to breathe, the air seemed to catch in her lungs.

"Maryanne." Her name was little more than a whisper.

"Yes?"

He raked his hand through his hair, then looked away. "Nothing. Never mind."

"What is it?" she pressed, unwilling to let the matter drop.

The muscles along the side of his jaw clenched. "I said it was nothing," he answered gruffly.

Maryanne gazed down at her hands, feeling an overwhelming sense of frustration and despair. The tension between them was so thick she could practically touch it, but nothing she could say or do would make any difference. If anything, her efforts would only make it worse.

"Hey, Nolan," Eddie called out, loping toward them. "What's with you, man?" He laughed, tossing his basketball from one hand to the other. "You nearly lost that game 'cause you couldn't take your eyes off your woman."

Nolan scowled at him. "You looking for a rematch?"

"Any time you want."

"Not today." Shaking his head, Nolan slowly pushed the sleeves of his sweatshirt past his elbows.

"Right," Eddie said with a knowing laugh. "I didn't think so, with your woman here and all."

"Maryanne isn't my woman," Nolan informed him curtly, his frown darkening.

"Right," Eddie responded. "Hey, dude, this is me, Eddie. Can't fool me! You practically went comatose when you saw her. I don't blame you, though. She ain't bad. So when are you two getting married?"

Nine

"I've changed my mind," Barbara announced at closing time Monday evening.

Maryanne was busy refilling the salt and pepper shakers and reloading the napkin holders. "About what?" she asked absently, stuffing napkins into the small chrome canisters.

"You and Nolan."

If Barbara hadn't had Maryanne's attention earlier, she did now. Nolan had left the restaurant about forty minutes earlier, after having his customary meal of chili and coffee. He'd barely said two words to Maryanne the whole time he was there. He'd buried his face in the evening edition of the *Sun* and done a brilliant job of pretending he didn't know her.

"What about us?" Maryanne's expression might have remained aloof, but her heart was pounding furiously.

"Since the night of our pity party, I've had a change of heart. You're exactly the right kind of woman for Nolan. The two of you…balance each other. At first I agreed with Carol. My opinion of Nolan isn't as negative as hers, but you have to remember that those two work for rival papers. At any rate, I was concerned. You *are* really sweet."

Maryanne winced at the "sweet." It rather sounded as though friendship with her was like falling into a jar of honey.

"And now?"

"I don't know exactly what changed my mind. Partly it was watching Nolan when he was here. I got quite a kick out of him."

"How do you mean?"

Barbara's grin was broad as she continued to wipe the counter. "I swear that man couldn't keep his eyes off you."

Maryanne was puzzled. "What are you talking about? Nolan didn't look my way even once."

"Oh, he'd scowl every time you were close, but behind that cross expression of his was an intensity I've never seen in him before. It was like he had to come in and get his daily fix of you."

Maryanne's heart couldn't decide whether to lift with happiness or sink with doubt. "You're wrong. Other than ordering his meal, he didn't speak to me at all. I might as well have been a robot."

"That's what he'd like you to believe."

"He was reading the paper," Maryanne said. "The same way he reads it every time he comes here."

"Correction," Barbara said, and her face broke into a spontaneous smile. "He *pretended* to be reading the paper, but when you weren't looking his eyes were following you like a hawk."

"Oh, Barbara, really?" It seemed almost more than she dared hope for. He'd hardly spoken to her in the past few days, and he seemed to be avoiding her. The kids in the park had taken to teasing them about being "in love" and asking pointed questions, and Nolan had practically fallen all over himself denying that they were anything other than friends.

"It's more than just the way he was watching you," Barbara said, slipping on to a stool. "Have you read his columns the past couple of weeks?"

Naturally Maryanne had, more impressed by his work every time she did. The range of his talent and the power of his writing were unmistakable. Within a few years, if not sooner, she expected his newspaper column to be picked up for syndication.

"Lately, I've noticed something unusual about his writing," Barbara said, still clutching the dishrag. "That cynical edge of his—it isn't quite as sharp. His writing's less sarcastic now. I heard one of my customers comment earlier today that Nolan's going soft on us. I hadn't thought about it much until then, but Ernie's right. I don't know what's made the difference, but I figure it must be love. Oh, I doubt there's much in this life that's going to change Nolan Adams. He'll always be stubborn as a mule, headstrong and temperamental. That's just part of his nature. But mark my words, he's in love."

"What you said earlier, about us being so different…"

"You are, with you so nice and all, and Nolan such a grouch. At least he likes to pretend he's one. You and I know better, but most folks don't."

"And?" Maryanne probed.

"And, well, it seems to me the two of you fit together perfectly. Like two pieces of a puzzle."

It seemed that way to Maryanne, too.

"You heard, didn't you?" Barbara muttered, abruptly changing the subject.

Maryanne nodded. Mom's Place was going to close in a month for remodelling.

"What are you going to do?"

Maryanne didn't know yet. "Find a temporary job, I suppose. What about you?" By then, she should have sold a few of the articles she'd submitted. At least she hadn't been rejected yet. She should be hearing any time.

"I'm not that worried about taking a month or so off work," Barbara returned, her look thoughtful. "I could use a vacation, especially over the holidays. I was thinking of staying home and baking Christmas gifts this year. My fudge is out of this world."

"I suppose I should start looking for another job now." Maryanne was already worried about meeting expenses. Mom's Place couldn't have chosen a worse time to close.

A half hour later, she was waiting for the bus, her mind spinning with what Barbara had said. The diner's closing was a concern, but Barbara's comments about Nolan gladdened Maryanne's heart.

Nolan did feel something for her, something more powerful than he'd let on.

She supposed she should confront him with it, force him to acknowledge his feelings. A brief smile crossed her lips as she envisioned what would happen if she actually did such a thing. She nearly laughed out loud at the thought.

Nolan would deny it, of course, loudly and vehemently, and she'd have to counteract with a loud argument of her own. The smile appeared again. Her decision was made.

Feeling almost light-headed, Maryanne glanced down the street, eager for the bus to arrive so she could get home. The first thing she intended to do was march into Nolan's apartment and demand the truth. If he tried to ignore her, as he usually did, then she had the perfect solution.

She'd kiss him.

A kiss would silence his protests in the most effective way she could imagine. Maryanne almost melted at the memory of being kissed by Nolan, being held in his arms. It was like walking through the gates of an undiscovered paradise. Just remembering those moments made her feel faint with desire, weak with excitement. He seemed to experience the same emotions, Maryanne remembered hopefully.

Cheered by the thought, she nearly applauded when her bus arrived. The ride passed quickly and she hurried into the building, eager to see Nolan.

Consumed by her sense of purpose, she went directly to his apartment. She stood in front of his door, took several deep breaths, then knocked politely. No answer. She tried again, harder this time.

"Who is it?" Nolan growled from the other side.

"Maryanne. I want to talk to you."

"I'm busy."

She was only a little discouraged by his unfriendliness. "This'll just take a minute."

The door was yanked open with excessive force. Nolan stood before her, dressed in a black tuxedo and white cummerbund, looking so handsome that he caught her completely by surprise. Her mouth sagged open.

"Yes?" he asked crossly.

"Hello, Nolan," she said, aware that her mission had been thwarted. Nothing he could've said or done would have affected her as profoundly as finding him dressed like this. Because it meant he was going out on a date.

"Hello," he said, tugging at the cuffs of his jacket, adjusting the fit. He frowned, apparently waiting for her to say something.

"Uh…" She tried to gather her scattered composure, and finally managed to squeak, "You're going out?"

He scowled. "I don't dress like this for a jaunt to the corner store."

"No, I don't suppose you do."

"You wanted something?"

She'd been so confident, so sure she was doing the right thing. But now, seeing Nolan looking more dressed up and formal than he'd ever looked for *her*, she found herself speechless.

She couldn't help wondering where he was going— and with whom. The "with whom" part bothered her the most.

He glanced pointedly at his wristwatch. "How long is this going to take?" he asked coolly. "I'm supposed to pick up Prudence in fifteen minutes."

"Prudence?" His face, tight with impatience, drew her full attention. *Prudence,* her mind repeated. Who was this woman?

Then in a flash, Maryanne knew. It was all she could do not to laugh and inform him that his little plan just wasn't working. No imaginary date was going to make *her* jealous.

He wasn't seeing anyone named Prudence. Good grief, if he had to invent a name, the least he could've done was come up with something a little more plausible than Prudence.

In fact, Maryanne remembered Nolan casually mentioning a week or so earlier that he'd been asked to speak at a Chamber of Commerce banquet. There had also been a notice in the paper. Who did he think he was kidding?

Of course he wanted her to believe he was dating another woman. That was supposed to discourage her, she guessed. Except that it didn't.

"It wasn't important..." she said, gesturing vaguely. "The radiators were giving me trouble this morning, but I'll manage. I was planning to go out tonight myself."

His eyes connected with hers. "Another pity party?"

"Not this time." She considered announcing she had a hot date herself, but that would have been carrying this farce a little too far. "Barbara and I will probably go to a movie."

"Sounds like fun."

"I'm sure it will be." She smiled up at him, past the square cut of his jaw to his incredibly dark eyes. "Have a good time with...Prudence," she said with a bright knowing smile.

Holding back a laugh, she returned to her own apartment. The rat. The low-down dirty rat! He was pretending to escort some imaginary woman to a fancy affair. Oh, he'd like nothing better than for Maryanne to think he considered her a pest. But she knew that wasn't quite the case.

Where was the man who'd rushed to her rescue when the pipes needed a little coaxing? Where was the man who'd nearly been run over on a basketball court when he saw her standing on the sidelines? Where was the man who'd tried to set her up with someone else he thought more suitable? Nolan Adams had just proved what she'd suspected all along. He was a coward—at least when it came to love.

Suddenly depressed, Maryanne slowly crossed the living room and sank on to her sofa, trying to gather her wits. Ten minutes later, she still sat there, mulling things over and feeling sorry for herself, when she heard Nolan's door open and close. She immediately perked up, wondering if he'd had a change of heart. He seemed to pause for a moment outside her door, but any second thoughts he might be having didn't last long.

Barbara phoned soon after, full of apologies, to cancel their movie plans, so Maryanne spent the evening drowning her sorrows in television reruns and slices of cold pizza.

She must have fallen asleep because a harsh ringing jolted her awake a couple of hours later. She leapt off the sofa and stumbled dazedly around before she realized the sound came from the phone. She rushed across the room.

A greeting had barely left her lips when her father's booming voice assailed her.

"Where the hell are you?"

"Hello, Dad," she muttered, her heart sinking. How like him to get to the subject at hand without anything in the way of preliminaries. "How are you, too?"

"I want to know where you're living and I want to know right now!"

"I beg your pardon?" she asked, stalling for time. Obviously her father had discovered her small deception.

"I talked to the managing editor of the *Seattle Review* this morning and he told me you haven't worked there in weeks. He said you'd quit! Now I want to know what this craziness is you've been feeding your mother and me about a special assignment."

"Uh…" By now, Maryanne was awake enough to know her father wasn't in any mood to listen to excuses.

"You lied to us, girl."

"Not exactly…" She paused, searching for the right words. "It was more a case of omission, don't you think?"

"You've had us worried sick. We've been trying to get hold of you all afternoon. Where were you? And who the hell is Nolan Adams?"

"Nolan Adams?" she echoed, playing dumb, which wasn't all that difficult at the moment.

"Your mother mentioned his name, and when I called the paper, some woman named…Riverside, Carol Riverside, claimed this was his fault."

"Dad, listen, it's all rather complicated, so I think—"

"I don't want excuses, I want facts. You decided to work on the other side of the country. Against my better judgment, I arranged it for you with the promise that I wouldn't intrude—and look where it's gotten me! To have you deceive us by—"

"Dad, please, just settle down."

He seemed to be making an effort to calm himself, but more than likely the effort was thanks to her mother. Maryanne could hear her arguing softly in the background.

"Can I explain?" she asked, waiting a minute for the tension to ease, although she wasn't sure what to say, what excuses she could possibly offer.

"You can try to explain, but I doubt it'll do any good," he answered gruffly.

Now that she had the floor, Maryanne floundered.

"I take it this all revolves around that columnist friend of yours from the *Sun*?" her father asked. "That Adams character?"

"Well, yes," Maryanne admitted reluctantly. But she didn't feel she could place the whole blame on him. "Leaving the paper was my decision—"

"Where are you living?"

That was one of several questions Maryanne was hoping to avoid. "I—I rented an apartment."

"You were in an apartment before. It doesn't make the least bit of sense for you to move. The Seattle has a reputation for excellence."

"Yes, Dad, I know, but moving was necessary." She didn't go on to explain why. She didn't want to mislead her father more than she already had. But at the same time, if she told him she couldn't afford to continue living at The Seattle, he'd certainly demand to know why.

"That doesn't explain a damn thing," Samuel Simpson boomed.

Maryanne held the phone away from her ear and sighed heavily. She was groggy from her nap and discouraged by her relationship with Nolan. To complicate matters, she was truly in love for the first time in her life. Loving someone shouldn't be this difficult!

"I insist you tell me what's going on," her father said, in the tone she remembered from childhood confrontations about missed curfews and other transgressions.

She tried again. "It's not that easy to explain."

"You have three seconds, young lady, to tell me why you've lied to your parents."

"I apologize for that. I've felt horrible about it, I really have, but I didn't want to say anything for fear you'd worry."

"Of course we'd worry! Now tell me exactly what it is we should be worrying about."

"Dad, honestly, I'm over twenty-one. I should be able to live and work where I please. You can't keep me your little girl forever." This conversation was not only reminiscent of several she'd had with Nolan, it was one she should have had with her father years ago.

"I demand to know why you quit the paper!"

Maryanne refused to be intimidated. "I already explained that. I had another job."

"Obviously you're doing something you're too ashamed to tell your parents."

"I'm not ashamed! It's nothing illegal. Besides, I happen to like what I do, and I've managed to live entirely on what I make, which is no small feat. I'm happy, Dad, really happy." She tried to force some cheerful enthusiasm into her voice, but unfortunately she didn't entirely succeed. How she wished she could brag about selling her articles. Surely she'd receive word soon!

"If you're so pleased about this change in jobs, then why do you seem upset?" her mother asked reasonably, joining the conversation from an extension.

"I—I'm fine, really I am."

"Somehow, sweetie, that just doesn't ring true—"

"I don't like the sound of this," her father interrupted impatiently. "I made a mistake in arranging this Seattle assignment for you. It seems to me it'd be best if you quit whatever you're doing and moved back to—"

"Dad, I refuse to quit now."

"I want you to move back home. As far as I can see, you've got one hell of a lot of explaining to do."

"It seems to me," Maryanne said after a moment of strained silence, "that we should both take time to cool down and think this over before one of us says or does something we're all going to regret."

"I'm calm." The voice that roared over the long-distance wires threatened to impair Maryanne's hearing.

"Daddy, I love you and Mom dearly, but I think it would be best if we both slept on this. I'm going to hang up now, not to be rude, but because I don't think this conversation is accomplishing anything. I'll call you first thing in the morning."

"Maryanne... Maryanne, don't you dare—"

She didn't allow him to finish, knowing it would do no good to argue with him when he was in this frame of mind. Her heart was heavy with regret as she replaced the receiver. Knowing her father would immediately call again, she unplugged the phone.

Now that her family had discovered she wasn't working at the *Review*, everything would change. And not for the better. Her father would hound her until she was forced to tell him she'd taken a job as a waitress. Once he discovered that, he'd hit the roof.

Still thinking about what had happened, she put on her flannel pyjamas and pulled out her bed. With the demanding physical schedule she kept, sleeping had never been a problem. Tonight, she missed the clatter of Nolan's typing. She'd grown accustomed to its comforting familiarity, in part because it was a sign of his presence. She often lay awake wondering how his mystery novel was developing. Some nights she even fantasized that he'd let her read the manuscript, which to her represented the ultimate gesture of trust.

But Nolan wasn't at his typewriter this evening. He was giving a speech. Closing her eyes, she imagined him standing before the large dinner crowd. How she would have enjoyed being in the audience! She knew beyond a doubt that his eyes would have sought her out....

Instead she was spending the night alone. She lay with her eyes wide open; every time she started to drift off, some small noise would jerk her into wakefulness. She finally had to admit that she was waiting to hear the sounds of Nolan's return.

Some time in the early morning hours, Maryanne did eventually fall asleep. She woke at six to the familiar sound of Nolan pounding on his typewriter.

She threw on her robe, thrust her feet into the fuzzy slippers and began pacing, her mind whirling.

When she could stand it no longer, she banged on the wall separating their two apartments.

"Your typing woke me up!" Which, of course, wasn't fair or even particularly true. But she'd spent a fretful night thinking about him, and that was excuse enough.

Her family had found out she'd quit her job and all hell was about to break loose. Time was running out for her and Nolan. If she was going to do something—and it was clear she'd have to be the one—she'd need to do it soon.

"Just go back to bed," Nolan shouted.

"Not on your life, Nolan Adams!" Without questioning how wise it was to confront him now, Maryanne stormed out of her apartment dressed as she was, and beat hard on his door.

Nolan opened it almost immediately, still wearing the tuxedo from the night before, without the jacket and cummerbund. The sleeves of his shirt were rolled past his elbows and the top three buttons were open. His dishevelment and the shadows under his eyes suggested he hadn't been to bed.

"What now?" he demanded. "Is my breathing too loud?"

"We need to talk," she stated calmly as she marched into his apartment.

Nolan remained standing at the door. "Why don't you come in and make yourself at home?" he muttered sarcastically.

"I already have." She sat on the edge of his sofa and waited until he turned to face her. "So?" she asked with cheerful derision. "How'd your hot date go?"

"Fine." He smiled grimly. "Just fine."

"Where'd you go for dinner? The Four Seasons? Fullers?" She named two of the best restaurants in town. "By the way, do I know Prudence?"

"No," he answered with sharp impatience.

"I didn't think so."

"Maryanne—"

"I don't suppose you have coffee made?"

"It's made." But he didn't offer her any. The fact that he was still standing by the door suggested he wanted her out of his home. But when it came to dealing with Nolan, Maryanne had long since learned to ignore the obvious.

"Thanks, I'll get myself a cup." She walked into the kitchen and found two clean mugs in the dishwasher. "You want one?"

"I have some," he said pointedly, stationing himself in the kitchen doorway. He heaved a long-suffering sigh. "Maryanne, I'm busy, so if you could get on with—"

"My father knows," she said calmly, watching him closely for some sort of reaction. If she'd been looking for evidence of concern or regret, he showed neither. The only emotion she was able to discern was a brief flicker of what she could only assume was relief. That wasn't encouraging. He appeared all too willing to get her out of his life.

"Well?" she probed. "Say something."

"What the hell have you been telling him?"

"Nothing about you, so don't worry. I did mention you to my mother, but you don't need to worry about that, either. She thinks you and I... Never mind."

"*What* does your father know?" Nolan asked.

She sipped from the edge of the mug and shrugged. "He found out I wasn't on special assignment for the paper."

"Special assignment? What does that have to do with anything?"

"That's what I told my mother when I moved."

"Why the hell would you tell her something like that?"

"She was expecting me to send her my columns, and call every other day. I couldn't continue to do either of those things. I had to come up with some excuse."

He cocked an eyebrow. "You might have tried the truth."

Maryanne nodded her agreement. If she'd bungled any part of this arrangement, it had been with her parents. However, there wasn't time for regrets now.

"Dad learned I moved out of The Seattle. I didn't tell him where I was living, but that won't deter him. Knowing Dad, he'll have all the facts by noon today. To put it mildly, he isn't pleased. He wants me to return to the East Coast."

"Are you going?" Nolan's question was casual, as though her response was of little concern to him.

"No."

"Why not?" The impatient look was back. "For the love of heaven, Annie, will you kindly listen to reason? You don't belong here. You've proved your point. If you're waiting for me to admit I was wrong about you, then fine, I'll admit it, and gladly. You've managed far better than I ever dreamed you would, but it's time to get on with your life. It's time to move back into the world where you belong."

"I can't do that now."

"Why the hell not?"

"Because...I've fallen—"

"Look, Annie, it's barely seven and I have to go to work," he said brusquely, cutting her off. "Shouldn't you be getting dressed? Walking around the hallway in your pyjamas isn't wise—people might think something."

"Let them."

He rubbed his face wearily, shaking his head.

"Nolan," Maryanne said softly, her heart in her throat. "I know you didn't go out with anyone named Prudence. You made the whole thing up. This game of yours isn't going to work. It's too late. I'm...already in love with you."

The whole world seemed to come to an abrupt halt. Maryanne hadn't intended to blurt out her feelings this way, but she didn't know how else to cut through the arguments and the denial.

For one wild-eyed moment Nolan didn't say anything. Then he raised his hand, as though fending off some kind of attack, and retreated from the kitchen.

"You can't be in love with me," he insisted, slowly sinking to the sofa, like a man in the final stages of exhaustion. "I won't allow it."

Ten

"Unfortunately it's too late," Maryanne told him again, no less calmly. "I'm already in love with you."

"Now just a minute," Nolan said, apparently regaining his composure. "You're a nice kid, and to be honest I've been impressed—"

"I am not a kid," she corrected with quiet authority, "and you know it."

"Annie… Maryanne," he said, "listen to me. What you feel for me isn't love." His face revealed a bitterness she hadn't seen before. He walked toward her, gripped her shoulders and gazed down at her.

"That won't work, either," she said in the same quiet voice. She wasn't a poor little rich girl who'd only recently discovered who she was. Nor had she mistaken admiration for love. "I know what I feel."

She slipped her arms around his neck and stood on tiptoe, wanting to convince him of her sincerity with a kiss.

But before her mouth could meet his, Nolan jerked his head back, preventing the contact. He dropped his arms and none too gently pushed her away.

"Are you afraid to kiss me?"

"You're damn right I am," he said, burying his hands in his pockets as he hastily moved even farther away.

Maryanne smiled softly. "And with good reason. We both know what would happen if you did. You've done a good job of hiding your feelings, I'll grant you that much. I was nearly fooled."

"Naturally I'm flattered." His expression was darkening by the second. He stalked across the room, his shoulders hunched forward. He didn't say anything else, and Maryanne strongly suspected he was at a loss for words. Nolan was *never* at a loss for words. Words were his stock-in-trade.

But he was confronting emotions now, not words or concepts, and she knew him well enough to realize how uncomfortable that made him.

He'd hidden his feelings behind a mask of gruff annoyance, allowing her to believe she'd become a terrible nuisance in his life. He needed to disguise what he felt for her—to prevent her from learning what everyone else already knew.

Nolan was in love with her.

The mere thought thrilled her and gave her more courage than she'd ever possessed in her life.

"I fully expect you to be flattered," she said gently, "but I'm not telling you this to give your ego a boost. I honestly love you, and nothing my parents say is going to convince me to leave Seattle."

"Maryanne, please…"

He was prepared to push her away verbally, as he had so often. This time she wouldn't let him. This time she walked over to him, threw both arms around his waist and hugged him close.

He raised his hands to her shoulders, ready to ease her from him, but the moment they came to rest on her he seemed to lose his purpose.

"This is ridiculous," she heard him mumble. He held himself rigid for a moment or two, then with a muttered curse buried his face in her hair. A ragged sigh tore through his body.

Experiencing a small sense of triumph, Maryanne pressed her ear to his chest and smiled contentedly when she heard his racing uneven heartbeat.

"You shouldn't let me hold you like this." His voice was low and hushed. "Tell me not to," he breathed as his lips moved through her hair and then lower to the pulse point behind her ear and the slope of her neck.

"I don't want you to stop…" She turned her head, begging him to touch and kiss her.

"Annie, please."

"I want to be in your arms more than anywhere. More than anything."

"You don't know what you're saying…."

She lifted her head enough for their eyes to meet. Placing her finger on his lips, she shook her head. "I'm a woman, a grown woman, and there's no question of my not knowing what I want."

His hands gently grazed her neck, as though he was still hesitant and unsure. Kissing her was what *he* wanted—she could read it clearly in his dark eyes— but he was holding himself back, his face contorted with indecision.

"Go ahead, kiss me," she urged softly, wanting him so much her whole body seemed to ache. "I dare you to."

His breathing was labored, and Maryanne could

sense the forces raging within him. A fresh wave of tenderness filled her.

"You make it so hard to do what's right," he groaned.

"Loving each other is what's right."

"I'd like to believe that, but I can't." He placed his hand on her cheek and their eyes locked hungrily. He searched her face.

"I love you," she whispered, smiling up at him. She didn't want him to question her feelings. She'd say it a thousand times a day if that was what it took to convince him.

Flattening her hands against his hard chest, she leaned into his strength and offered him her mouth. Only moments earlier he'd pushed her away, but not now. His gaze softened and he closed his eyes tightly. He was losing the battle.

It was while his eyes were closed that Maryanne claimed the advantage and kissed him. He moaned and seemed about to argue, but once their mouths met, urgency took hold and Nolan was rendered speechless.

To her delight, he responded with the full-fledged hunger she'd witnessed in his eyes. He slid his hands through her hair, his fingers tangling with the thick auburn mass as he angled her head to one side. Maryanne felt herself savoring the taste of his kiss. It was so long since he'd held her like this, so long since he'd done anything but keep her at arm's length. She wanted to cherish these moments, delight in the rush of sensations.

So many thoughts crowded her mind. So many ideas. Plans for their future.

He tore his mouth from hers and nestled his face in the hollow of her neck as he drew in several deep breaths.

Maryanne clung to him, hugging him as close as humanly possible. "Nolan—"

"It isn't going to work—you and me together...it isn't right," he whispered.

"It's more right than anything I've ever known."

"Oh, Annie, the things you do to me."

She smiled gently. "You know what I think?" She didn't give him the opportunity to answer. "I love you and you love me and when two people feel that way about each other, they usually—" she paused and swallowed once "—get married."

"What?" Nolan exploded, leaping away from her as though he'd received an electrical shock.

"You heard me," she said.

"You're a crazy woman. You know that, don't you? Downright certifiable." Nolan backed away from her, eyes narrowed. He began pacing rapidly in one direction, then another.

"Marriage was just a suggestion," she said mildly. "I am serious, though, and if you're at all interested we should move fast. Because once my father gets wind of it there'll be hell to pay."

"I have no intention of even considering the idea! In fact, I think it's time you left."

"Nolan, okay, I'm sorry. I shouldn't have mentioned marriage. I was just thinking, hoping actually, that it was something you wanted, too. There's no need to overreact." He had already ushered her across the living room toward the door. She tried to redirect his efforts, turning in his arms, but he wouldn't allow it.

"We need to talk about this," she insisted.

"Oh, no, you don't," he said, opening the door and steering her into the hallway. "Your idea of talking doesn't seem to coincide with mine. Before I figure out how it happens, you're in my arms and we're—"

"Maryanne!" Her father's voice came like a high-intensity foghorn from behind her.

Maryanne whirled around to discover both her parents standing in the hallway outside her apartment door. "Mom... Dad..." Frantic, she looked at Nolan, hoping he'd do the explaining part.

"Mr. and Mrs. Simpson," Nolan said formally, straightening. He removed his arms from around Maryanne, stepped forward and held out his hand to her father. "I'm Nolan Adams."

"How do you do?" Muriel Simpson said in a brittle voice as the two men exchanged brief handshakes. Her mother's troubled gaze moved from the men to Maryanne, surveying her attire with a single devastating look.

Until that moment, Maryanne had forgotten she was still in her pyjamas. She closed her eyes and groaned.

"Samuel," Muriel Simpson said in a shocked voice. "Maryanne's coming out of...his apartment."

"It's not what it looks like," Maryanne rushed to tell them. "Mom and Dad, please, you've got to listen to me. I didn't spend the night at Nolan's, honest. We just happened to get into a tiff this morning and instead of shouting through the walls and—"

"Samuel." Her mother reached for her father's sleeve, gripping it hard. "I feel faint."

Samuel Simpson clamped his arm about his wife's waist and with Nolan's assistance led her through his open apartment door. Maryanne hurried ahead of them to rearrange pillows on the sofa.

Crouched in front of her mother, Maryanne gently patted her hand. Muriel wasn't given to fainting spells; clearly, she'd been worried sick about her daughter, which increased Maryanne's guilt a hundredfold.

"My little girl is safe, and that's all that matters," Muriel whispered.

"Listen here, young man," Maryanne's father said sternly to Nolan. "It seems you two have some explaining to do."

"Daddy, please." Jumping to her feet, Maryanne stood between her father and Nolan, loving them both so much and not sure which one to confront first. She took a deep breath and blurted out, "I'm in love with Nolan."

"Sir, I know the circumstances look bad, but I can assure you there's nothing between me and your daughter."

"What do you mean there's nothing between us?" Maryanne cried, furious with him. Good grief, she'd just finished spilling out her heart to the man! The least he could do was acknowledge what they shared, what they both felt. Well, if he wasn't so inclined, she was. "That's a bold-faced lie," she announced to her father, hearing Nolan groan behind her as she spoke.

Samuel Simpson, so tall and formidable, so distinguished and articulate, seemed to find himself dumbstruck. He slumped onto the sofa next to his wife and rested his face in both hands.

"Maryanne," Nolan said from between gritted teeth. "Your parents appear to think the worst. Don't you agree it would be more appropriate to assure them that—"

"I don't care what they think. Well, I do, of course," she amended quickly, "but I'm more interested in settling things between you and me."

Nolan frowned impatiently. "This is neither the time nor the place."

"I happen to think it is."

"Maryanne, please," her mother wailed, holding out one hand. "Your father and I have spent a long sleepless night flying across the country. We've been worried half to death about you."

"She didn't answer her phone," Samuel muttered in dire tones, his eyes narrowing suspiciously on the two of them. "If Maryanne had been at her apartment, the way she claims, then she would have picked up the receiver. We must've called fifteen or twenty times. If she was home, why didn't she answer the phone?"

The question seemed to be directed at Nolan, but it was Maryanne who answered. "I unplugged it."

"Why would you do that?" Muriel asked. "Surely you know we'd try to reach you. We're your parents. We love you!"

"That's it, young lady. You're moving back with us."

"You can't force me to leave Seattle. I refuse."

"This place…" Muriel was looking around as though the building was likely to be condemned any minute. "Why would you want to live here? Have you rejected everything we've given you?"

"The answer is obvious," her father bellowed. "She's living here to be close to *him.*"

"But why didn't her…friend move into her apartment building?"

"Isn't it obvious?" Samuel stood abruptly and stalked to the other side of the room. "Adams couldn't afford to live within a mile of The Seattle." He stopped short, then nodded apologetically at Nolan. "I didn't mean that in a derogatory way. You seem like a fine young man, but frankly…"

"I wouldn't care where Nolan lived," Maryanne informed them both, squaring her shoulders righteously. Any man she fell in love with didn't need to head a financial empire or be related to someone who did. "I'd live anywhere if it meant we could be together." Her eyes softened at her mother's shocked look.

"Don't you remember what it's like to be young and in love, Mom?" Maryanne asked her. "Remember all those things you told me about you and Dad? How you used to argue and everything? It's the same with Nolan and me. I'm crazy about him. He's so talented and—"

"That's enough," Nolan interrupted harshly. "If you're looking for someone to blame for Maryanne's living in this building and working at Mom's Place—"

"What's Mom's Place?"

"A very nice diner," Maryanne inserted quickly. "We do a brisk lunch trade and carry a limited dinner menu."

Her mother let out a cry of dismay. "You're…you're working as a waitress?"

Miserable, Maryanne nodded. "But I'm doing lots of freelance work. None of the feature articles I've written have sold yet, but it's too soon for that. I just found out the community newspaper's buying a couple of my shorter pieces, and I plan on selling them lots more."

"You might have warned me they didn't know about your being a waitress," Nolan muttered under his breath.

Samuel drew a hand across his eyes, as if that would erase the image of his daughter waiting on tables. "Why would you choose to quit the newspaper to work as a waitress?" Asking the question seemed to cause him pain.

"It's honest work, Dad. I don't understand why you're acting like this. You're making it sound like I'm doing something that'll bring disgrace to the family name."

"But your education is being wasted," her mother said, shaking her head. "You could have any job in publishing you wanted."

That much was true when it was her family doing the hiring, but when she was looking on her own her employers were more interested in her job skills than who her father was.

"I'm afraid I'm the one who started this," Nolan interrupted. "I wrote a column about Maryanne," he said bluntly. "It was unfortunate, because I was out of line in some of the things I said, but—"

"Nolan didn't write anything that wasn't true," Maryanne hastened to say. "He made me stop and think about certain aspects of my life, and I decided it was time to prove I could make it on my own."

"By denouncing your family!"

"I never did that, Dad."

Samuel's shoulders sagged with defeat. The long hours her parents had spent travelling were telling on them both. They looked at her blankly, as though they couldn't quite believe, even now, what she'd been doing for the past month and a half.

"I did it for another reason, too." All three of them were staring at her as if they suspected she'd lost her mind. "I'd met Nolan and we had dinner together and I discovered how much I liked him." She glanced at the man in question and saw him frown, knitting his brow, obviously searching for a way to stop her. "I'm sorry, Mom and Dad. I hated lying to you, but I couldn't see any way around it. I didn't want to worry you," she said, stepping next to Nolan and wrapping her arm around his waist. "I belong here with Nolan." There, she'd said it! "I won't be returning to New York with you."

"Maryanne, sweetie, you can't go on living like this!"

"I have a wonderful life."

Her father was pacing again. "You're in love with this man?"

"Yes, Daddy. I love him so much—enough to defy you for the first time in my life."

Her father's eyes slowly moved from his only daughter to Nolan. "What about you, young man? How do you feel about my daughter?"

Nolan was quiet for so long it was all Maryanne could do not to answer for him. Finally she couldn't stand it any longer and did exactly that. "He loves me. He may not want to admit it, but he does—lock, stock and barrel."

Her father continued to look at Nolan. "Is that true?"

"Unfortunately," he said, gently removing Maryanne's arm, "I don't return her feelings. You've raised a wonderful daughter—but I don't love her, not the way she deserves to be loved."

"Nolan!" His name escaped on a cry of outrage. "Don't lie. Not now, not to my family."

He took her by the shoulders, his face pale and expressionless. She searched his eyes, looking for something, anything to ease the terrible pain his words had inflicted.

"You're sweet and talented, and one day you'll make some man very proud—but it won't be me."

"Nolan, stop this right now. You love me. You're intimidated because of who my father is. But don't you understand that money doesn't mean anything to me?"

"It rarely does to those who have it. Find yourself a nice rich husband and be happy."

She found his words insulting. If she hadn't been so desperate to straighten out this mess, she would have confronted him with it. "I won't be happy without you. I refuse to be happy."

His face was beginning to show signs of strain. "Yes, you will. Now, I suggest you do as your family wants and leave with them."

Every word felt like a kick in the stomach, each more vicious than the one before.

"You don't mean that!"

"Damn it, Maryanne," he said coldly, "don't make this any more difficult than it already is. We don't belong together. We never have. I live in one world and you live in another. I've been telling you that from the first, but you wouldn't listen to me."

Maryanne was too stunned to answer. She stared up at him, hoping, praying, for some sign that he didn't mean what he was saying.

"Sweetie." Her mother tucked an arm around Maryanne's waist. "Please, come home with us. Your friend's right, you don't belong here."

"That's not true. I'm here now and I intend to stay."

"Maryanne, damn it, would you listen to your parents?" Nolan barked. "What do you intend to do once Mom's Place closes for remodeling?"

"Come home, sweetie," her mother pleaded.

Too numb to speak, Maryanne stared at Nolan. She wouldn't leave if he gave the slightest indication he wanted her to stay. Anything. A flicker of his eye, a twitch of his hand, anything that would show her he didn't mean the things he'd said.

There was nothing. Nothing left for her. She couldn't go back to the newspaper, not now. Mom's Place was closing, but the real hardship, the real agony, came from acknowledging that Nolan didn't want her around. Nolan didn't love her.

She turned her back on him and walked to her own apartment. Her mother and father joined her there a few minutes later, trying to hide their dismay at its bleakness.

"I won't need to give my notice," she told them, sorting through the stack of folded clothes for a fresh uniform. "But I'll stay until Mom's closes. I wouldn't want to leave them short-staffed."

"Yes, of course," her mother answered softly, then suggested, "If you like, I can stay with you here in Seattle."

Maryanne declined with a quick shake of her head, trying to conceal how badly Nolan's rejection had hurt. "I'll be fine." She paused, then turned to her family. "He really is a wonderful man. It's just that he's terribly afraid of falling in love—especially with someone like me. I have everything he doesn't—an education, wealth, and perhaps most importantly, parents who love me as much as you do."

Maryanne hadn't known it was possible for two weeks to drag by so slowly. But finally her last day of work arrived.

"The minute I set eyes on Nolan Adams again, I swear I'll give him a piece of my mind," Barbara declared, hands on her hips.

Nolan hadn't eaten at Mom's once in the past two

weeks. That didn't surprise Maryanne; in fact, she would've been shocked if he'd decided to show up.

"You keep in touch, you hear? That Nolan Adams—he's got a lot to answer for," Barbara said, her eyes filling. "I'm gonna miss you, girl. Are you sure you have to leave?"

"I'm sure," Maryanne whispered, swallowing back her own tears.

"I suppose you're right. That's why I'm so furious with Nolan."

"It isn't all his fault." Maryanne hadn't told anyone the embarrassing details that had led to her leaving Seattle.

"Of course it is. He should stop you from going. I don't know what's got into that man, but I swear, for two cents I'd give him—"

"A piece of your mind," Maryanne finished for her.

They both laughed, and hugged each other one last time. Although they'd only worked together a short while, they'd become good friends. Maryanne would miss Barbara's down-to-earth philosophy and her reliable sense of humor.

When she arrived home, her apartment was dark and dismal. Cardboard boxes littered the floor. Her packing was finished, except for the bare essentials. She'd made arrangements with a shipping company to come for her things in the morning. Then she'd call a taxi to take her to Sea-Tac Airport in time to catch the noon flight for New York.

The next morning, dressed in jeans and a loose red sweatshirt, Maryanne was hauling boxes out of her living room and stacking them in the hallway when she heard Nolan's door open. She quickly moved back into her own apartment.

"What are you doing?" he demanded, following her in. He was wearing the ever-present beige raincoat, his mood as sour as his look.

"Moving," she responded flippantly. "That was what I thought you wanted."

"Then leave the work to the movers."

"I'm fine, Nolan." Which was a lie. How could she possibly be fine when her heart was broken?

"I guess this is goodbye, then," he said, glancing around the room, looking everywhere but at her.

"Yes. I'll be gone before you get back this afternoon." She forced a trembling smile to her lips as she brushed the dust from her palms. "It's been a pleasure knowing you."

"You, too," he said softly.

"Someday I'll be able to tell my children I knew the famous Nolan Adams when he was a columnist for the *Seattle Sun*." But those children wouldn't be his....

"I wish you only the best." His eyes had dimmed slightly, but she was too angry to see any significance in that.

She didn't reply and the silence stretched, tense and awkward.

"So," she finally said, with a deep sigh, "you're really going to let me go."

"Yes." He spoke without hesitation, but she noticed that his mouth thinned, became taut.

"It may come as a surprise to learn you're not the only one with pride." She spoke as clearly and precisely as she could. "I'm going to do what you asked and leave Seattle. I'll walk away without looking back. Not once will I look back," she repeated, her throat constricting, making speech difficult. She waited a moment to compose herself. "Someday you'll regret this, Nolan. You'll think back to what happened and wish to hell you'd handled the situation differently. Don't you know it's not what you've done that will fill you with regret, but what you haven't done?"

"Annie—"

"No, let me finish. I've had this little talk planned for days and I'm going to deliver it. The least you can do is stand here and listen."

He closed his eyes and nodded.

"I've decided to haunt you."

"What?" His eyes flew open.

"That's right. You won't be able to go into a restaurant without believing you see me there. I'll be hiding behind every corner. I'll follow you down every street. And as for enjoying another bowl of chili, you can forget that, as well." By now her voice was trembling.

"I never meant to hurt you."

She abruptly turned away from him, wiping the tears from her cheeks with both hands.

"Be happy, Annie."

She would try. There was nothing else to do.

Eleven

"Have you had a chance to look over those brochures?" Muriel asked Maryanne two weeks later. They were sitting at the breakfast table, savoring the last of their coffee.

"I was thinking I should find myself another job." It was either that or spend the rest of her life poring over cookbooks. Some people travelled to cure a broken heart, some worked—but not Maryanne. She hadn't written a word since she'd left Seattle. Not one word.

She'd planned to send out new queries, start researching new articles for specialty magazines. Somehow, that hadn't happened. Instead, she'd been baking up a storm. Cookies for the local day-care center, cakes for the senior citizens' home, pies for the clergy. She figured she'd gone through enough flour in the past week to take care of the Midwest wheat crop. Since the holiday season was fast approaching, baking seemed the thing to do.

"But, sweetie, Europe this time of year is fabulous."

"I'm sorry, Mom, I don't mean to be ungrateful, but travelling just doesn't interest me right now."

Her mother's face softened with concern. "Apparently, baking does. Maryanne, you can't bake cookies for the rest of your life."

"I know, I know. If I keep this up I'll look like the Goodyear blimp by Christmas."

Her mother laughed. "That obviously isn't true. If anything, you've been losing weight." She hesitated before adding, "And you've been so quiet."

When she was in pain, Maryanne always withdrew into herself, seeking what comfort she could in routine tasks—such as baking. She was struggling to push every thought of Nolan from her mind. But as her mother said, she had to get out of the kitchen and rejoin the world. Soon she'd write again. Maybe there was a magazine for bakers—she could submit to that, she thought wryly. It would be a place to start, anyway, to regain her enthusiasm. Soon she'd find the strength to face her computer again. Even the sale of three articles hadn't cheered her. She'd stared at the checks and felt a vague sense of disappointment. If only they'd arrived before she left Seattle; then she might have considered staying.

"Is it still so painful?" Muriel asked unexpectedly. Nolan and Maryanne's time in Seattle were subjects they all avoided, and Maryanne appreciated the opportunity to talk about him.

"I wish you and Dad had known him the way I did," she said wistfully. "He's such a contradiction. Rough and surly on the outside, but gentle and compassionate on the inside."

"It sounds as though you're describing your father."

She pondered her mother's words. "Nolan *is* a lot like Daddy. Principled and proud. Independent to a fault.

I didn't realize that in the beginning, only later." She laughed softly. "No man could ever make me angrier than Nolan." Nor could any man hope to compete when it came to the feelings he evoked as he kissed her. She came to life in his arms.

"He drove me crazy with how stubborn he could be. At first all I could see was his defensiveness. He'd scowl at me and grumble—he always seemed to be grumbling, as if he couldn't wait to get me out of his hair. He used to look at me and insist I was nothing but trouble. Then he'd do these incredibly considerate things." She was thinking of the day she'd moved into the apartment and how he'd organized the neighborhood teens to haul her boxes up four flights of stairs. How he'd brought her dinner. The morning he'd fixed her radiator. Even the time he'd tried to find her a more "suitable" date.

"There'll be another man for you, sweetie, someone who'll love you as much as you love him."

A bittersweet smile crossed Maryanne's lips. That was the irony of it all.

"Nolan does love me. I know it now, in my heart. I believed him when he said he didn't, but he was lying. It's just that he was in love with someone else a long time ago and he was badly hurt," she said. "He's afraid to leave himself open to that kind of pain again. To complicate matters, I'm Samuel Simpson's daughter. If I weren't, he might've been able to let go of his insecurities and make a commitment."

"He's the one who's losing out."

Maryanne understood that her mother's words were meant to comfort her, but they had the opposite effect. Nolan wasn't the only one who'd lost. "I realize that and I think in some sense he does, too, but it's not much help."

Her mother was silent.

"You know, Mom," Maryanne said, surprising herself with a sudden streak of enthusiasm. "I may not feel like flying off to Paris, but I think a shopping expedition would do us both a world of good. We'll start at the top floor of Sak's and work our way straight down to the basement."

They spent a glorious afternoon Christmas shopping. They arrived home at dinnertime, exhausted yet rejuvenated.

"Where was everyone after school?" Mark, the older of the Simpson boys, complained. At sixteen, he was already as tall as his father and his dark eyes shone brightly with the ardor of youth. "I had a rotten day."

"What happened?"

Every eye was on him. Mark sighed expressively. "There's this girl—"

"Susie Johnson. Mark's bonkers over her," fourteen-year-old Sean supplied, grinning shrewdly at his older brother.

Mark ignored him. "I've been trying to get Susie's attention for a long time. At first I thought she'd notice me because of my brains."

"What brains? Why would she do anything as dumb as that?"

Samuel tossed his son a threatening glare and Sean quickly returned to his meal.

"Some girls really go for that intelligent stuff. You, of course—" he looked down his nose at Sean "—wouldn't know that, on account of only being in junior high. Which is probably where you'll stay for the rest of your life."

Samuel frowned again.

"Go on," Maryanne urged Mark, not wanting the conversation to get sidetracked by her two brothers trading insults.

"Unfortunately Susie didn't even seem to be aware I was in three of her classes, let alone that I was working my head off to impress her. So I tried out for the soccer team. I figured she'd have to notice me because she's a cheerleader."

"Your skills have been developing nicely," Samuel said, nodding proudly at his eldest son.

"Susie hasn't noticed."

"Don't be so sure," Maryanne said.

"No, it's true." Mark sighed melodramatically, as if the burden of his problem was too heavy to bear. "That was when I came up with the brilliant idea of paying someone—another girl, one I trust—to talk to Susie, ask her a few questions. I figured if I could find out what she really wants in life then I could go out of my way to—" he paused "—you know."

"What you were hoping was that she'd say she wanted to date a guy who drove a red Camaro so you could borrow your mother's to take to school for the next week or so." Samuel didn't succeed in disguising his smile as he helped himself to salad.

"Well, you needn't worry," Mark muttered, rolling his eyes in disgust. "Do you know what Susie Johnson wants most in this world?"

"To travel?" his mother suggested.

Mark shook his head.

"To date the captain of the football team?" Maryanne tried.

Mark shook his head again.

"What then?" Sean demanded.

"She wants thinner thighs."

Maryanne couldn't help it; she started to smile. Her
eyes met her younger brother's, and the smile grew into
a full-fledged laugh.

Soon they were all laughing.

The doorbell chimed and Maryanne's parents exchanged brief glances. "Bennett will get it," Samuel
said before the boys could vault to their feet.

Within a couple of minutes, Bennett appeared. He
whispered something to Maryanne's father, who ex-
cused himself and hurried out of the dining room.

Maryanne continued joking with her brothers until
she heard raised voices coming from the front of the
house. She paused as an unexpected chill shot down
her spine. One of the voices sounded angry, even de-
fensive. Nevertheless Maryanne had no difficulty recognizing whose it was.

Nolan's.

Her heart did a slow drumroll. Without hesitating,
she tossed down her napkin and ran to the front door.

Nolan was standing just inside the entryway, wearing
his raincoat. Everything about him, the way he stood,
the way he spoke and moved, conveyed his irritation.

Maryanne went weak at the sight of him. She noticed
things she never had before. Small things that made her
realize how much she loved him, how empty her life
had become without him.

"I've already explained," her father was saying. Samuel managed to control his legendary temper, but obviously with some difficulty.

Nolan's expression showed flagrant disbelief. He looked tired, Maryanne saw, as if he'd been working nights instead of sleeping. His face was gaunt, his eyes shadowed. "You don't expect me to believe that, do you?"

"You're damn right I do," Maryanne's father returned.

"What's going on here?" she asked, stepping forward, her voice little more than a whisper. She was having trouble dealing with the reality that he was here, in New York, in her family's home. But from the look of things, this wasn't a social call.

"My newspaper column's been picked up nationally," Nolan said, his gaze narrowing on her. "Doesn't that tell you something? Because it damn well should!"

Maryanne couldn't conceal how thrilled she was. "But, Nolan, that's wonderful! What could possibly be wrong with that? I thought it was a goal you'd set yourself."

"Not for another two years."

"Then you must be so pleased."

"Not when it was arranged by your father."

Before Maryanne could whirl around to confront her father, he vehemently denied it.

"I tell you, I had nothing to do with it." Samuel's eyes briefly met Maryanne's and the honesty she saw there convinced her that her father was telling the truth. She'd just opened her mouth to comment when Nolan went on.

"I don't suppose you had anything to do with the sale of my novel, either," he said sarcastically.

Samuel Simpson shook his head. "For heaven's sake, man, I didn't even know you were writing one."

"Your novel sold?" Maryanne shrieked. "Oh, Nolan, I knew it would. The little bit I read was fabulous. Your idea was wonderful. I could hardly force myself to put it down and not read any more." She had to restrain the impulse to throw her arms around his neck and rejoice with him.

"For more money than I ever thought I'd see in my life," he added, his voice hard with challenge. Although he was speaking to Samuel, his eyes rested on Maryanne—eyes that revealed a need and a joy he couldn't disguise.

"Oh, Nolan, I'm so happy for you."

He nodded absently and turned to her father again. "Do you honestly expect me to believe you had nothing to do with that?" he asked, more mildly this time.

"Yes," Samuel answered impatiently. "What possible reason would I have for furthering your career, young man?"

"Because of Maryanne, of course."

"What?" Maryanne couldn't believe what she was hearing. It was ridiculous. It made no sense.

"Your father's attempting to buy you a husband," Nolan growled. Then he turned to Samuel. "Frankly, that upsets me, because Maryanne doesn't need any help from you."

Her father's eyes were stern, and he seemed about to demand that Nolan leave his home.

Maryanne stepped directly in front of Nolan, her hands on her hips. "Trust me, Nolan, if my father was going to buy me a husband, it wouldn't be you! Dad had nothing to do with your success. Even if he did, what would it matter? You've already made it clear you don't want anything to do with me."

His only response was silence.

"I may have spoken a bit…hastily about not loving you," Nolan said a moment later, his voice hoarse.

Samuel cleared his throat, murmuring something about giving the two of them time to talk and promptly left the room.

Maryanne stood gazing up at Nolan, her heart shining through her eyes. Nolan *did* love her; she'd known that for a long time. Only he didn't love her enough to discard the burden of his self-doubts. The boy from the wrong side of the tracks. The self-educated, self-made newsman who feared he'd never fit in with the very people who were awed by his talent.

"You were right," he grumbled, the way he always grumbled, as if he felt annoyed with her.

"About what?"

His smile was almost bitter. "About everything. I love you. Heaven knows I tried not to."

Maryanne closed her eyes, savoring the words she'd never expected to hear. Her heart was pounding so furiously that her head spun. Only…only he didn't say he loved her as though it pleased him.

"Is that such a terrible thing?" she asked. "To love me?"

"No…yes."

He seemed trapped by indecision, dragged down by their differences, yet buoyed by the need to see her again, hear the sound of her voice, gaze at her freckle-dotted nose and run his fingers through her hair. Nolan didn't have to say the words for Maryanne to realize what he was thinking.

"When everything started happening in my life, I thought—I assumed—your father was somehow involved."

"Did you really?" she asked skeptically. The excuse was all too convenient.

Nolan lowered his gaze. "No, I guess I didn't believe he really had anything to do with the sale of my book. But having my columns picked up nationally came as a surprise. For a while I tried to convince myself your family had to be behind that, but I knew it wasn't true. What *really* happened is exactly what you said would happen. You haunted me, Annie. Every time I turned around I could've sworn you were there. I've never missed anyone in my life the way I've missed you."

She smiled shakily. "That's the most beautiful thing you've ever said to me."

Nolan's look was sheepish. "I tried to tell myself your father was out to buy you a husband. Namely me. Think about it, Annie. He got you that job with the *Review*, and for all I knew he could've made it his primary purpose in life to give you everything you want."

"I thought I'd proved otherwise," she said. "My parents went out of their way to make sure none of us was spoiled. I was hoping I'd convinced you of that."

"You did." He slid his hands into the wide pockets of his raincoat. "I guess what I'm trying to say is that if your father's willing to have me in the family, I'd be more than happy to take you off his hands."

"Take me off his hands. How very kind of you," Maryanne snapped, crossing her arms in annoyance. She was looking for romance, declarations of love and words that came straight from his heart. Instead he was handing out insults.

"Don't get all bent out of shape," he said and the smile that stole across his lips was so devastating Maryanne's breath caught. "The way I figure it," he continued, "you need someone…"

Maryanne turned to walk away from him. Not any great distance, of course, just far enough for him to know he wasn't getting anywhere with this argument.

"All right," he amended, catching her by the hand and urging her around to face him again. "*I* need someone."

"Someone?"

"You!" he concluded with a wide grin.

"You're improving. Go on."

"Nothing seemed right after you left. There was this giant hole inside me I couldn't seem to fill. Work didn't satisfy me anymore. Nothing did. Gloria and Eddie asked about you and I didn't know what to say. I was grateful Mom's Place was closed, because I couldn't have eaten there."

A part of her longed for all the romantic words a woman wanted to hear from the man she loved. But it wasn't too likely she'd get them from Nolan. He wasn't telling her he'd heard her name whispered in the wind or seen it written in his heart. Nolan would never say things like that.

"You want me to move back to Seattle so I'll quit haunting you," she finally said.

"No. I want you to come back because I love you."

"And need me?"

He nodded. "I still think you could do a hell of a lot better than marrying an ornery guy like me. I promise to be a good husband—that is, if you're willing to put up with me…" He let the rest fade. His eyes grew humble as he slowly, uncertainly, pulled her into his arms. "Would you…be willing?"

She smiled, and hot tears gathered in the corners of her eyes. She nodded jerkily. "Yes. Oh, you idiot. I could slap you for putting us through all of this."

"Wouldn't a kiss do just as well?"

"I suppose, only…"

But the thought was left unspoken. His kiss was long and thorough and said all the tender words, the fanciful phrases she'd never hear.

It was enough.

More than enough to last her a lifetime.

Epilogue

It was Christmas morning in the Adams household.

The wrapping paper had accumulated in a small mountain on the living-room carpet. The Christmas tree lights twinkled and "Silent Night" played in the background.

Maryanne sat on the sofa next to Nolan with her feet up, her head on her husband's shoulder. The girls were busy sorting through their stash of new toys and playing their favorite game—"being grown-ups." Bailey was pretending to be a young college graduate determined to make a name for herself in the newspaper business. Courtney played a jaded reporter from a rival newspaper, determined to thwart her. It was Maryanne and Nolan's romance all over again. The girls had loved hearing every detail of their courtship.

"They don't seem *too* disappointed about not getting a puppy," he said.

"I'm so proud of them." Maryanne smiled. Both

Courtney and Bailey were thrilled about the new baby, and although it had been hard, they'd accepted that there wouldn't be a puppy in the family, after all. Not for a few years, anyway.

"They're adorable," Nolan agreed and kissed the top of her head. "Just like their mother."

"Thank you," she whispered.

"When did you say your parents would—" Nolan didn't get a chance to finish the question before the doorbell rang. "Is that them?" Samuel and Muriel Simpson had come from New York to spend Christmas week with the family.

Maryanne nodded. Sitting up, she called to her oldest daughter, "Courtney, could you please answer the door?"

Both girls raced to the front door, throwing it open. They were silent for just a second, then squealed with delight. "Grandma! Grandpa Simpson!"

"Merry Christmas. Merry Christmas."

Maryanne's parents stepped into the house, carrying a large wicker basket. Inside slept a small black-and-white puppy.

"A puppy?" Courtney said in a hushed voice. She stared at her grandparents, who grinned and nodded.

"We think every family needs a dog," Maryanne's father said.

"Oh, he's *so* cute," Bailey whispered, covering her mouth with both hands.

"He's perfect," Courtney said, lifting the squirming puppy from his bed. "Is he ours? Can we keep him?"

"Oh, yes, this is a special-delivery Christmas gift for my two beautiful granddaughters."

Maryanne came over to take the puppy from Courtney. She cuddled the small, warm body and looked into sleepy brown eyes. "I guess you've come a long way, haven't you?" she murmured. The puppy gazed up at her, unblinking, and Maryanne fell in love. Just like that, all her concerns disappeared. At least this baby would be house-trained well before their son was born. And the girls could help look after him. She looked up to meet Nolan's eyes, and he nodded. So, despite everything, there'd be *two* new additions to the family this next year.

Nolan ushered her parents inside and took their coats. "Sit down and make yourselves comfortable. Maryanne and I have a Christmas surprise, too."

"As good as a new puppy?" her father asked.

"Oh, yes," Courtney told him after a whispered consultation with her sister. She stroked the puppy, still cradled in her mother's arms. "I don't know what we're naming *that* surprise, but we're calling this one Jack."

* * * * *

Also by JoAnn Ross

The Inheritance

Honeymoon Harbor

Summer on Mirror Lake
Snowfall on Lighthouse Lane
Herons Landing
Second Chance Spring

For a complete list of books by JoAnn Ross,
visit her website, www.joannross.com.

ONCE UPON A WEDDING

JoAnn Ross

One

Once upon a time, in the early 1900s, a newly married royal couple of a small European principality decided to take a tour of America on their honeymoon. When the King and Queen of Montacroix had learned of the lush green majesty of the Olympic National Monument from their friend former President Theodore Roosevelt, they'd added it to their itinerary. As soon as that news reached Washington State's Olympic Peninsula, the residents of the once prosperous but dying Victorian seaport town nestled up against the mountains had immediately voted to rename the town Honeymoon Harbor in hopes of using the royal visit to garner publicity.

It worked. As the years passed, the town became a popular wedding and honeymoon destination. Honeymoon Harborites had long grown accustomed to seeing brides decked out in white princess dresses and grooms in tuxedos exchanging vows in the town center's lacy white Victorian gazebo, on the sand beside impossibly blue water, and barefoot in mountain meadows carpeted with wildflowers dancing on the breeze.

But they really perked up when the couples were

locals. And any wedding became an event when it
involved the Mannions or the Harpers, whose feud,
mostly long past—but still occasionally simmering—
had begun when Nathaniel Harper was the sole person
to vote against the name change. Or, as some old-timers
claimed, when, generations ago, Nathaniel and Gabriel
Mannion were both courting the same woman, who'd
ended up choosing Gabriel.

Today's wedding between Kylee Campbell and Mai
Munemori involved both families. Seth Harper had remodeled the Folk Victorian house for Kylee and Mai
to live in, and they had chosen the back garden as the
perfect location to exchange their vows. Meanwhile
Seth's fiancée, Brianna Mannion, had stepped in as
wedding planner when the couple found attempting to
coordinate events while learning the ropes of mothering
their newborn adopted daughter more time-consuming
and exhausting than they'd expected. Although the last
wedding Brianna had organized had involved two King
Charles spaniels, as a former executive concierge to the
top rollers at the Las Vegas Midas Resort and Casino,
she had no doubt that the small, intimate garden wedding would go off without a hitch. Little did she realize that she was about to learn the unfortunate lesson
of best-laid plans.

Desiree Marchand had loved baking ever since
she'd been old enough to stand on a stool in her grand-
mère Dupree's kitchen, learning the many variations of
French pastry dough, beginning with the basic distinc-
tion between *viennoiserie* and *patisserie*. "The Vien-
nese may have given us pastry," her grand-mère would
say, "but we French are the ones who put the magic into

the dough." According to family lore, an old-line Creole ancestor, who could trace his roots directly back to France, had started the family's first *boulangerie* in 1736, making bread for the patients at New Orleans's Charity Hospital, which had continued to operate until Hurricane Katrina.

Today Desiree was in Kylee and Mai's kitchen, singing to herself as she put together the happiest of pastries, a wedding cake. She was spreading French buttercream frosting on the three layers of cake, when an all-too-familiar baritone voice from her past began singing along. Spinning around, she found herself looking straight into a pair of dark chocolate-brown eyes.

"What are you doing here?"

Bastien Broussard lifted his hands. "Apparently I'm here to get stabbed with whatever that weapon is that you're holding."

She glanced down at the stainless-steel bench scraper she'd been using to smooth the buttercream. And lowered her hand. "I meant here." She inadvertently swung it again as she waved her hand around the kitchen. "In this town. In this house."

Before he could answer, Brianna came rushing into the kitchen, appearing nearly as flustered as Desiree felt. "Don't tell Kylee and Mai, but we have a problem."

She was not alone. What was the man Desiree had loved with all her heart, then walked away from, doing here, in the far northwest corner of the country?

"What is it?" she asked, trying for a reasonably calm voice. But from the way a corner of Bastien's mouth quirked, he knew that he'd rattled her. As he'd always been able to do. In so many ways.

"We've lost our musician."

"Lost, lost? As in you can't find her? Or lost as in she's not showing up?"

"The second. She's in the hospital getting stitches for a cut she got opening a can of dog food," Brianna answered on something close to a wail. She closed her eyes, took a deep breath, seemed to be counting to ten, then opened her eyes again. "I don't know what's wrong with me. I've dealt with being stuck in an elevator with snarling little dogs trying to rip each other's tulle brides-maid's dresses off. I don't know why I'm panicking over a musician."

"Because this wedding is personal. Kylee's been your friend all your life. You want everything to be perfect."

"I always expect everything to be perfect," Brianna returned sharply, then pressed her fingers against the bridge of her nose. "I'm sorry. I've been working on that." She took another breath. Let it out. "It's not the end of the world." Desiree couldn't quite decide whom she was trying to convince. Her? Or herself? "If I can't find a wedding singer in the next ninety minutes, I'll simply have Seth figure out how to hook up my phone to a sound system. He's a genius at that tech stuff. It won't be the same as an actual performer, but it's bet-ter than nothing."

Do. Not. Say. A. Word. Desiree was afraid to even look at the man standing behind her for fear that he'd know that she knew what he was thinking, and she didn't want to encourage him.

"What type of wedding singer was she?" he asked.
Damn.

"Marian Oberchain's very versatile. She can sing pop, the oldies, ballads, even country. She could also play a classical harp, an acoustic guitar and the ukulele, which I really wanted because Mai's from Hawaii, and Marian was going to play the 'Hawaiian Wedding Song'... I'm sorry. I don't believe we've met."

"I'm an old friend of Desiree's," he said. "Bastien Broussard."

"You're French?"

"Cajun." He gifted her with one of his knee-melting smiles. Not the full-out sexy kind he used to turn on Desiree, but it was enough to bring a bit of color to the usually cool and composed Brianna's cheeks. "A few centuries removed from France. But I lived in Paris for a while."

As if that smile had emptied her head, a feeling which Desiree had experienced too many times in the past, Brianna appeared to have forgotten her immediate problem.

"Perhaps you'd better go find Seth so he can hook up that system," Desiree suggested.

"I suppose I should. Oh, I'm sorry, I just realized that I was so distracted that I didn't introduce myself. I'm Brianna Mannion."

"And *your* family would have come here from the auld sod," he said, somehow pulling off what sounded to Desiree like an actual Irish accent.

"Like yours, from a few generations back," she confirmed. "It's good to meet you, Mr. Broussard. Enjoy your visit. In fact, I just had a wonderful idea."

No! Desiree begged inwardly. *Don't go there.*

"Why don't you stay for the wedding? I know Kylee and Mai would welcome having you here and that way you and Desiree can catch up."

Damn. She'd gone there.

"I'd enjoy that," Bastien said. "Although I'm afraid I'm not dressed formally enough for the occasion."

Both women skimmed a look over him in his dark, slim-cut indigo jeans, a white button-down linen shirt worn open over a black body-hugging T-shirt, and cobalt-blue loafers that looked so soft they had to be pricey Italian leather to allow him to go without socks. He still looked like a Cajun bad boy blues rocker, but he had taken on a definite Parisian flair since she'd last seen him. His hair, as black as her own, was no longer down at his shoulders, but had been cut to a shaggy style that just reached his collar and begged a woman's hands to run through it.

"You look great," Brianna said. "We're very casual here in Honeymoon Harbor. The only reason I'll be dressing up is that I'm the maid of honor."

"*Bien*, then," he said. "I'd be honored to accept your invitation. But I do have another suggestion that might solve your problem."

"Oh?" Brianna lifted a perfectly arched blond brow.

"As it happens, I'm a singer. And a musician."

"Really. What instrument do you play?"

"A tenor sax typically. Which is in my rental car. But I can also play the alto sax, keyboard and guitar. And once, while I was in Hawaii, I had a lesson in the ukulele. Coincidentally, it was the 'Hawaiian Wedding Song.'"

In full official wedding coordinator mode, Brianna folded her arms. "I don't want to risk insulting you, Mr. Broussard, but are you any good? Because this wedding is the most personal event I've ever planned."

"*Je comprends.* I'd feel the same way myself." He reached into the pocket of his dark jeans, pulled out a cell phone and opened YouTube. "This was at a live concert in Australia."

He hit Play and there he was standing alone in the spotlight onstage, wearing much the same outfit as he was wearing now, but with a black leather jacket and black rocker boots, his beautiful voice crooning a blues ballad about love and loss Desiree knew that he'd written about them. Bastien had played it for her in Paris, on the balcony of their room in the Hôtel Plaza Athénée with its perfect view of the Eiffel Tower their last night together.

"Oh. Now I feel really foolish." Brianna looked up at him. "You're famous."

He shrugged in that casual Gallic way he had. "A bit," he allowed. "In my own circle. There's no reason you should know of me."

"He won a music award," Desiree heard herself saying before she could stop herself.

"Three," he corrected her with a self-deprecating grin that was sexier than any male swagger. "But who's counting?" He turned back to Brianna. "If you'd like to give me the bride's playlist…"

"It's right here." Brianna pulled it out of a white binder and handed it to him. "I'll have to talk to Kylee and Mai, but I'm sure they'll agree that you should feel free to play whatever you'd like. And what feels appropriate. I don't know what you usually charge, but—"

"Consider it my gift to the happy couple," he said. Then tilted his head and looked at Desiree, who knew very well what was coming. "Desiree sings, too. In fact, we were in a band together. She was the front singer, of course."

"You were in a band?" Brianna looked at Desiree as

if she'd been keeping some big secret from everyone in Honeymoon Harbor.

"It was a very long time ago. I was nineteen, working in my father's bakery as an apprentice with plans to attend culinary school in France. Then I got sidetracked for a few years."

Plans which she'd put off after Bastien had approached her in New Orleans's Jackson Square, where she'd been singing Christmas carols with a choral group. And hadn't her father exploded when she'd told him that she'd agreed to join the band of a stranger whom she'd met that very same night? That had caused a split between them for two weeks, until Augustin Dupree had thrown in the towel. Only after threatening to slice Bastien into pieces with a filet knife and feed him to the gators if he ever hurt his baby girl.

"I was three years older," Bastien said. "Mood Indigo, that was our band. It was blues rock, but to be honest, we'd play whatever someone would pay us to play. Including our share of weddings, until Desiree decided that baking would provide her a steadier income. Which, at the time, she was correct about." He touched her with his melting dark gaze. "What do you say, *cher*? Want to relive our young and foolish past for a couple hours?"

"Oh, that would be so romantic!" Brianna actually clapped her hands. The outward display of excitement from the warm but usually composed woman was like a brass Mardi Gras band marching through the kitchen. "Would you, Desiree? I know it would mean so much to Kylee and Mai."

"Your cake appears nearly finished," Bastien noted.

"It just needs the topper," she said. "Which I'm going to wait to add until right before rolling it outside."

"Wonder Women." He nodded his approval, not that she needed it. "I like that."

"You like all women," Desiree retorted.

Brianna's brow furrowed again. "Mr. Broussard—"

"Bastien," he said easily.

"Bastien it is," Brianna said in an outwardly casual tone that didn't fool anyone for a moment. "Perhaps you could get your saxophone from your car while Desiree and I go over a few last-minute details about the cake cutting?"

"Fine." He met Desiree's gaze. "I'm parked down the street. I'll be back soon.'

They both watched him walk away. "I've always been mad crazy in love with Seth," Brianna murmured. "But looking never hurt, did it?"

"Every other woman always has," Desiree said, sounding a bit too sharp to her own ears. "I'm sorry. That sounded snarky and I certainly didn't mean it that way."

"I'm the one who should apologize, inviting him to stay without talking with you alone first. Is there a problem?"

"No." She wouldn't allow it. "Don't worry, nothing's going to screw up Kylee and Mai's special day."

"You loved him," Brianna guessed.

"Yes." Desiree sighed. "I was young and naive."

"I've been there. It's hard. Are you sure…"

"It'll be fine." She forced a smile. "I haven't sung in public for years. It could be fun." Right up there with a root canal.

"Being a wedding, there are going to be a lot of love songs."

"As long as I can avoid singing 'Unchained Melody.' Because that always makes me cry when I think of Patrick Swayze getting murdered."

"You're not alone. That one's not on the list because Kylee cries like a baby whenever we watch *Ghost*. Jolene would be really upset if we ruin the makeup she spent so much time applying."

"Then it'll be fine," Desiree said.

"Perhaps this could turn out to be a romantic reunion for the two of you."

"Nope," Desiree said as Bastien walked back into the kitchen, looking good enough to scoop up with a spoon. "Not happening."

Two

Once she'd calmed down, Brianna, who was no longer in the kitchen, had reminded Bastien of one of those old Hitchcock movie blondes. Like Grace Kelly. Cool and calm in a crisis.

Desiree, on the other hand, sticking with the '50s/'60s movie theme, was more Natalie Wood. He'd always found her more stunning than the girl-next-door, with an undercurrent of recklessness and sensuality humming beneath the surface that her strict and proper New Orleans Catholic French upbringing usually kept hidden. Until she was onstage. Or, he thought, as bittersweet memories caused both his body and his heart to ache, in bed.

"What are you doing here?" she asked as she finally put the possible weapon down on the counter.

"I came to see you."

What else could have brought him to this small, quaint town that was nothing like Paris? Nor New Orleans. He found it interesting that she'd kept her singing career a secret from a woman who appeared to be a friend. Bastien had always known that of the two of them, she could have been the true star. But she'd given up her chance for fame to bake croissants and, apparently, wedding cakes. He'd stopped by her bakery on the way here, where a young woman had sent him to this house. The *boulangerie* had matched her personality. Tidy and organized, as baking required, yet the desserts in the window and glass display case were lovely, even sensual, and enticing. Just like her.

"How did you find me?" She made it sound as if he'd discovered her in the witness protection program. Nor did she seem at all happy to see him. Bastien could have taken that as a sign he stood no chance of winning her back, but he had always been an optimist. He decided that there'd be no reason for her to put up that protective wall if she weren't susceptible to being won over.

"Well, I could have Googled you, but decided that could be considered a bit stalkerish, so I simply asked your father."

"You asked Papa? I don't understand. Did you call him all the way from Paris to ask, 'Hey, Augustin, where can I find your daughter? I know you've always believed she's much too good for me, but I want to see her.'"

He found it interesting that she knew he'd been living in Paris. True, he did appear in music magazines like *Rolling Stone* and on various entertainment shows, from time to time, and had even written a song for a Disney movie, but perhaps she'd occasionally checked up on him. As he admittedly had her.

"No, I asked him where to find you while having coffee and beignets at the Café du Monde, which is admittedly touristy, but nevertheless, they do make great beignets. And it's conveniently near the French Market where we both happened to be shopping for greens, boudin and shrimp."

Her eyes—a vivid clear blue of the Caribbean Sea that contrasted so sharply with tawny skin that was a beautiful blend of her Creole father and islander mother—widened. They'd always had a way of focusing in on you as if you were the only person in the room. He wasn't the only man to get lost in those thickly lashed eyes. He'd witnessed audience members react the same way when, after looking for an individual to sing directly to, she'd single one out.

"What were you doing at the market?"

"Like I said, shopping… I've been living in New Orleans for the past two years."

"But I was visiting Papa just a few months ago and he never said a thing."

"I doubt he wanted to encourage a reunion. Also, I asked him not to."

"Why? Were you still angry about me leaving? Not just about having broken up the band, but after that night in Paris, two years later?"

After playing a gig in Madrid, he'd taken a train to Paris, where he knew she should be finishing up her two years of culinary training. Bastien called the number he'd never gotten out of his head, suggesting they meet for coffee at a café not far from the school. They hadn't bothered with the coffee, but had instead gone straight to his balcony room at the Hôtel Plaza Athénée, which by then he could almost afford.

They'd been drinking champagne on the balcony when he'd sung her the song he'd written just that morning, about the love of a man for a woman, and the loss Bastien knew was going to break his heart.

Afterward, they'd made love in the deep soaker tub that had a perfectly framed view of the Eiffel Tower, and then went on to spend the night making up for all the time lost since she'd left the band. The next morning, they'd shared a continental breakfast in bed. As if it were yesterday, he could picture her plucking an elegant, golden crusty croissant from the basket, biting into it, intently studying it as if preparing for the Superior Pastry Certificate she'd only just achieved at Paris's Le Cordon Bleu school.

"I could make a better one," she'd decided. "But the hint of almond admittedly marries well with the buttery flavor." She'd held it out to him, inviting him to take a bite.

"I'd rather take a bite of you," he'd said, nevertheless tasting the croissant because he'd never been able to deny Desiree anything. "Good," he'd decided. "But not as tasty as my angel." Putting their mimosa glasses on the table beside the bed, he'd pulled her down on top of him.

Bastien suspected, from the way Desiree's gaze moved from his to out the French doors of the cottage toward the garden, that she too was remembering those golden twenty-four hours. After breakfast, they'd wandered the streets of Paris, had lunch at a little bistro next to the Seine before going up into the Eiffel Tower to look out over the city, which was in full, glorious spring bloom. At the end of the sun-brightened day, the flowers he'd bought her from a small stand outside the Jardin de Tuileries still in hand, she'd boarded a night flight to New York City. She was going to work for the man who'd go on to be named the best pastry chef in the world. Bastien had stayed behind in Paris, having decided to use the city for his home base.

"I wasn't angry about you leaving the band," he said, bringing both his mind and the conversation back to the present. "Truthfully, I was surprised you stayed as long as you did. Every morning of those five years we toured, I'd wake up thinking, 'This will be the day Desiree leaves.' I understood that you did what you had to do. For yourself and your career. And I've done okay for myself going solo."

"You've done more than okay. You truly are a star."

He shrugged. "It's a living. I'm not going to lie and say it didn't hurt, watching your plane fly away, off to New York, but the same way we were destined to first meet, I consoled myself with the knowledge that eventually we'd meet again when the time was right, and stay together forever."

A dark brow lifted over those expressive eyes, which had begun to spark with a bit of temper he'd always enjoyed uncovering. "You were that sure of yourself?"

"No. I was that sure of us," Bastien said mildly. "Unfortunately, due to contractual concert agreements, I couldn't follow you to New York. Also, if you want me to be perfectly honest—"

"Of course I do."

"All right. The truth was that I didn't know how many more chances we'd get, and I didn't want to risk screwing up what could have been our last time together."

"You were always superstitious."

Bastien grinned as he shrugged. "What can I say? It's the Cajun in me." He was also the more romantic of the two of them, but decided this wasn't the time to bring that up. "But like I said, my situation, when you were visiting your father, was complicated."

"Because of your concert schedule?"

"No. I'd stopped playing live concerts by then."

"But I bought… Never mind."

Ah. Desiree was talking about the new album he'd had engineered at a studio in New Orleans. Bastien liked that she still listened to him sing and wondered if she'd ever realized that all the love songs he wrote were always for her.

"I stopped because of my grand-mère."

"I've always liked Abella."

"As she liked you. I always wondered how she and your father could be so close, while at the same time he disapproved so strongly of me."

"My mother died when I was born," she reminded him. "And although my grand-mère lived with us and took care of me as if I were her own daughter, we lost her to cancer when I was twelve. Along with the understandable grief at his mother's death, I suspect Papa was at a total loss on how to handle a hormonal adolescent girl who was growing up faster than he would have wished. He was merely being protective."

Looking back on the young man he'd been when they'd first met, Bastien decided that if he ever had a daughter, he'd feel the same way.

"Also," she continued, "they undoubtedly grew close because they were both in the business of making people happy with their food. And your grand-mère Abella always bought the bread for her restaurant from my family."

"That's why he called me."

"My father called you? In Paris? When?"

"A little over two years ago. He found me through my manager. He wanted to let me know how ill Abella was becoming. I knew she was growing older, but she'd always had such strength, you know? And she'd raised me, much as yours did you, after my parents took off."

Bastien's father had been a blues musician who, like many musicians, had unfortunately become too fond of drugs and alcohol. Because LeRoy Broussard had left the family when Bastien was a toddler, he had no memory of him. He did remember his mother, who was also too fond of her "hot and dirty" Cajun martinis, taking off with an oil man who'd had no use for children. The memory of watching her drive off in that big fancy car when he was seven years old had been burned into Bastien's mind as if by a red-hot branding iron. Over the years, it had lost its power to wound. But it had made him vow that when he settled down, he'd only wed a woman he'd want to live with forever. Like the woman who was standing so near. And yet so far.

"Of course I knew she was growing older. But she'd always been so strong," Bastien said. "I'd call her every Sunday, from wherever I was, timing the call between when she got home from early mass and before she opened the restaurant for the after-church crowd. Not once had she so much as hinted that she had a heart condition. I learned about that from your father, who, like I said, tracked me down in Paris, where I was living in the Oberkampf—"

"Where, despite making a good enough living to live in one of the pricier arrondissements, you preferred to hang out with musicians."

"That would only be natural since I *am* a musician," he said. Although he only played in public occasionally these days. "The only time I ever was comfortable with pricey things was when I wanted to show off for you. Rather than take you to my very plain room with a cranky old landlady who watched with an eagle eye for me to bring home a woman, or a man, if I were so inclined, both of which were against my rental agreement, I splurged and booked that hotel room."

The color in her cheeks and the way her eyes turned a little dreamy told him that he wasn't the only one who had bittersweet memories of that twenty-four hours they'd spent together.

"At any rate, Augustin told me that the restaurant was wearing her heart out, but she refused to sell. She insisted that she'd keep working until they put her in a box. Which was exactly what she did until last month, two years after I came home to help her run it. In truth, at the end, she spent her last six months sitting in a chair, bossing me around her kitchen as if I were a mere line cook, but despite her failing health, we passed a good time together, her and me."

"I'm so sorry." She reached out and touched the bare skin beneath his rolled-up sleeve, warming Bastien all the way to the bone. "But at least you had that special time together."

"True. It's a debt I owe to your father. Have you ever thought what a coincidence it was that we both grew up so many years with our grandmothers taking on our mothers' roles? I've often wondered if that was another reason why we connected."

"But I never knew my mother, so I suspect that was easier for me. And my father was always there." Unlike either of his parents.

"Grand-mère's passing put a lot of things in motion.

I'd already hired my cousin Octave as a sous chef. She left the restaurant to me, so, after staying a few months to make sure he could handle it, I sold it to Octave, whose wife is having their second child this fall. And voilà." He lifted his hands. "Here I am."

"Why?" Desiree asked again.

"To see you, *cher*."

"And do you have plans beyond that?"

"*Bien sur*. I'm opening a restaurant. I checked this town out online and it's definitely lacking in dining choices. So I decided it would be a perfect location to open a Cajun café."

She tilted her head, and put her hands on her hips. "You're opening a restaurant here? In Honeymoon Harbor?"

"I am. I find the name prophetic. I saw a couple getting married in that pretty little gazebo as I drove by. What would you think of us exchanging our vows there? Or would you prefer being married in New Orleans, where your father can walk you down the aisle in the same cathedral where you received your First Communion and confirmation?"

"I'm certainly not going to marry you."

"Of course you are," he said easily. "Because we're soul mates. But don't worry, I'll give you all the time you need to get used to the idea."

"You gave me that soul mate line that day you asked me to join your band. After you'd heard me sing."

"It wasn't a line then. And it isn't now. It's the God's own truth. And while I'm being truthful, here's another fact for you. I wouldn't have cared if you could sing or not. I just wanted an excuse to be with you every day. That, by the way, has not changed."

"You're out of your crazy Cajun mind."

"Over you," he agreed. "And here's the best part."

She folded her arms over her white apron with *Ovenly* written in pretty script on the bib part. "I can't wait to hear it."

"I'm opening up that café in the space next to your *boulangerie*. Which will make us neighbors."

"You are not." Her remarkable eyes were now shooting flaming daggers. "That space only became open last week and I'm expanding Ovenly into it."

"Have you signed a lease?"

"No, but—"

He flashed her his most sincere smile. The one that had usually charmed Sister Mary Constance out of assigning him to detention.

"I'm sure a compromise can be worked out. But why don't we discuss that later, *cher*?" He glanced down at his watch. "We're running out of rehearsal time and you wouldn't want to disappoint the brides."

Three

While Desiree and Bastien were going through the song choice list Brianna had given them, editing it to take out a few that they felt had been overdone and adding others, two of the bedrooms were a hive of activity. Gloria Wells, owner of Thairapy Salon, was styling the bridal parties' hair, as well as that of many of Mai's family members who'd flown in from Hawaii for the occasion. In the other bedroom, Gloria's daughter, Jolene, who'd arrived the previous day from Los Angeles, was using her pots, pencils and powders to create her own kind of magic.

"I love it that you kept me looking like myself," Kylee Campbell said, closing her eyes as instructed while Jolene spritzed the rose water setting spray on her face. "But so much better! We need to add credits at the end of the wedding video. Just like in the movies!" She held up her hands as if framing it on a screen. "Makeup by award-winning Jolene Wells!"

"Being nominated is a long way from winning. It's a long time until the awards ceremony in September."

"But there were so many TV movies and series made

last year," Kylee said. "And you ended up making the top tier! I'd vote for you to win in a heartbeat."

"Me, too," Mai, her fiancée and about-to-be wife, said. "Besides, how many more Tudor-period TV series does the world need? There is no competition."

And wasn't that exactly what Jolene had thought when she'd seen the list? "I love you," she told Mai. "You, too," she assured Kylee.

"Love is all around!" Kylee, who seemed to be talking in exclamation marks today, said.

"We probably *should* have credits," Mai seconded Kylee's suggestion. "How many people have not only a famous makeup artist, but also a three-time award-winning singer at their wedding? I can't imagine how you pulled that off," she told Brianna, who'd arrived to get her makeup done for her role as maid of honor.

"Bastien Broussard fell into my lap," Brianna said. "Actually into your kitchen. It turns out he's an old friend of Desiree's who's in town to visit her. From New Orleans, by way of Paris."

"I love Paris," Kylee said with a sigh. "I once dreamed of living there, in some little attic apartment on the Left Bank."

"You'd definitely fit in with all the other artists and bohemians," Brianna agreed.

"I would have back then. But I don't regret a thing. Because if I *had* settled in Paris, I might not have met Mai, and we wouldn't have Clara." She laughed. "Of all the ways I imagined my life turning out while I was growing up, I never, in a million years, would've guessed I'd be happy as a typical suburban mom."

"In the first place, this cottage is not in the burbs. Honeymoon Harbor doesn't even *have* suburbs. And you'll never, ever, be typical. You still do beautifully creative photography, so it isn't as if you've been completely domesticated."

"That would certainly be true," Mai said as she left the room with Kylee to get their hair styled, then be helped into their gowns.

"You're my next victim," Jolene said, turning to Brianna. "Not that you need much work. Fortunately, not everyone has your perfect skin, or I'd never get my makeup line launched."

"I've been using the night cream I bought from your mom at the salon. And the day cream with the sunscreen," Brianna said. "They're so light, I can't even feel them on my skin. When you do launch it, it's going to be a smashing success."

"From your mouth to God's ear," Jolene said as she spritzed a lavender rosemary toner on Brianna's face. "This will keep your skin hydrated when you're spending so much time in the sun," she said. "The lavender is mostly to relax you. You've been running around like the Energizer Bunny all day."

"I want Kylee and Mai's day to be perfect. As maid of honor, it's my responsibility to make it happen."

"It'll be wonderful. Beautiful. And as perfect as everything you always do."

If Brianna hadn't been so nice to her during those high school bullying days, Jolene could have been jealous of her ability to multitask seemingly a gazillion things at once without so much as having a honey-blond hair slip out of place. She began smoothing a moisturizer on her face. "And even if you messed everything up, Kylee's so high up in the gilded happy clouds, I don't think she'd even notice."

"She's definitely dialed her usual enthusiasm level up to eleven," Brianna agreed.

Jolene dabbed on a bit of foundation. "I don't want to gossip, but is Amanda Barrow always so quiet?"

"She's not the chattiest person in the world, but then again, I'm usually not, either, so I've never noticed. But now that you mention it, she might be a bit more subdued today. Why?"

"She had what looked like the last stage of a bruise on her right cheek. And it was a little swollen, like a bruise tends to be. So, not wanting to bring it up, since we don't know each other at all, I massaged her face, to help break up the blood, with Arnica gel. It's a homeopathic herb that I've found works very well with bruises after face lasering."

"Ouch." Brianna's hands lifted to her own cheeks. "I can't imagine doing that."

"You're not in a business that requires women to remain forever young," Jolene said.

"Thank God. My problem used to be just the opposite. I was young enough that sometimes it was hard to be taken seriously. Especially by older wealthy men who were used to more staid, gray-haired butler types."

"You were young, blonde and pretty. Like nearly every other woman, you've undoubtedly encountered your share of unwanted male attention."

"And isn't that a polite way to put it," Brianna said, confirming Jolene's statement. "Getting back to Amanda—who, by the way, created a fairyland out in that garden—she's a landscaper. Although she has a crew, while she was doing the work on Herons Landing, I watched her carrying big rocks around and planting trees and shrubs. I suppose bruises could be part of that."

"Makes sense," Jolene agreed. "So, I noticed your brother arrived a while ago," Jolene casually commented.

"Seth came because his mom's officiating. I sort of coerced Aiden to come to catch up with him. He's been staying at the coast house for a few weeks."

"Really?" Jolene was proud of how her voice showed none of the nerves that had been tangling ever since she caught sight of the one man she'd rather never see again, talking with Seth and Caroline Harper in the back garden. "Is he on vacation?"

"More like decompressing. He recently came back from Los Angeles—"

"Aiden's been in LA?" What would she have done if she'd known? And the second question: Had he known *she* was living there?

True, she didn't have her face on a billboard on Sunset Boulevard, but the announcement of the award nomination was listed in the *Los Angeles Times*, *LA Weekly*, *Los Angeles Magazine* and *Variety*. And other papers she hadn't even known about until she'd discovered her mother had gone online, downloading and printing out every mention of the nomination she could find. Jolene made a note never to go to a movie she'd worked on with her mother. Gloria would probably take a photo of the screen when her name appeared. Way, way down toward the end, after nearly everyone had left the theater.

"Aiden joined the LAPD right out of the Marines. He started in SWAT, then moved to different departments. Funny, I was so caught in my own career at the time, I didn't make the connection about both of you being there. I guess you never ran across one another?"

Jolene shrugged. "It's a big city. The odds would have been against it."

"I imagine that's so," Brianna said. "Las Vegas wasn't nearly as large, but I know how we all run in our own worlds and spaces. But now you'll have an opportunity to catch up."

Fortunately, Brianna went on to talk about how wonderful Mai's family was, most of whom were staying at Herons Landing, which saved Jolene from responding.

Four

"You can't deny that we still blend together perfectly," Bastien said after he and Desiree had sung for thirty minutes.

"Our voices," she qualified. "Though you never sang all that often when we were a four-person band."

"We put you in the front because you were the prettiest," he said. He glanced out the doors again at the gathering guests. "I'm going to run out and see if any one of those guys in the Hawaiian shirts happened to have brought a uke. That'd be cool if we could sing the 'Hawaiian Wedding Song' to that."

"I doubt they'd have it here at the house, even if they'd brought it on the plane."

"True. But this is a small town, so wherever they're staying can't be that far away."

"They're all either at Brianna's bed-and-breakfast or the Lighthouse View Hotel. Neither of which are very far away."

"I thought Brianna Mannion was a wedding planner."

"She's helping out today. The brides recently adopted

a baby, so their lives got too busy to take care of details, which was when Brianna stepped in. She used to be a concierge for the mega-rich at some of the best hotels in the country, then decided to slow her life down and come back home from Las Vegas. To make a long and somewhat winding story short, she and the contractor helping to restore the Victorian house she was renovating are now engaged."

"Long and winding stories that end up happily are my favorite," he said.

She refused to fall into that conversation snare. Their own road might have been long and winding, but she wasn't going to allow her heart to tumble again. She'd done the right thing breaking up with Bastien. She'd have to remember all the reasons why leaving had been for the best. And why their lives were still not compatible.

"I mostly know the melody to the 'Hawaiian Wedding Song,'" she said. "Enough to keep up if I knew the words. Which I don't. And I really can't wait for you to try to track down a ukulele. I have to go change into the dress I'm wearing to the wedding. Jolene, a Hollywood makeup artist, insists on doing my makeup along with all the other women's. She's the daughter of Gloria, who runs the salon and is in charge of hair today."

"It's going to take me some time to catch up on all the small-town connections," he said, as if he was actually going to be staying here in Honeymoon Harbor. He wouldn't last a month. "You're gorgeous just the way you are," he said, unaware of her thoughts, "but you should have time to go online and check it out while she fancies you up. You always were the quickest of us to memorize lyrics." He flashed her another of those damn cocky grins, then went off in search of a ukulele.

Shaking her head, she went off to get "fancied" up. Since baking in a hot kitchen could melt off makeup, it had been years since she'd worn anything but a bit of moisturizer. When Gloria Wells had started selling her daughter's organic products at Thairapy, she'd fallen in love with the light and smooth lotion.

"Well," Jolene said, as Desiree sat down in the chair in front of the dressing table. "I've been gilding a lot of gorgeous lilies today. But it's still fun."

"Other than a bit of lipstick and sometimes a touch of powder for New Orleans humidity, I haven't worn makeup since I used to sing, which was years ago," Desiree said.

"Brianna told me you were in a rock band." Jolene swept a moisturizer over her face, then followed up with a light-as-air primer. "That must have been fun."

"It was blues rock. And it had its moments." Desiree smiled for the first time since Bastien had appeared in the kitchen. "Who am I kidding? It was fun. For a few years. Then I decided it was probably time to grow up and get a job where I could earn a living down the road. The music business, like Hollywood, was and still is extremely sexist. Not every woman can have a career for as long as Cher or Carly Simon."

"I suppose you can probably do makeup as well as I do."

"Stage makeup is different," she said. "As you probably know from working in Hollywood. The bright lights take more. I layered it on with a trowel."

"You're striking enough to get away with going over the top." Jolene stood back and studied her. "Your eyes hold such a wonderful element of surprise when contrasted with your skin. What would you say to a smoky cat eye with some glitter?"

"That it might be a bit much for an afternoon garden wedding."

"True." Jolene sighed. "But it'd be fabulous. If I weren't leaving after the wedding to Ireland for a shoot, I'd want to really get creative with you so Kylee could take your portrait. But for today, we'll skip the cat eyes and glitter and just go with a bit of smoke."

As she got busy with her artistry gathering up her brushes and colors, Desiree went online and looked up the lyrics for the song. Which, fortunately, were short and simple. And perfect.

"I'd imagine your work allows for a lot of travel," she said, after she'd committed them to memory over two readings.

"At times," Jolene said. "But even with films set in fabulous places, many of the interior shots are done in studios in LA, so there's not as much as you'd think. Though sometimes the constant traveling for work makes it difficult to have a relationship. I'm going to be in Ireland for three months, while my boyfriend, I guess that's what you'd call him, although it sounds so high school, will be shooting in Australia and Hawaii."

"I didn't want to say anything, because you probably get tired of answering the question, but since you brought him up, I've seen the photos of the two of you on magazine covers at the checkout in the market—is it difficult dating an actor?"

"I'd never dated one before Mark," Jolene said, sweeping color across Desiree's lids. "I always stuck with guys in the trade. Electricians, carpenters, the occasional camera operator. But yes, I'll admit that it can get bothersome having paparazzi cameras in your face whenever you go out to the grocery store."

"I can imagine. When Bastien and I were together, women would send notes and even nude photos to him. Sometimes they'd even have them delivered to the dressing room we shared, or they would wait outside the club door and hand him envelopes with their phone numbers. It was hard on our relationship because, being young, I'd get jealous... I can't believe I just told you something I've never admitted to anyone."

"Hairdressers and makeup artists are like bartenders," Jolene said cheerfully. "Clients always tell us everything. We're also like priests in a confessional. We're sworn to keep all secrets. And if I had to put up with that behavior, it would really upset me. But to be honest, my relationships never last long enough for me to get jealous." She drew a line with a black pencil and smudged it with her fingertip. "My mother said I was born leaving. She's probably right."

"I envy you," Desiree admitted. "Being able to move on so easily."

"It has its pluses." She looked into the mirror. "So, what do you think?"

"I have never, in my entire life, looked this good. No wonder you were nominated for an award."

"*Nominated* is the operative word," Jolene said. "The awards aren't until September."

"It doesn't matter. I'd vote for you in a heartbeat."

"Too bad your vote doesn't count. Close your eyes." She spritzed Desiree's face with setting water. "And if I weren't leaving right after the wedding, I think we could become besties. Now that my BFF back in LA is engaged, I suspect I'll come back from Ireland to discover I've lost her to her fiancé." She took a mascara brush and swept it across Desiree's lashes. "I don't know a woman in Hollywood who has lashes as thick and long as yours," she said. "And I'm including those who paid big bucks for extensions. This mascara is waterproof, just in case you end up crying at the wedding."

"I don't cry," Desiree said.

"Never?"

"Not since my grandmother passed when I was twelve. My mother died when I was born. There were complications with the birth. So I ended up having only my father through my teens. It didn't take me long to realize that tears really upset him, since he had no idea what to do with a girl. I just learned, the night of my grandmother's funeral, to cry into a pillow. By the time I graduated, I'd lost the tears, I suppose," she said, meeting Jolene's eyes in the mirror. "A bit like your ability to move on."

That wasn't entirely true. She had cried in the restroom on the flight to New York from Paris, but that was more information than she cared to share.

She was, Desiree told herself as she left the room to change into her dress, going to have to gather up all her strength to resist Bastien Broussard. Or she'd be right back where she'd been when the most delicious man she'd ever seen had sauntered up to her after she'd finished singing "Joyeux Noël" and, without so much as an introduction, asked, "Hey, *cher*, want to be in my band?"

It was the first time in her life she'd understood that "near occasion of sin" the nuns were always warning girls against. It was also the first time she'd wanted to experience it. In that frozen moment in time, if Bastien Broussard had asked her to fly to the moon with him on gossamer wings, she'd have accepted on the spot.

She had assured the rest of the choral group that she'd be fine, and although she'd known it would be considered foolish, she had gone with him down Pirate's Alley, where the famed Privateer Jean Lafitte and Andrew Jackson had formed an unlikely alliance to plan the successful defeat of the British at the Battle of New Orleans. Unlike the noisy holiday mood throughout the Quarter, the bar had been reasonably quiet. He'd ordered a beer for himself, a Coke for her, and he'd explained about how he had a three-piece band that needed a front girl and since she was not only the most beautiful girl in the Crescent City, but also sang like an angel, she'd be perfect.

She'd been vaguely aware of him saying something about not making much money, but she needn't worry, he'd be sure she'd be taken care of, and he'd protect her against any drunk guys who might want to harass her, and how he'd promised her they'd pass a good time together.

By then she'd already been swept away by his smooth, deep voice and dark brown eyes, and, with their fingers linked together, she'd walked with him to a little hole-in-the-wall bar on Royal, where he introduced her as his new front girl, and within five minutes they'd left with a gig that had been only two nights away.

"I don't know any of your songs," she'd complained at the time.

He'd stopped, framed her worried face in his beautiful hands and said, "Don't worry, *cher*. We have two whole days. I'll teach you." And hadn't he? About a great deal more than singing the blues.

Five

Desiree had always been a beauty, but whatever magic Jolene, daughter of Gloria, had done had turned her into a goddess. "No one will notice the brides."

"I strongly doubt that," she said dryly. "I saw them getting dressed. They're stunning."

"There must be something in the water, here," Bastien said. "Because all the women are beautiful."

"You've always had an eye for women." She didn't say it in the angry, sulky way she once had. Bastien hoped that was because she'd grown older and belatedly realized that he'd had no reason to look at anyone but her.

"For the record, all the years we were together, I never, *ever*, looked, touched or had any kind of sex with any of those groupies. Or any other woman."

"I knew that," she said. "Well, most of the time." She shrugged shoulders bared by a dress with a floaty, longish skirt that looked as if it had washed off a painting of Monet's garden at Giverny, but sadly didn't show off her long legs he could still, during long dark nights, remember wrapped around him.

"But you were always waiting for me to cheat." She hadn't trusted him then. He wondered if she'd trust him now. If not, it may take longer than expected to win her over. But fortunately, she wasn't going anywhere. And now that he'd come up with a plan, neither was he.

"Perhaps," she admitted. She shrugged those bare shoulders that gleamed as if they'd been polished. "I was young and insecure. So, did you find your ukulele?"

"I did. But I also found something, or someone, better. One of the bride's cousins has a job playing at one of those big resort luaus. He's agreed to play the 'Hawaiian Wedding Song' during the ceremony."

"That's good news."

"It would be. But he insists he can't carry a tune, and from his demonstration, he's right, so we'll have to sing it."

"That's okay. I have it memorized."

"I knew you would. Now here's the cool thing. I was talking to Caroline Harper, she's the mother of Seth, who's the fiancé of Brianna, the wedding-planner-slash-B-and-B owner."

"I know that."

"Of course you do. I was just trying to connect all the dots. Apparently, Kylee's mom died. And her dad rejected her when she came out to him."

"That I didn't know. But since Mai's dad is going to walk both brides down the aisle, I suspected something like that might have happened."

"You suspected right. So, since Mai's entire family is essentially going to become Kylee's family, Mrs. Harper, who's officiating, planned a Hawaiian ceremony. A surprise for the both of them, which she hid from them during yesterday's rehearsal. Mai's family brought leis that have been stashed in Amanda Barrow's cooler. She's apparently the landscaper who created this garden and is also one of the attendants."

"Oh." Desiree's right hand went over her heart. "That is so lovely. And thoughtful."

"She seems like a lovely woman," he agreed. "If we get married here, perhaps we ought to consider her. Unless you'd like to get married in the church I drove by on the way to Herons Landing. Or, like I said, back home in New Orleans."

"This is my home now. But that doesn't matter because you won't be staying because we're not getting married and I'm going to be the one to move into that space next to my bakery. So, since you're wasting time, what aren't you telling me?"

"There's a song Honi, the cousin, sang for me, that would be perfect for the brides' first dance. But they're not doing that, so we thought it'd make a nice song for the exchange of leis."

"I thought you said her cousin couldn't sing."

"He can't. And, just so you won't think I planned this, he swears the entire family is tone deaf. Since it's a song for a guy, we thought he could play it on the ukulele while I sang it."

"I'm still not getting the problem."

"It's a love song called 'I'll Weave a Lei of Stars for You.'"

"Oh, that sounds beautifully romantic." Then she caught on to the possible problem. "You want to sing it to me."

"Well, if there weren't two of us, I suppose I could sing it by myself. But it would look a little odd and take away from the romanticism of the day if you suddenly either walked away, or just stood there not looking at me, while I sang it by myself."

He watched as she ran both those scenarios through her mind. "You're right. So obviously you'll sing it to me."

"It won't bother you?"

"Not at all. Believe me, I'm impervious to your Cajun charms."

"Ouch." It was his turn to cover his heart. "Direct hit."

"I'm sorry if that wounds your male ego. But you don't have to worry about my delicate sensibilities. It won't be any different than if we were two singers who'd never had a relationship."

"But we did. For five years." When he'd watched her become more and more unhappy touring with the band. "And that one night three years ago."

Score one for him. He watched her eyes soften and knew that she was sharing the same memories of that twenty-four hours that had so often haunted both his waking moments and his dreams.

"Well," she said finally, "I guess we should both just think of it this way... We'll always have Paris."

They decided that Bastien would play from the list that Kylee and Mai had compiled as the guests gathered, while Desiree brought out the pastry trays and attached the Wonder Women to the base she'd already secured to the top tier of the cake with straw dowels before covering it with more buttercream frosting. She'd also volunteered to help the bridal party with any last-minute needs. Not that they seemed to need her help, since Brianna had everything running perfectly.

Caroline Harper, who would by this time next year be Brianna's mother-in-law, reminded Desiree of a wood nymph in her flowing deep green dress with a moonstone on a black cord around her neck. Her streaked blond hair, cut in a smooth, jaw-length bob, was evidence she hadn't gone *completely* New Agey during this lifestyle transformation that had had all of Honeymoon Harbor buzzing. Though she was wearing a crown of flowers around her head.

Her smile was warm as she greeted old friends and Mai's family before the ceremony started. She and her husband had been traveling the country, but had returned to Honeymoon Harbor for this wedding.

One of Mai's many cousins, who was wearing a beautiful white silk Aloha shirt with red flowers that was definitely superior to the cheaper ones sold in tourism shops, led everyone to their seats. Because of Kylee lacking an immediate family, there were no sides. There were only family and friends gathered together in this magical fairy garden Amanda Barrow had created for them.

After everyone was seated, Seth Harper rolled out the white runner that led from the second patio outside the master bedroom's French doors to the arch covered with summer wisteria, under which the brides would exchange their vows.

Her work completed until it was time to cut her cake, Desiree went to stand beside Bastien. Although it had been years since they'd sung together, as he paused to smile down at her, it was as if time had spun backward and she was precisely in the place she was meant to be. Dangerous thinking, that, she reminded herself as an older man came forward to stand at the end of the runner.

Brianna's attention to detail was demonstrated by Mai's three brothers, who were accompanying Brianna; Chelsea Prescott, Honeymoon Harbor's librarian; and Amanda Barrow down the aisle wearing Hawaiian shirts in the same colors as the dresses worn by the women they walked beside.

Brianna, maid of honor, had chosen a sapphire blue that brought out her blue eyes. Amanda had gone with a sunny yellow that worked with skin tanned from years of working outdoors, while Chelsea's bright purple was a perfect choice for her burnished brunette hair. They looked like beautiful flowers in this lush summer garden Amanda had created.

They walked up the aisle, carrying small bouquets of tulips in the colors of their gowns mixed with white, to "All You Need Is Love."

It was such a positive song, one that was often requested at weddings, and one Desiree wished could be true. But she'd learned that love, while sometimes wonderful, could also be painful. And it wasn't always enough. Still, when she got to the part about it being easy to be where you're supposed to be, her voice faltered just a little. The guests didn't notice, but she felt Bastien's knowing glance, as if reinforcing the song's message.

As they split when they reached Caroline, the men to the right, women to the left, there was a momentary pause, allowing for suspense as everyone waited for the brides.

Then an older man, who'd been introduced to Desiree last night at the rehearsal dinner as one of Mai's uncles, stood at the end of the runner and lifted a conch shell, and blew a deeply rounded tone that spiraled over the garden and could probably be heard all over the harbor, announcing the arrival of the brides. Watching the bridal couple carefully, Desiree saw Mai's gasp of surprise as she touched her cheek, as if wiping away a tear.

While they might have gone a bit old-school with Elvis's "Can't Help Falling in Love with You" for the processional, there was nothing ordinary or expected about their gowns.

While getting dressed earlier, Desiree had been awed by Kylee's beautiful black fitted strapless midi dress embroidered with oversize red, yellow and purple beaded flowers. Dottie and Doris, who'd come to help the women into their gowns, had told her they'd ordered the dress from a designer Kylee had met on a photography trip through Italy. The more flamboyant of the two, she was wearing a pair of red sequined low-top Converse tennis shoes.

According to Dottie, the more talkative of the elderly twin sisters, it was traditional for Japanese brides to wear white for the ceremony, then change to red for the reception. Wanting to be modern, while paying homage to all the women in her family who'd married in the traditional style, Mai had embraced both looks in a Western-style white strapless sheath gown, with a red sash embroidered with gold butterflies that fell down her back instead of a train. She'd chosen to wear simple white ballet-style flats. They were accompanied by Mai's Japanese-Hawaiian father, who walked down the aisle with a bride on each arm. He kissed both their cheeks, then sat down next to his wife in the front row.

"Greetings. And *aloha*," Caroline said. "We're gathered here today to celebrate the love of Kylee and Mai as they exchange vows in this very special union of marriage. Before we begin, I'd like to ask all the family and friends here today to take the hand of the person next to you and unite with us with one heart as we close our eyes and picture those who could not be here with us today. The Hawaiians have gifted us with the lovely knowledge that when the breeze stirs in a wedding, as it's doing lightly at this very moment in this garden, it's the presence of their *ohana*, or family, who are physically absent but are surrounding the brides at this moment with their love, support and blessing."

As she felt her eyes moisten at the thought of her mother and grandmother, Desiree was glad Jolene had brought along that big waterproof mascara tube, especially when Bastien's fingers lightly brushed the back of her hand. The touch was as quick and light as a butterfly's wings, but it struck like a gilded arrow straight to the center of her carefully guarded heart.

"The traditional Hawaiian lei signifies love and respect," Caroline said as she continued the ceremony. "Like a wedding ring, it's an unbroken circle that represents your eternal commitment and devotion to one another. Just as the beauty of each individual flower isn't lost when it becomes part of the lei, but enhanced by the strength of its bond, so will you, Kylee and Mai, remain unique individuals, enhanced by the strength of *your* bond."

"May the lei of life you weave together as wife and wife be as beautiful and fragrant as these two you give to each other here today," Caroline said as Mai and Kylee exchanged leis. Singing the song he'd learned from Mai's cousin, Bastien looked deep into Desiree's eyes and when he got to the part about always greeting her with a kiss each time she wore her lei of stars, she knew that she wasn't alone in remembering all those kisses they'd shared.

The blessing of the rings involved dipping them in a Koa wood bowl filled with water from the Pacific Ocean, meant to represent the cleansing of past relationships to a new beginning. As Caroline explained *Ho'oponopono* signified a reconciliation, a letting-go, Desiree felt Bastien glance down at her, but she steadfastly kept her eyes on the couple.

While Kylee poured water from the harbor and Mai poured the water her family had brought from the ocean outside their home into a wooden bowl, Mai's cousin came forward with his ukulele to play the "Hawaiian Wedding Song." As Bastien and Desiree sang the lyrics, she couldn't help noticing they were, as they'd once been both onstage and off, in perfect harmony.

Kylee spoke her vows first. "My darling Mai, when I went to France to take photos for my book of World War Two American soldiers' cemeteries, I never expected to find my best friend and the love of my life. As a family, with our daughter, Clara, we will create a home filled with laughter and compassion. I promise to respect you and cherish you as an individual, a partner and an equal, knowing that we do not complete but complement each other. May we have many adventures and grow old together." She took Mai's hand in hers, and said, "I give you this ring as I give you myself, with love and affection. Wear it in peace always."

A collective sigh rippled through the guests as she slipped the ring on Mai's extended finger. The open love shining in her gaze as she looked into Mai's eyes reminded Desiree of the way she'd once looked at Bastien.

And then it was Mai's turn. "Dearest Kylee, when I took my grandmother to visit my grandfather's grave in France, I never expected to find *my* best friend and the love of *my* life. I promise to laugh with you, cry with you and grow with you. I promise to share my whole heart with you and Clara and love you loyally as long as I shall live." She slipped the ring onto Kylee's extended finger. "I give you this ring as I give you myself, with love and affection. Wear it in peace always."

At that moment the breeze blowing in from the water picked up, stirring the air as it sighed in the tops of the tall fir trees and set the garden's flowers to swaying.

Caroline returned the wooden bowl to a small table draped in white linen. "Dearest Kylee and Mai, as you embark upon this wonderful shared life, I ask that you remember this special day in your beautiful garden with joy and thanksgiving. May your love and understanding grow throughout the years. May yours always be a shared adventure, rich with moments of serenity as well as excitement. May your home be like a peaceful island where the pressures of the world can be sorted out, brought into focus and healed. And may you love to live, and live to love.

"To all present, I invite you to remain after the ceremony, for the christening of the couple's beautiful daughter, Clara, who has brought such joy into all the lives of those who've met her.

"And now, with the blessings of everyone who is present here today, and by the power vested in me by the State of Washington, it is my pleasure to pronounce you legally married. You may kiss your bride."

As the conch shell sounded and the brides shared their wedding kiss, the guests stood and applauded. All stayed standing as Mai's mother, Tamami, walked down the runner in a pink kimono embroidered with white lotus flowers, carrying a baby girl whose white christening dress, Desiree had learned as the women dressed, was the same one Mai had worn.

The christening was brief but meaningful, and it was impossible not to see the love and wonder in both Kylee's and Mai's eyes as they gazed at their adopted baby girl. This time, when Bastien looked down at Desiree and smiled, she smiled back. It was impossible to keep a closed and guarded heart when she was surrounded by so much joy and love.

Then the brides, followed by the grandmother and daughter, walked down the aisle to "From This Moment On" as the guests showered them with white rose petals.

Her heart feeling so much lighter, Desiree began flirting with the harmony, which had Bastien winking at her, the way he would those times onstage, when their eyes would meet, and it would feel as if they were the only two people in the world. Once again, time spun backward, to that first Christmas they'd met, when this Cajun sax player had stolen her heart.

Oh, yes, Desiree admitted, she could feel herself falling all over again. And even as her wary head warned her she could be in trouble, her newly emboldened heart didn't care.

Six

The reception was buffet-style, catered by Luca's Kitchen, and with Desiree's bakery providing not just the cake but various pastries and cookies. Bastien played his sax and Desiree sang for the gathered guests while they ate.

Brianna was finally breathing a sigh of relief at how well everything had gone when Kylee, who'd changed into more casual attire, came up to her.

"That was amazing," she said, throwing her arms around Brianna. "Thank you for providing memories for a lifetime."

"It was truly my pleasure," she said. "Although I'll admit Mai's family made it easy. Once Caroline came up with the idea to make her feel more at home, they'd arranged for so much of the ceremony. Including bringing the leis, bowl and conch shell."

"It made Mai cry a bit. In a good way... I was glad to see Aiden here," Kylee said. "I haven't seen him since he returned to Washington."

"I wasn't certain he'd show up," Brianna admitted. "He's hidden away like a hermit at the coast house. But

I played the Catholic guilt card and pointed out how important it was for him to get out with people again. Also, quite honestly, Seth has been worried about him."

It had been painful for Brianna to watch Aiden suffering and Seth worrying about not being able to get through to his best friend.

"It had to have been hard on him, having his partner killed. Not to mention being shot himself." Kylee glanced over to where Aiden was standing across the lawn, talking with his older brother Quinn. His expression was nowhere near as happy as the rest of the guests.

"It was also good to see Jolene again, and thank goodness she used that waterproof mascara, because I got so emotional during the wedding, I was on the verge of weeping like the willow Amanda planted in our front yard. And speaking of Jolene, would you have ever guessed someone from Honeymoon Harbor would end up on the cover of *People* for dating a movie star?"

"I'm happy for her," Brianna confided. Jolene had been the subject of bullying through middle school and up until she'd suddenly dropped out of high school at sixteen.

"Me, too. So, what's going on between her and your brother?"

"Which brother?"

"Aiden."

"I had no idea anything was going on." Brianna's gaze turned toward Jolene, who was currently amusing Clara with funny faces. "What do you mean?"

"I've been watching them. They've stayed on the outskirts of the crowd the entire reception, seeming to make sure they're on opposite ends of the yard. If she moves, he moves. And vice versa. It doesn't seem accidental and I'm definitely picking up vibes."

"I haven't a clue. Although Jolene would come over for the occasional sleepover during middle school, before she suddenly dropped out of high school, I never noticed Aiden paying any attention to her."

"Well, he sure is now."

"They both live in Los Angeles. She told me they hadn't run into each other, but maybe their paths have crossed in the past few years and she didn't want to talk about it for some reason."

Before Kylee could comment, one of the young women hired to keep the tables cleared and the buffet table looking tidy came over to ask Brianna a question and the subject was forgotten.

Bastien went into the kitchen, in search of Luca Salvadori, who was taking a fresh antipasto platter from the refrigerator.

"Hey, man," Luca said, "that was some wicked-cool music you two pulled off at the last minute. I was surprised Desiree sang. She's never mentioned a word about singing to anyone in town that I know of. And believe me, if she had, it would've been in bold print on the town's Facebook page."

"We were in a band together for five years. That was some time back."

"You didn't record anything?"

"I scraped up enough dough to pay for studio time to have an album engineered. But it's a catch-22. You need a name to be signed. And you can't be signed if you haven't gotten enough attention to get a label interested. So it never went anywhere."

"I'll bet it would now," Luca said, putting the tray on the counter. "I'm a fan, by the way. I've got all your blues rock albums. I was wondering about that gap of time. Between albums."

"Thanks. As for the time…" Bastien shrugged. "Life happens."

"I know about that," Luca said. "The question of the moment is how you let her get away."

Another shrug. "Stupid also happens. But life on the road wasn't ever for Desiree. She's been baking all her life and decided it was a more dependable way to earn a living."

"She could work in any high-end restaurant in the country, and from what I hear, she turned down a bunch before settling down here. I buy some of my pastries from her, although I make the tiramisu myself from my grandmother's recipe."

"Speaking of grandmothers, the reason for the gap is that I quit the road to go home to New Orleans and help my grand-mère run our family restaurant. But she recently passed, so I sold the restaurant to my cousin, and now that I'm free, I intend to win Desiree back."

"A man with a plan," Luca said with an approving nod. "Good for you."

"The thing is, I don't want to go back on the road. So I thought I'd open a restaurant here."

Luca's dark brows rose. "Why would you open a restaurant here in this small town when you could probably put your name on one in any city in the country and fill the place every night?"

"Because Desiree isn't in any other city. She's here."

"Wow. You *are* serious. But I don't get what that has to do with me."

"I wanted to make sure there wasn't going to be a problem with me giving you some competition."

"Hell, no, I think it's great. You may be able to tell from the town's name that we're a destination wedding town. Not like Vegas, but we get our share of tourists. A bigger variety of places for people to go out to eat can only make the town more appealing, which in turn brings in more visitors with dollars to spend. Right now, for dinner choices, there's Mannion's, which is a great pub; Taco the Town's food truck; Leaf, which, as it sounds, is vegetarian, and me. Adding you to the mix will help people get into the habit of going out more. Especially in the winter when tourism slows down and the locals start getting cabin fever. What are you going to name it?"

"Sensation Cajun."

"I like it." Luca held out his hand. "So welcome to Honeymoon Harbor, and good luck. With both the restaurant and Desiree." He picked up the tray again to take it out. "She's a helluva woman."

"Thanks. You called that one right."

Although they'd stopped singing, the wedding reception showed no signs of slowing down. And, as long as Kylee and Mai seemed to be enjoying themselves, why should it? The best thing about summer was the long days when the sun wouldn't set until after nine o'clock and the twilight glowing with shades of gold and amber would last for another thirty or forty minutes.

During that time, Honeymoon Harborites expressed surprise to learn that the town's baker had once been in a band.

"It's as if you two had been singing together all your lives," Dottie enthused.

"It was five years," Desiree repeated what she'd been saying for the past twenty minutes. "A long time ago."

"Well," Dottie's twin, Doris, said, "it may have been long ago, but it's obvious the connection between the two of you is still there. I suspect we'll be fitting you for a wedding dress before this time next year."

"I wouldn't bet the store on that," Desiree said with a laugh. A laugh that faded as she saw Bastien heading toward her, setting off those all-too-familiar butterflies in her stomach.

After greeting the elderly twins and accepting their compliments, he took Desiree by the elbow and led her to the far end of the garden. How could such an innocuous touch send heat flowing through her entire body?

"I talked with Luca Salvadori," he said. "I wanted to make sure he was okay with me opening up a restaurant. He thinks it's a great idea that will create more business for everyone."

"I'm delighted he approves," she said, folding her arms to steel herself against the charm offensive she knew would be directed her way. "Perhaps you may have thought to ask me how *I* felt before you made your plans to attempt to steal my building space."

"What would you say to taking this conversation somewhere more private, before we start garnering even more attention?"

She narrowed her gaze. "Where?"

"First to the building in question. I have an idea. I also have a question. When was the last time you ate?"

"I've been busy." She thought back. "A croissant this morning."

"Then you should be hungry. Let's take off. I'll show you my idea, then cook you dinner."

"Where are you staying?"

"At the Lighthouse View Hotel. I was lucky to get the only available room. It seems that you were right about Mai's family filling both Brianna's B and B and the hotel."

"I didn't realize they had kitchenettes at the hotel."

"They don't." There it was. That slow, devastating smile she'd been expecting. "I thought maybe I could use your kitchen."

Her initial thought was to turn him down on the spot. Then again, if he actually did intend to stick around, and Desiree sincerely doubted it, since small towns weren't his style, there were other spaces Seth could remodel for him. He didn't need hers. Which was what she was going to convince him of. Over his damn dinner.

"I could use something to eat. And I've missed New Orleans food. Also you're right about it giving us an opportunity to discuss the flaws in your impulsive plan in private."

"Believe me, *cher*," he said, his eyes turning as serious as she'd seen him since he'd put her on that plane to New York, "there was nothing impulsive about it."

And didn't that have her thinking about how he'd been spending the past two years? Family was important to Cajuns, and Bastien was no different. The fact that he'd give up a successful career to take over his grandmother's popular, but small, restaurant proved that under that hot, sex-on-a-stick exterior was a huge and caring heart.

Bastien had never been a bad man. He'd just proven

to be the wrong man for her. Or perhaps they'd met too soon and she hadn't been ready for him.

"So, what do you say?"

"I don't have anything in the house to make a meal with," she said. "We'll have to stop by the market." And wouldn't that have Mildred Marshall posting about Desiree buying dinner groceries with the hot new stranger in town on the Facebook page before they'd left the parking lot?

"Sounds good to me. I'm guessing, since we're on a harbor, there's a fish shack?"

Desiree glanced down at her watch. "Kira's Sea House should still be open. For another twenty minutes."

"*Bien*. We'll start there."

He was a fast shopper who knew what he wanted. Kira packed up some Dungeness crab and Gulf shrimp. He wanted the ones with shells, he told the fishmonger, to make stock.

Which admittedly impressed Desiree. And apparently Kira, who asked for the recipe.

"I'll have Desiree write it down for you as I fix it," he said. "I learned to cook in my grandmother's restaurant, and neither of us have ever been the type to use recipes."

"That must have been an adventurous experience for diners," Kira said as she wrapped the shrimp in white waxed paper and put them with the crab in a bag with ice to keep them cool.

"Food should be an adventure," he said. "Otherwise, what's the point?"

"You won't get any argument from me," Kira agreed

cheerfully. Then turned to Desiree. "But please, write down what Chef Adventurous here does, okay?"

"I'll try," she agreed. "Just remember. I'm a baker, not a cook."

The farmer's market was down the street, and although the stands were beginning to close up for the day, Desiree was not surprised when both men and women stopped to sell him what he needed. Charm. Say what you want about it, Bastien was definitely born with more than his fair share. And when you tossed in that slow, sexy Cajun accent, well, he was pretty much irresistible.

One of the buskers, playing an alto sax for tips at the front of the market, recognized him immediately and looked on the verge of having a seizure from excitement. Especially when his alleged musical hero signed an autograph, then invited him to perform with him at the preopening trial run dinner at Sensation Cajun. By the time they escaped, Desiree was worried about the kid driving home safely.

The rice, unfortunately, had to be bought at Marshall's Market, where Bastien had the usually stone-faced Mildred Marshall giggling like a schoolgirl as he laid on a Cajun accent as heavily seductive as Dennis Quaid's in *The Big Easy*. But a great deal more authentic.

"You're like the Pied Piper," she said as they walked out of the market to their cars. Having driven to the wedding alone, they had to take two cars to each of the stops. Which kept her from being in a confined space with him before she worked out her feelings about him appearing so unexpectedly.

"Just being friendly," he said. "Bein' as I'm going to be part of the community."

"You are not."

"Of course I am. And for old time's sake, your first dinner at Sensation Cajun will be on the house."

Ovenly was painted a soft green the color of pine needles with white trim and double doors that looked as if they'd been taken from some old building in France. A green awning extended over the sidewalk, allowing for three bistro tables and chairs. Since she didn't serve dinner, the bakery had closed for the day.

"There's a brick patio in back," she said. "Normally I'd only be able to use it about two or three months a year, but I extend the season into fall with portable post heaters."

"That's a good idea. And something I'll have to consider for my place."

"I still can't believe you'll actually build a restaurant here in Honeymoon Harbor."

"Want to bet?"

"I'm not a betting person."

"You took a bet on me," he reminded her.

"And look how that turned out," she snapped, then pressed her fingers to her forehead, where a headache was beginning to throb. "I'm sorry. I didn't mean that the way it came out."

"You're hungry," he said. "And undoubtedly tired. Besides, your leaving was partly my fault. I was young, too cocky and we clicked so well, in every way, I forgot to let you know how much I loved you."

"That's all in the past."

"The past isn't dead. It's not even past," he said,

quoting William Faulkner. From his outward appearance, Desiree never would have taken him for a serious reader, but in all their years together, she'd never seen him without a book. "But here we are, *cher*. So, let's deal with who and where we are now, and the rest will fall into place."

He'd always been that way, looking for the positive in a situation. Despite having been abandoned first by the father he'd never known, then his mother, Bastien Broussard had somehow remained the most optimistic person she'd ever met. She also wasn't all that surprised that he would have given up a career, just as it was skyrocketing upward into the stratosphere, for family.

"Tell me about your idea," she said. She still didn't believe he'd stay, but she was willing to listen.

"First off, I want to paint my part pink."

"Pink?" She'd been about to point out that it wasn't yet *his* part, and wouldn't be if she had anything to say about it, when his words sunk in. "Tell me you're kidding."

"This town came of age during the Victorian Era. Pink was a popular color for houses back then. They're scattered all over New Orleans."

"But not here in the Pacific Northwest," she said.

"That's exactly my point. I don't want people thinking of being in the Northwest, as stunning as the scenery is. I want them to feel as if they've been whisked away to the Big Easy. I want Sensation Cajun to be, well, a sensational experience."

"Okay. I get that. But why pink?"

"Brennan's is pink. It's also been a destination landmark for decades. Tourists who go to New Orleans are willing to wait in line to get in for a meal. And mine wouldn't be Barbie pink. I'm thinking of a deeper rose that will stand out when people are coming in on the ferry. With big arched windows on either side of the door with an awning over it. I'd already thought of green, which works perfectly with yours. It would also be great if you extended the exterior color to yours, so they'd be more uniform."

She folded her arms. Tried to picture Ovenly painted pink. "Why would I want to do that?"

"Because along with the larger windows on both the street and harbor side to let in more light, I'd like to take out that wall between our places."

"You want to invade my bakery?"

"*Invade*'s a bit harsh. My idea was to have Brianna's fiancé build some sort of archway between the two, keeping the old brick. New Orleans and French styles aren't that different."

"That's true enough, given that New Orleans is the closest you'll come to France in the States, thanks to our ancestors."

"You're getting it. Our styles could blend well together, Desiree. And not just outside, but on the menu. Luca told me he buys pastries from you."

"He does. And Brianna buys cookies and croissants for her B and B."

"See? You'd have a new outlet. We could set up the dessert cart with items you chose for each day. After diners taste how good your pastries are they could go into your bakery after their meal and take some more home for their evening dessert, a late-night snack, or even breakfast the next morning.

"And," he pressed on, "you said you wanted to expand. There's plenty of space for you to do it. Especially since I'm putting smaller, more intimate dining rooms upstairs. I believe together we'll draw from neighboring towns along with visitors to the National Park. I'm also going with green shutters on either side of the windows across the second floor and putting wrought iron on a little extension. Not an actual balcony, but to give the impression of one."

"This is sounding more and more like Brennan's exterior."

"I doubt I'll be taking any business away from them. But for those who've been to New Orleans, dining at Sensation Cajun could feel like reliving their time there. And for others who've never been, it'll give them a Big Easy experience.

"You've thought this through."

"I have, ever since your father complained that you hadn't come home to work in the family business. Luca thinks my name will bring in some people, too, though I'm not sure that this is blues rock country."

"You'd be surprised. Don't forget, Jimmy Hendrix was from Washington State. You wouldn't, by the way, be the only famous person in town. Brianna's uncle Mike is an artist."

"Michael Mannion lives here?"

"He has a studio and a gallery. Like me, he lives above the store on the third floor of a building he bought. But he's turning the second floor into space for various local artisans. Brianna talked him into doing wine painting evenings which have proven quite popular."

"I went to a showing of his work at a gallery on Julia Street. He'd done a book of paintings from each of the fifty states. We hit it off, and though his original paintings are above my budget, I could definitely use some of his Louisiana prints. With little tags beneath stating his name, with the address of the gallery. It might even drive some business his way."

He smiled at her, obviously pleased with that idea. "Small-town interconnections," he said. "This isn't turning out to be that different from New Orleans, which is, in its way, several small, close-knit communities within one city."

She couldn't deny that. Still, as they entered her bakery, Desiree wondered if a man whose dream was once to play concerts all over the world could truly be happy running a restaurant here, in a town that didn't get the number of tourists in a year that New Orleans or Paris did in a day.

"I realized I've dropped a lot on you today," he said.

"Whatever gave you that idea?" The sarcasm didn't have the edge she'd intended. He was getting to her, the sane, sensible voice in her head warned. *Be strong.*

"Just think about it," he suggested easily. "What could that hurt?"

"Nothing." But her hopeful heart, as tended to happen whenever she was anywhere around Bastien, was disagreeing with her head. "I suppose."

"I'd never make you do anything you don't want, Desiree," he said, just as he'd told her that first night he'd made love to her. Damn. That memory had long-neglected body parts jumping into the interior conversation, siding with her heart. *Dinner,* she reminded herself. Then he'd be on his way, back to the Lighthouse Hotel, and hopefully New Orleans, or Paris, or wherever the gypsy musician might roam.

"I've mostly given up making bread," she said as

they passed the pastry case, which her two employees had emptied for the night. "I prefer the art of pastry making. But I do bake bread once a week for Luca. He uses whatever he needs for that night, then vacuum freezes the rest and warms it as he needs it. I kept out a loaf to eat with some cheese along with Roma tomatoes and basil when I got home tonight. So, I can contribute that to our dinner."

"Great plan. We'll have bruschetta while the sauce simmers.

"I do have another idea that we can talk about over dinner," he said after she'd retrieved the bread from the back workroom and they were walking up the stairs that Seth had insisted on replacing.

"I'm not going to bed with you," she said, wanting to get that settled right off.

"Did I say anything about sleeping with you? That wasn't my idea. Well, not one I wanted to talk about quite yet. Though anytime you want to ravish me, I wouldn't say no."

"There will be no ravishing."

"Whatever you say, *cher*," he agreed cheerfully. Too cheerfully, Desiree warned herself.

Seven

"Wow," Bastien said now, as they entered the apartment that took up the entire floor. "I wasn't expecting this."

"What were you expecting?" she asked as she put her purse on a small curved table painted in a pastoral scene by the front door. A gilded bronze mirror in one of the Louis styles—she forgot which one—hung on the buttery-yellow wall above the table.

Desiree was well aware that her apartment didn't fit in with the typical Northwest design style. Or the heavy, and to her mind cluttered, historical Victorian homes throughout town that always showed up on the annual home tour circuit. Fortunately, Seth, who'd remodeled both what had once been Fran's Bakery and this upstairs apartment, which had only been used for storage and, it had turned out, a home for mice and spiders the size of her hand, had caught on to her vision right away.

"I don't know because I hadn't given it a lot of thought," Bastien said, taking in the buttery-yellow walls that brightened up the long, dark days of winter and the rains of spring. "But it wasn't this."

Tall blue draperies hung from the tops of fifteen-foot-high walls boasting wide white crown molding to puddle on the floor. Desiree never would've been able to afford that luxury if Sarah Mannion hadn't sewn those drapes herself. There were prints and paintings in a variety of frames and eclectic styles—scenes of Paris, of New Orleans, bright and colorful modern art and more classic art prints, like the mother bathing her child in a porcelain bowl—all of which she'd unearthed at various garage sales and flea markets Sarah had taken her to visit.

"I knew wherever you lived would be pretty, like you. And feminine. Again like you." He swept a long, slow look over her that once would've had her panties melting on the spot. But not tonight, she sternly told the rebellious, reckless body of her youth. "But I didn't expect to find myself back home. Though this is more like the Garden District than my grand-mère's double shotgun house."

There were times, whenever she'd have people over for the first time, when she'd watch their eyes open wide and she'd wonder if she'd perhaps overdone the formality. But that feeling would only last a moment as her guests would immediately settle in and she'd watch the cares of their day fall away, just as hers did whenever she came upstairs from the bakery.

"Brianna's mother, Sarah, designed it for me. She's principal of the high school, but is taking design classes at the community college so she can have a new career in retirement. She used this apartment as a class project that entailed adding residential space to a commercial building. Usually people go industrial loft style in these old places. But I don't feel at home in that type of space.

"Some of the things, like the Mardi Gras masks on the bookshelves, we ordered online, and the art on the walls were all my choices, but it was as if she somehow was inside my head, reading the thoughts I couldn't quite put into words."

She definitely wasn't going to put into words the thoughts she was having now. Like how much she wanted him to lift up her skirt and take her hard and fast against the door. *Stop that*, she told her bad, bad head, dragging it back to a safer topic.

"Both Seth and Sarah had understood that as much as I love Honeymoon Harbor, I wanted a blend of New Orleans and Paris."

Bastien stuck his hands in his back pockets, looking up at the oversize bronze-gold chandelier dripping with crystals that created rainbows on the walls. "That looks like an authentic plaster medallion."

"It is. Seth found it down in Portland. It was badly chipped, but his father, Ben—"

"Who would be the husband of Caroline."

"That would be him." She smiled at the way he kept mapping out the connections between all the people he'd met today. "He's one of the few remaining old-time master plasterers. His family built most of the original buildings in town and, as you can see, he managed to repair it beautifully."

Sarah had covered a reproduction curved Louis XV–style sofa in a deep blue velvet. Desiree had decided against sanding and repainting the cracked and peeling paint that gave the piece character and enjoyed imagining all the families who'd owned it before her. As they passed the sofa, an unwanted image of making love to

him on that soft velvet flashed through her newly sex-
crazed mind.

An archway through the tall brick, much like the one
Bastien had suggested to connect her bakery to his restaurant, led to her kitchen, where she'd replaced the top
cabinets with open shelves, and had Seth install a deep
farm sink, marble countertop and a vintage, butcher-
block-topped wheeled table to use as an island.

Bastien put the groceries down on the marble countertop while she went out onto the wrought iron–railed
balcony that allowed her to keep a small kitchen garden
in pots and sit with her morning coffee, breathe in the
aroma of fresh herbs and watch the boats on the water.

"Nice setup," he said when she'd returned with a tomato and leaves of basil. "I like the espresso machine."

"During the day, I'll run down to Cops and Coffee.
But this is my sanctuary, so I like my coffee French.
And before you ask, I do leave out the chicory."

"Not a bad call, in my opinion," he agreed. "It took
a while, but I talked grand-mère out of putting it in the
café coffee."

"Would you like some wine?" she asked.

"I wouldn't turn it down. I'd say we earned it today.
Especially you, who, along with stepping in to perform,
also did all that baking."

"Ah, but you're cooking dinner when we could have
ordered out. Or picked up an already cooked chicken
at the market."

"Bite your tongue," he said as he laid out his ingredients. "So you still don't sing at all, *cher*?"

"Only to myself." She got out a bottle of an Ore-
gon Sauvignon Blanc that always reminded her of the
Pouilly-Fumé they'd drunk with that lunch at the little

bistro beside the Seine and poured them each a glass. "When I'm alone baking."

"Thanks," he said. "You still have some amazing pipes."

While she got the ingredients for the bruschetta out of the refrigerator, Bastien washed the vegetables, then began chopping carrots, green pepper and onion—the "Holy Trinity" of Cajun food. "The first time I heard you, singing that solo for 'Joyeux Noël,' I thought I'd died right there in Jackson Square, because I knew only an angel could sound so sweet."

He looked up from peeling the shrimp. "You looked like an angel come down from heaven, too."

"It's not going to work this time, Bastien." Oh, but it was. As it had been more and more all day. She sliced the bread on the diagonal and rubbed it with a garlic clove.

"What?"

"The famous Broussard charm offensive," she answered as she brushed olive oil onto the bread, then put it beneath the broiler.

"It's the truth." Behind her, shrimp shells boiled in a pot along with leftover bits of vegetables to make stock.

He'd always been as serious about his cooking as she was about baking. The difference, she thought now, was that baking was chemistry, while cooking, at least how he did it, was more art. Each fit their personalities. Except when it came to this man, her head tended to rule her heart, while he'd always worn his heart out in the open on his sleeve.

"It's good to be back in the kitchen together," he said. "The same way it was good to sing together at the wedding."

There was no point in lying about the connection; it had felt like that first night they'd strolled through the Quarter, singing together. On Bourbon Street, as they'd stood on a corner, waiting for the light to change, a man had come up and handed Desiree a dollar. "You're a true professional now," Bastien had told her, making her laugh. But it had still felt rewarding.

"I'm sorry the musician Brianna hired cut her hand, but it was fun to sing again," Desiree admitted. The bread had browned. She put it on the butcher-block island counter, cut up the tomato, rolled up the basil leaves and cut them *en chiffionade* from either side up to the bitter stem, which she tossed away. "Especially at such a happy occasion." She spread on the goat cheese, then topped the bread and cheese with tomato, basil and capers.

"That was a nice story about how they met at that World War Two cemetery in France," he said. "And each knew, at that moment, that they were meant for each other."

"I suspect it was more lust at first sight," she said, her tone as dry and crisp as her wine.

"I don't remember you being so cynical. I believe it was true love. I certainly fell in love when I heard you, even before I turned around and saw you. But I'm not going to deny that while you looked and sounded an angel, my thoughts had nothing to do with heaven. Perhaps lust is merely fate's way to get us to pay attention to the person we're supposed to fall in love with."

"I've never met a man who says the *L* word so easily," she said.

"Known a lot of men, have you, *cher*?" Bastien took a bite of bruschetta she held out to him.

"Most of the students in pastry classes admittedly tend to be women. But I've met my share of male bakers, and both students and restaurant chefs tend to sit around and drink late into the night talking about all sorts of different personal things. Sex included, naturally. But love is never mentioned."

"Now see, that's the difference. It's not like I throw it around like confetti or Mardi Gras beads. Had I been with other women before you? Yes. Had I ever told any other woman that I loved her? That would be a hard no. It was a word I was saving. When I went back to the guys in the band the next morning, I told them that I'd not only found our front girl, I'd found the girl I was going to marry."

It had been the same for her. Except she'd been a virgin when, the third night after she'd joined the band, they'd made slow, tender love on a lumpy double bed in his small, three-floor walk-up studio apartment on Dauphine Street.

"Sometimes I wonder if I moved too fast," he mused. "Being that I was your first lover, perhaps you thought sex always felt that special, that right, and maybe took our love, not for granted, exactly, but as something you could feel for any man you were attracted to. Any other man who you might want to be with."

"You have it backward," she said. "You're right about me always connecting sex with love. I still do. I used to think it was my Catholic upbringing, but now I believe I'm just hard-wired that way. I always knew that when I did have sex with a man, he'd have to be someone I loved. And could see myself loving forever."

"Okay." He blew out a breath. "I promised myself that this time, I'd tell you how I felt and give you time to get used to the idea. So, demonstrating that I do have a degree of self-control where you're concerned, I'm not going to make love with you tonight."

"Well, for once we're on the same page," she said, not quite truthfully, remembering that flash of fantasy about him taking her up against the door.

"We always have been, *cher*." He looked at her over his wineglass. "Sometimes we just get a bit lost in translation." He turned down the stock pot. "We've a while yet before I need to make the roux. Why don't we enjoy our wine outside on that pretty little New Orleans balcony and enjoy the sunset?"

It was a perfect evening. The sun had turned the blue water to gold and copper. Sailboats skimmed across the gilded water, while more energetic kayakers paddled closer to shore.

"I've been thinking of taking sailing lessons," she said. "It looks so freeing."

"Maybe we could take them together, and then I could sail you to some hidden cove where we could drop anchor and make love in the moonlight."

"I thought we weren't going to talk about sex."

"I said we weren't making love," he corrected her. "But I don't remember you saying we couldn't talk about it." He took another bite of the crunchy bruschetta. "This is delicious."

"It's simple," she said. "But fresh herbs make it so much better. I was thinking of putting my garden on the patio, but then I'd have to go all the way downstairs any time I wanted something, and the pots would take up room I needed for customers. The balcony was Seth's idea."

"He's very talented. I'm glad there's someone local with the talent and vision to create my space for Sensation Cajun."

"As I said, his family built most of this town. Each generation has taught the next. They and the Mannions *are* Honeymoon Harbor." She told him of the ancient feud.

"So now he and Brianna Mannion will be connecting the family in a more personal way," he said.

She smiled, then took a sip of wine. "I've been told there have been inter-family marriages over the years, but John and Sarah Mannion beat them to it. She was Sarah Harper before she married John. He's mayor, she's the principal, and together they run the Mannion family Christmas tree farm. They have a big festival from the day after Thanksgiving to until Christmas Day. It's a wonderful community tradition."

"We'll have to go and celebrate my first Northwest Christmas together."

"If you're still here."

His eyes met hers and held. Her hormones were pinging around like steel balls in a pinball machine, and he was positively radiating testosterone. "I told you," he said. "I'm not going anywhere."

"What if I leave? I had some very good offers in Seattle and Portland before deciding to settle here after a visit."

"Then I'll move to Seattle or Portland."

"Even if you've finished building your restaurant?"

He lifted his broad shoulders and took another, longer drink of wine. "I'm betting that you have no intention of leaving. It's obvious you've woven yourself into the fabric of this town's life. But, it's only a building, Desiree. To be with you, I could walk away from it, as I did the one I sold to my cousin to come here, without a backward glance."

He put his glass on the little bistro table between them, turned toward her and took her hand. "Here's the thing you need to understand," he said. "I already let you leave twice."

"You never asked me to stay. Not even after Paris." And hadn't that hurt?

"Only because I was afraid you might. I knew band life wasn't for you, even though you could have been a star."

"You don't have to say that."

"It's true. You were the whole package, Desiree. But you hated the touring. Being crowded into that old van before we could afford to lease a decent bus. Never having a moment to yourself. The crowds, the fans. They weren't for you."

"You enjoyed them."

"I did," he admitted. "More so after you left."

"Well, if you're trying to make me feel better, that certainly doesn't."

"I didn't mean it the way it sounded. It was because I didn't have to watch you fight your growing stage fright every night. And I no longer woke up every morning wondering if that was the day you'd leave."

"I never told you I had stage fright. And it was more anxiety. I'm a quiet person at heart, Bastien. That's one of the things I love about baking. I do it early in the morning, when it's dark and the town is still sleeping. It's a special, silent time when I can have my thoughts to myself."

"Not so silent, I suspect," he said. "Since you sing while you work."

"You've caught me," she admitted with a smile.

"You hid the anxiety well," he said. "But I knew. There were so many times I thought I should lie and tell you that I didn't love you because I knew how we'd eventually turn out. But I was selfish and wanted every minute I could have with you.

"The first time you left, I understood that you needed to go to school and learn your craft. Having grown up working in a kitchen, I totally got that. Which is why I didn't say a word to discourage you. The second time, you were flush with your shiny new culinary diplomas and ready to spread your wings in the big city. No way was I going to try to deny you that...

"But now you've reached the stage in your life when you need a place to settle. Nest. Make a home."

How well he knew her. As she gazed at Bastien, Desiree felt all her excuses leave her heart with the setting sun.

"And I'm going to do everything I can to convince you to allow me to be part of your home. To let me back into your heart."

"You've never left." The admission in her soft voice vibrated with emotion.

He closed his eyes, drew in a deep breath, and although she hadn't realized that he'd been stressed, she could see the tension leaving his body. "I made a promise. Back there in the kitchen."

"You did," she said. "And I had every intention of holding you to it." She laid her free hand on the one that was holding hers. "But haven't you heard? It's a woman's prerogative to change her mind."

He stood up, bringing her with him. "The shrimp stock gets better the longer it simmers," he said.

"Then it's going to be the best stock ever made," she said, lifting her lips to his.

Eight

"I had a fantasy," she admitted as they walked, hand in hand, into her bedroom. She'd painted it an eggshell buff that added a golden glow. A wrought iron four-poster bed added to the antique feel, while the draped netting created a lush, dreamy vibe. The room looked like it was bathed in champagne.

"I'm a big fan of fantasy," Bastien said in a voice as silky as her duvet. "What a coincidence," he said as she confessed the sex-against-the-door scenario. "I had the same one when I walked in. Perhaps because I attacked you the moment that bellman had left our hotel room in Paris." The sex had been quick, hot, and the memory of that ravishment possessed the ability to thrill after all these years apart.

"I attacked you right back," she reminded him.

"That you did," he said as he closed the bedroom door. He pressed Desiree against it, causing every muscle in her body to quiver with memory. "Brace yourself, *cher*."

Before she could respond, his head swooped down and his mouth was on hers, the kiss hard, deep, erotic.

There was no soft, slow seduction as there'd been their first night. No playful sex as they'd had so often shared, too high on life from performing to go to sleep. This was what she wanted. She needed him to take her, to claim her, to break through the last of those emotional protective barricades she'd built during their years apart.

She couldn't tell if the room or her head was spinning as his mouth broke away from hers and nipped first one bare shoulder, then the other, just sharp enough that she knew her skin would show his marks in the morning.

Then, just as he had in her fantasy, he caught her wrists, lifted her arms above her head, pressing them against the wood of the door as his other hand dove beneath her pretty flowered tea-length dress, pushing aside the bit of lace she wore beneath it to slide his fingers into her. She was already wet, needy and ready. Desiree arched her hips to that wicked hand as his mouth reclaimed hers, swallowing a sound that was part moan, part laugh at how, yet again, their minds and bodies were in perfect sync.

"There are some men, with lesser egos, who might find being laughed at in such a moment emasculating," he said. "But I take it as a challenge." He thrust deeper, bringing her to climax with a flick of his thumb.

"That's one."

He released her arms, turned her around so she was facing the door and unzipped her dress, allowing it to fall in a flowered puddle to the floor. Her bra was next with a single snap of the hook, and then he slowed the pace, kissing a line from the nape of her neck, down her spine, and lower, as he pulled her undies down her legs.

"Step out of your shoes," he instructed. The lace

underwear that was down around her ankles was next. Then he kissed his way up her body again, his mouth tasting what his fingers had readied.

"I want to watch you." He nipped at her inner thighs, the way he had her shoulders, branding her with his teeth, then soothing the skin with his tongue. "I want to see your eyes, watch your face, when I take you."

Her knees were weak as he turned her yet again, to face him. As he did, she saw herself in the tall mirror leaning against the wall. She was naked, and her skin, deepened to a dusky rose, gleamed with moisture, while Bastien remained fully dressed. The erotic contrast had her feeling helpless as his hands moved over her, cupping her breasts. His fingertips, roughened from years of guitar strings, scraped her nipples, causing an ache between her thighs.

"Tell me you want me," he said, his hands growing more possessive, more arousing, as they moved over her, demanding more.

"I do," she managed.

"Say it." He pressed the straining zippered placket of rough denim against her bare flesh. "Say my name."

Lost in a world of slick, sinful sensation, she could deny him nothing. The ability to trust completely, to give every bit of herself, was born from knowing she was deeply, truly loved. "I want you, Bastien. I *need* you."

She gripped his shoulders and moved her hips against him, drawing forth a ragged male groan that was the sexiest thing she'd ever heard. He reached between them, freeing himself, then, taking a condom from the pocket of his jeans, tore the wrapper open. He was big, stone hard and, miraculously, hers.

"I'm going to take you," he said as he rolled the latex over himself.

"Finally." She panted the word.

It was his turn to laugh. Then as Desiree clasped his shoulders, he drove into her, filling her, ravishing her against the door of her pretty champagne-colored room, setting off an orgasm that streaked through her like flaming, brightly colored Mardi Gras fireworks.

They finally made it to the bed. Lying on the one-thousand-count Egyptian cotton sheets Sarah had given her for a housewarming gift, Desiree watched Bastien pull his T-shirt off to reveal a deeply tanned chest with the same mouthwatering abs she'd loved to run her hands over. She could easily spend the rest of her life watching him undress over and over again. Like a GIF, she thought with a laugh. She could use it as a screen-saver on her laptop, although she'd never get any work done.

"You're laughing again," he said, as his hands pushed down his unfastened jeans.

"Not at you." As her wandering eyes followed his happy trail down to his obliques, she wondered how anyone who cooked for a living could maintain such an amazing body. "I'm just happy."

"I'm glad." He kicked off those pricey Italian loafers, leaving his long, lean feet bare. She'd never realized how sexy bare feet could be until today. He pushed a pair of navy boxers down his legs, stepped out of them and joined her in the bed. "Now that we've taken the edge off and fulfilled that fantasy, let's see if I could make you even happier."

* * *

Much, much later, after he'd proven to be a man of his word, they were sitting in her kitchen eating the best étouffée she'd ever had in her life. And having grown up in New Orleans, that was saying something.

"Your grandmother taught you well," she said. She'd claimed his linen shirt as her own and was wearing it with her undies, while he had, sadly, put that T-shirt and jeans back on for cooking. "You also chose the name of your restaurant well. This is truly sensational."

"Thanks, but the company is what really makes the meal. I've missed being with you."

"Me, too. With you. And not just for the mind-blowing sex. When I left Paris, it felt as if I'd torn off a limb. I kept waiting for you to show up in New York." She took a piece of bread and spread it over the plate to mop off the last bit of sauce. "You never did."

"You weren't ready."

"You had no way of knowing that."

"You're right. I didn't. But it was the opportunity of a lifetime for you," he said. "It'd be like me being able to study under Lester Young, John Coltrane or Charlie Parker. How many people can say they were there, in that very kitchen, creating pastries with arguably the most famous pastry chef in the world?"

She laughed. "I don't think that's the type of thing that will make it into my obituary. Fortunately, I have no desire to be famous. While you, on the other hand, are a world-renowned musician."

"For songs I wrote for you."

"I wondered about that," she admitted. She'd also sung along while baking, which had made her heart ache, at the same time the songs had her feeling as if he was still with her. Just a little. "You know how the French call an orgasm *la petite mort*?"

"The little death."

"That's it. That's how I felt. But not in the amazing orgasm way. But in a lonely way. As if you'd died to me. I grieved for a long time."

"I'm sorry."

"It's not your fault," she said. "I was the one who left."

"If it's any consolation, I felt the same way. Which is why I wrote the songs. They served as somewhat of a catharsis as I'd imagine I was singing them to you."

"Once again we're so in sync," she murmured, no longer fighting the fact that in so many ways, they fit together perfectly, like two pieces of a beautiful puzzle. "Because I'd sing along and imagine I was singing with you." She blew out a long breath. "So here we are. Where we belong, if you're honestly set on building your restaurant here."

"I never say anything I don't mean," he said. He gathered up their plates, took them over to the dishwasher, then made two cups of espresso with hearts in the foam.

"How long did it take you to learn that?" she said, duly impressed.

"I've been practicing awhile," he admitted. "To show off for you. Here's the idea I was thinking about earlier and was going to mention to you before we got sidetracked… What would you say to us singing again?"

"Professionally? Even I if wanted to, which I don't, what would we do with our businesses?"

"You mentioned Brianna's uncle is renting out space to artisans."

"I did and he is."

"What if I had a studio built there? That album you bought, my last one? I produced it at a studio in New Orleans and had it engineered there. We could do the same thing."

She thought about that. "Wouldn't we have to tour to promote it?"

"It's a new world. We can put some selected singles on a website. I already have live performances on You-Tube."

"I know." She sighed. "I've watched. Along with thousands of other people."

"Who bought the album while I was in New Orleans working in grand-mère's café. The only singing I've done in public over the past two years has been in a few local clubs. That performance on YouTube was at the House of Blues. We could make some extra bucks doing what we'd enjoy anyway. Pay for some trips, put some away for our kids' college—"

"Aren't you getting a little ahead of yourself, Bastien Broussard?"

"You talked about wanting children. Did you change your mind? Because it's okay if you have."

"No. I just believe we should wait until the restaurant is up and running and we've adjusted to living a normal life together."

"We've plenty of time," he agreed. "That's totally your call. I was at the airport, waiting for my flight, when CNN ran an article about women in their fifties having children."

She slapped his arm. "I don't want to wait *that* long. I've watched Kylee and Mai with Clara and as darling as that baby is, she defines high-maintenance. Also, while

I realize there's nothing wrong with having a baby without a formal marriage, Papa's a little old-fashioned."

"That's like saying the Pope is Catholic," Bastien said with a touch of laughter in his eyes. "I was getting to that. I should have waited to mention the college part. The reason I came here was to propose. I had it all planned out. But then I found you bustling around with cake for the wedding, and the next thing I knew I was off looking for a uke. Then we were singing, and the reception didn't seem the right place."

"It would have taken away from the brides' day," she agreed.

"Then I wanted to show you my restaurant first, so you'd know what you were getting into, and then there was the sex—which was mind-blowing, don't get me wrong. But that got me sidetracked again with the conversation about maybe singing together again, and kids, and the plan fell apart. But the most important thing of all is that I wanted to propose, Desiree Marchand, heart of my heart."

"That was on your latest album." He'd sung it in both English and French, *"couer de mon couer."*

"So what do you say?"

"How about just asking me straight-out?" she suggested.

He dropped to one knee, took her hand in his and placed it over his beating heart. "Desiree Marchand, will you be my wife and let me love and cherish you all the days of my life?"

"Yes," she said. "I can't think of anything that would make me happier than becoming your wife and loving and cherishing you all the days of *my* life."

"Thank God." He blew out a breath.

Bastien stood up, drawing her into his arms as they sealed their pledge with a kiss.

Then, as Desiree laughed, her now-freed heart felt so light that she could feel it floating up and out the French doors, over the moonlit harbor.

* * * * *

Also by Jennifer Snow

Wild Coast

Sweet Home Alaska
Alaska for Christmas

Wild Coast Novellas

Love on the Coast

Wild River

Alaska Dreams
Alaska Reunion
Stars Over Alaska
A Sweet Alaskan Fall
Under an Alaskan Sky
An Alaskan Christmas

Wild River Novellas

An Alaskan Christmas Homecoming
Wild Alaskan Hearts
A Wild River Match
A Wild River Retreat
An Alaskan Wedding

For additional books by Jennifer Snow,
visit her website, www.jennifersnowauthor.com.

AN ALASKAN CHRISTMAS HOMECOMING

Jennifer Snow

To all the fans of Wild River, Alaska—
thank you for your support! Happy reading!

One

It wasn't the sight of her sister blissfully in love that bothered Jade Frazier. Or the fact that Maddie was in love with a guy Jade had dated first. She'd gladly given her blessing on that union. Heck, she'd been responsible for setting them up on the Valentine's Day Blind Date Ice Fishing event hosted by SnowTrek Tours the year before. No. It wasn't her sister's happiness driving Jade to the brink. It was *her* single status after the last several failed relationships. Staring at another upcoming holiday alone was depressing.

Ho ho, holiday loneliness.

It was this damn small town. She'd lived in the ski resort town in Alaska her entire life. Which meant she knew every man in town and had dated at least half of them. The ones her age, the ones a few years older… If she kept climbing the age scale, she'd either be dating divorcés or look like she had daddy issues.

She scanned The Drunk Tank, the local watering hole on Main Street, hoping for new blood… She'd even settle for a holiday fling with a tourist. But the faces illuminated by the string of Christmas lights decorating the bar were all far too familiar.

She sighed. Loudly.

Loudly enough to catch the attention of her sister and Mike in the booth across from her. They slowly peeled away from one another and turned to face her.

"So, how's the fashion degree coming along?" Mike asked politely. He didn't see Maddie shake her head beside him.

"Jade switched courses to interior design," Maddie said.

Her sister's encouragement was unyielding, and Jade appreciated the support, but she could hear in Maddie's tone that this switching subjects for her online degree was getting old. From makeup artistry to special effects to fashion design to interior design… At twenty-eight years old, Jade had to get serious about her future career.

But this was it. Interior design was her calling. And it wasn't as though she'd switched from rocket science to botany. At least her attempts to find her "thing" had been in the same vein. And this final term assignment would prove that to everyone.

"It's going great, actually. We have a really fun assignment that accounts for fifty percent of our grade— decorating a business for the holiday season."

Mike glanced around. "It's already December. Are there any businesses who haven't been decorated since October? Ow!" he said, glancing at Maddie, who'd obviously kicked him under the table.

Jade refused to acknowledge the truth of Mike's words or get discouraged. Sure, she was getting a late start, but there had to be some shop in town in desperate need of her help. Noticing a bandage on Mike's forearm, she changed the subject. "Did you hurt yourself on a tour?" Mike was a tour guide for SnowTrek Tours and often led wilderness expeditions in the unpredictable Alaskan backwoods.

"No. I got a new tattoo," he said.

Jade wrinkled her nose. She wasn't a fan of body modifications. "What is it?"

Mike lifted the edge of the bandage to display a watercolor design of an ice fishing hut with the aurora borealis in the background. Obviously, a tribute to how he'd met her sister. As much as Jade disliked tattoos, the gesture was romantic, she'd give him that.

And it looked really well done, unlike the messy, unprofessional-looking ones that often left the Black Heart tattoo shop in town. "It looks good. Where did you get it done?"

"Redemption Tattoo—the new shop on Main Street."

Her mouth dropped. "The one opened by the ex-con?"

Mike shot her a look. "How about less judgment and more open-mindedness? Griffin's a good guy. A Wild River local who did some time for falling in with the wrong crowd, that's all. He's here to get his life back on track."

Maddie looked admiringly at Mike, but Jade wasn't so sure. Wild River was an accepting place, but she suspected Griffin would have an uphill battle in gaining back the respect of his hometown.

He was living in a holiday television special.

Wild River, Alaska, was a quaint tourist town, and

despite it being his hometown, Griffin Geller stuck out like a sore thumb.

As he prepared his tattoo gun with fresh black ink, he stared out at the snow and the white mountaintops in the distance. He missed Las Vegas, the year-round mild weather, the bright lights of the city and the exciting, fast-paced lifestyle…but that wasn't the future he needed.

Moving there ten years ago right after high school graduation had felt like a dream. Striking out on his own, working his way up by apprenticing in local tattoo shops, learning the craft from artists he'd admired from afar, he'd been living his best life. Tattooing was the only thing he was ever good at.

Unfortunately, he hadn't had the opportunity to do much of it since opening his shop on Main Street the month before. He'd figured there was a market for his services, given that the only tattoo shop in town had been shut down twice in the last year for health code violations. But it seemed no one was looking for new ink…

The only customers he'd had all week were the two women sitting side by side, treating the experience like a spa day.

He snapped on his plastic gloves and rolled his stool toward them. "What are we getting, ladies? Matching roses? Inspirational quotes?"

"We actually just want our existing tattoos redone. They've faded," Cassie Reynolds, the owner of SnowTrek Tours, said. He recognized her from the one business association meeting he'd attended before vowing never to return again. The stares and judgmental looks had been too much.

He examined the faded *Best* and *Friend* tattoos on each woman's wrist. This would take all of three minutes and he could charge maybe ten dollars for the work.

Jail had been less painful.

His business would struggle to survive here in this small town, but if it meant living on the straight and narrow, staying far away from the trouble of his past, this was where he needed to be. He was lucky to be getting this new start.

Three minutes and forty-six seconds later, he removed the plastic gloves and forced a smile. "All done."

"We love them. Thank you," Cassie said as they approached the counter.

The other woman with her was some sort of doctor at Wild River Community Hospital. He'd nearly gagged as he'd worked when she filled her friend in on an angioplasty she'd performed the night before. She was looking at the tattoo with appreciation, but she'd barely looked at him the entire time she'd been here. This had obviously been Cassie's idea.

The adventure tour owner scanned the shop as she paid. "You haven't decorated yet."

"Decorated?" He took the cash and handed her back change from the twenty.

She waved it away. "For Christmas. Not sure if you've noticed the abundance of holiday spirit all over town…"

He'd noticed. Just been desperate to avoid it. He cleared his throat. "Christmas isn't exactly my thing."

"Shocking," the doctor said under her breath.

It might actually shock her to know it used to be his thing. He'd loved everything to do with the holidays—the sights, sounds and smells. His family owned the local diner on Main Street, which was open every day of the year, so they hadn't celebrated in the traditional sense, but they'd gathered with the community on Christmas Eve and Christmas Day, families meeting up to eat together or lonely residents with nowhere to go. It had been a special time of year. One he'd looked forward to.

Getting arrested on Christmas Eve had quickly changed that.

"You at least need to decorate the window for the local business association competition," Cassie said, sliding back into a thermal winter jacket.

He shook his head. "I don't think I'll enter."

The doctor sighed and tried a more direct approach. "Look, if you want to draw in business, people need to be less afraid of you."

"Erika," Cassie hissed at the woman before sending him an apologetic look.

"What? It's true," Erika said. "The holiday decorations will show them you're one of us. You're not whatever embellished rumor they think you are."

He sighed. He'd rather tattoo a Christmas tree on his forehead, but she had a point. "I'll think about it."

Cassie smiled. "Great. If you need any decorations, I have a ton left over from my reindeer display."

"Thank you." Her kindness wasn't unappreciated. He suspected their tattoo touch-ups were more to help his struggling new business than because they'd really needed them.

Cassie offered an encouraging smile as they headed toward the door. "Hang in there. The first year is always the hardest."

She had no idea.

The bell above the door chimed as they exited onto Main Street, and Griffin sat on one of the plush leather waiting room chairs and stared out at the falling snow. How the hell had he let his life turn out this way?

Two

Had *everyone* in town gotten an early start to their decorating?

Bundled warmly in her faux fur winter jacket and fashionable yet practical heeled leather boots, Jade carried her interior design portfolio down Main Street, eager to show off her holiday-themed ideas. But every business had their storefront displays completed already. She'd tried the local seniors' home, thinking they'd appreciate her help, but the decorating committee—a group of adorable, feisty little old ladies—had shooed her out of the complex quicker than she could say *Bah, humbug!* The Wild River Resort Hotel had claimed that they were going with the same decorators as last year. The fancy five-star accommodations boasted the same white trees and silver accents throughout the common areas every year, and Jade hadn't been successful convincing them to try something new.

Improving her sales skills would be her biggest challenge in this career. She was confident in her decorating skills, but her pitch to potential clients was somewhat lacking. She didn't have the experience, so she needed the work, but how did she get work without the experience?

Acquiring a location and gaining a business's trust were part of the assignment and she couldn't fail. She was personable, well-liked in town… She just needed to find a procrastinator who was too busy to do their own decorating.

As she passed Redemption Tattoo, she paused, seeing a man hanging fake sparkly green garland that looked like it had been reused over and over since the eighties from one corner of the window to the other.

Ho ho, hell no.

She hesitated briefly before squaring her shoulders and opening the door. That tacky eyesore of a decoration would bring down the property value on Main Street, and obviously this guy needed her expert advice as much as she needed the job.

A blast of heat hit her as she entered and looked around. It wasn't at all like the other tattoo shop in town. This one was clean and nicely furnished in leather and chrome. Tattoo designs were framed and hung on the wall, not held up with duct tape or displayed in faded old binders. The air smelled fresh and sterile as well. Definitely not what she'd been expecting.

"Can I help you?" the man from the window asked.

Confidence radiated from her as she said, "Actually, I'm here to help you."

"Doubt it. Look, whatever you're selling, I'm not interested," he said, his gaze landing on her portfolio.

"Is the owner here?" she asked. She wouldn't waste her sales pitch on an employee…no matter how attractive he was. She took in the dark brown hair, combed to one side, partially shaved underneath, the thin, muscular frame and eyes that were so dark they looked almost black from this distance. She didn't recognize him. New in town? Someone Griffin Geller had brought back from Las Vegas?

Maybe, if she secured the decorating opportunity here at the shop, the two of them could get to know one another...

Nope. She wasn't here for a date. She was here for a job.

"I'm the owner," the guy said.

She blinked. "What?"

"Let me guess—you were expecting some big, bald, burly guy with teardrop tattoos on his face?"

"Yes," she said honestly.

He laughed and her stomach was a field of fluttering butterflies at the gentleness of the sound. What the hell? This guy who looked like he couldn't harm a wasp if it was stinging him in the eyeball was an ex-con? Again, definitely not what she'd been expecting.

"What are you selling?" he asked in her silence.

Obviously, her blunt honesty had earned her thirty seconds of his time.

Repressing her surprise, she took a deep breath. "I'm an interior designer and I'd like to offer you my services to create your holiday window display."

He shook his head. "Nah, I got it covered."

"You certainly do not," she said, eyeing the box of mismatched decorations in an old SnowTrek Tours box. Obviously, Cassie Reynolds's discards.

"It's not a big deal. I'm not really trying to win the contest or anything." He waved a hand.

Crap, this was her only shot unless she wanted to

decorate a back alley. She thought fast. "But you are trying to build a business here in town?"

He tossed the ugly green garland back into the box. "I'd prefer to attract clients because of my tattooing skills, not because of my holiday spirit."

She sensed the holiday spirit wasn't something he had much of. "You need to get them in the door first."

He sighed. "Look, I can't afford your services. This space on Main Street is already depleting my savings and, well, business so far hasn't been great."

"I'll do it for free." She wasn't doing this for money, yet.

"That's bad business sense."

She sighed. "Look, I'm a student of interior design and I need to display my skills with an actual client as part of my term grade. Everyone else in town has already finished their displays. I'm running out of options." Maybe she sounded desperate, but she was willing to play that card if she had to.

Griffin looked like he was considering it, but then he shook his head. "I don't think it's a good idea."

Still, he'd been considering it, which gave her the courage not to take no as his final answer. "Give me one good reason why not."

He cleared his throat. "I'm sure you've heard who I am by now and all about my past... Do you want your first client to be...?"

"Someone with bad taste in garland?" she finished quickly, picking up the strand he'd been about to hang.

His expression softened slightly, and he sighed. "Okay. You're right. This isn't my thing." He gestured toward the box of decorations. "It's all yours."

She laughed. "Yeah, no. Those aren't going to work.

I'll be back tomorrow morning at nine a.m." She headed for the door. "Your holiday display is going to blow your mind."

He nodded. "Okay…great…thanks, um…?"

"Jade. Jade Frazier."

"Thanks, Jade," he said, and the way he said her name had those damn butterflies doing cartwheels.

He didn't regret allowing Jade Frazier to volunteer to decorate his window. No, he was so far beyond regret that it was a distant dot in his rearview.

This was a bad idea for so many reasons.

He was a "bad apple," and despite hoping to reinvent his future, write a new narrative and all the other life-coach-y things his prison reformation officer had spouted, he still had a reputation that no one was going to forget so easily. Damn, his own family had refused to talk to him or acknowledge the existence of his new shop, a block away from the family diner, in the three months he'd been back.

Jade seemed like a nice woman. She was trying to start her own career. Associating herself and her interior decorating company with him wasn't a great idea.

Unfortunately, when he turned the corner the next morning at eight forty-five and saw her standing outside the shop with three large cardboard boxes on the ground next to her, he didn't have the heart to tell her he'd reconsidered. If only she wasn't so attractive, this might be easier, but since she'd walked into his shop the day before, he'd had a hard time getting the image of her dark emerald green eyes out of his mind.

He scanned the quiet street for a vehicle but didn't

see one. "Did you get dropped off?" Definitely harder to send her away now.

"Took the bus. I only live ten minutes away."

He eyed the boxes as he unlocked the door. "You took the bus with those?"

She grinned. "Not as weak as I look."

Determined, he'd give her that much. He opened the door and turned off the alarm as she bent to pick up the boxes. "Wait. I'll help." He went back out, stacked two and carried them inside.

She'd already removed her coat and scarf and hat, and his mouth went slightly dry at the sight of her in tight-fitting jeans and a snug holiday-red V-necked sweater that almost had him believing in Santa Claus again.

Damn, this was really not a good idea. He hadn't been with a woman in two years…

He cleared his throat. "So, how long do you think this will take?"

"Just a few days," she said, bending to open one of the boxes.

His eyes landed on her ass and he averted his gaze. A few days. He'd never last a few days. "That long? It's just some decorations."

"Great work takes time. Art takes time. Think of it as a full back piece. You can't do it all in one sitting, right? You do it over a few sessions, layer things in. Gain new perspective and inspiration as you work."

He swallowed hard. "I was just thinking it would only take an hour or two."

She waved a hand. "Don't worry. The contest judging isn't for another week and a half."

Right, 'cause that was what he was worried about.

"Okay, well, I'll leave you to it. There will be coffee and doughnuts in the back room if you want some."

"Thanks," she called over her shoulder as she took things out of the boxes. She began to hum a Christmas carol and he headed into the back room. He started the coffee and then he turned on the store music.

But even the sound of heavy metal blasting through the speakers couldn't drown out the voice in his head telling him that having Jade Frazier around for the next few days was the most dangerous situation he'd encountered in a long time.

Jade had spent all afternoon coming up with a theme for the tattoo shop window. She'd spent all evening buying the necessary items for her creation, and the window display was coming along exactly as she had envisioned it. The upside-down black Christmas tree adorned with flickering white lights—not twinkling, but actually flickering like goth candles—was the perfect spin on traditional Christmas decor. She'd been lucky to find it, as it had been the only one in stock at the department store in town…naturally. Not exactly a bestseller.

And the statue of the mythical creature Zanzibar, which she'd found at the local hobby and collectibles shop, was the perfect addition to the display. The gothic dragon climbing a tall winter castle was similar to the shop's logo, tying everything together nicely in dark red, silver and black metallic hues.

She was more than confident that she could pull off an A-grade design, but she hadn't anticipated how hard it would be to work so close to Griffin.

The shop had been quiet all morning. Only a few teenagers had stopped by, planning tattoos they weren't old enough to get, so it had been just the two of them. He'd sat at a desk, drawing and sketching new designs, and a few times she'd caught him glancing her way as she worked. Each time their gazes met, her heart pounded in her chest.

Reminding herself that he was not a good match for her only went so far when he was exactly her usual type. Clean-cut, clean-shaven, thin but muscular and not too tall. He was gorgeous and friendly. A professional business owner with artistic talent. The only thing she could list in the Con column was "ex-con."

Which was arguably a big one, but didn't everyone deserve a second chance?

She knew through the rumor mill that he was the son of Carla Geller, owner of Carla's Diner on Main Street. The fifties-style restaurant was a popular place in Wild River, thanks to the delicious food and the warm welcome Carla bestowed on all her customers. Carla's daughters, Molly and Gillian, worked as waitresses, and the business was a family affair.

Therefore, even Griffin's family was a checkmark in the Pro column. Having been raised by their father, who passed away several years before, leaving Jade and Maddie without any other family in Wild River, Jade always longed for a big, close-knit family like the Gellers.

Of course, she was getting far too ahead of herself. She needed to focus on this window display, and then, maybe, she could focus on the hot guy who was making it hard to focus.

He was drawing the line at holiday music. He played metal in his shop. Only metal.

But he was quickly losing the battle to the feisty, energetic woman standing in front of him. "It's Christmas. People expect to hear holiday music playing inside the stores."

He folded his arms across his chest. "Not in tattoo shops, they don't."

She sighed. "Maybe big, burly, bald men don't, but tattoos are more mainstream now. Everyone's getting one."

Didn't he know it. His only customer that day had been an eighty-two-year-old grandmother adding her third great-grandchild's name to the string of names already on her forearm. *She* might have appreciated the holiday music. She'd insisted he turn down the "crap" he was playing.

Still, he was holding firm to this. "Nope. Sorry. All of this is already too much." He gestured at the decorations all over his shop.

Jade sighed. "Okay, I can compromise."

Doubtful. He suspected she never had to. Those emerald green eyes could make a man do anything, if said man was in a position to allow himself to fall for her.

Lucky for Griffin, he was not that man.

He waited as she shuffled through the music on her iPod and then connected it to the speakers. The familiar tune of "We Wish You a Merry Christmas" started to play, and he folded his arms across his chest. "Sounds like the same old holiday music to me."

"Wait for it…"

He listened closer. Something was different in this remake. "Are they saying 'metal' instead of 'merry'?"

Jade grinned as the beat changed and the sound of screaming lyrics nearly blasted his eardrums.

Holy shit, she'd actually found a heavy metal Christmas album.

"So…we're good?" she asked with a cocky smile.

He sighed. "We're good." Unfortunately, he was far from good. He was falling for the sweetest, smartest, sexiest woman in Wild River, and he didn't deserve the chance to pursue her.

Three

Her delivery was here right on time.

"More stuff?" Griffin asked the next morning as Jade signed the delivery slip and carefully carried the box stamped Fragile to the window. She set it down and, using a box cutter, opened it.

"This is the best part," she said, reaching into the box and taking out a white frosted Christmas tree bulb. Even better than she'd hoped. She held the ornament up to show him. "What do you think?"

He squinted as he peered at the black-and-gray design on the bulb. Then his eyes widened. "Is that one of my tattoo designs?"

She nodded eagerly, handing it to him and then reaching into the box for another one. "Hope you don't mind. I took a few photos of the black-and-gray designs and had these rush ordered overnight from the imprinting store in town. They turned out so well!"

Griffin seemed slightly conflicted as he looked at the dozen bulbs inside the box. "You had these custom made? Overnight?"

She nodded, but her enthusiasm faltered. "You don't

like them? I thought they could serve a dual purpose. Nice, fitting decorations for the tree and a way to showcase your work in the window… But we don't have to use them."

He shook his head quickly. "No! I mean, of course we have to use them. They're incredible. I just can't believe you went to all this trouble."

Her smile returned. "I think it was worth it. It will really give the design a unique look." She was definitely taking a chance with the less-than-conventional color scheme, but she'd wanted to give Griffin a display that he'd be proud of. The bulbs would help elevate the overall design.

"They must have cost a fair bit," he said, looking at the rest of the bulbs.

A lot more than she was willing to admit, so she shrugged. "Gotta spend money to make money, right?" she asked, unloading the rest from the box.

"Well, at least let me cover the cost of these. You've spent enough and you're doing this for free."

"No way. I'm doing this for an A in my interior design class. Whatever it takes…" It was partially true, but she'd also wanted to do something nice for Griffin, to help generate more customers for the shop. His designs were fantastic. His artwork even had her contemplating a tattoo of her own… People just needed to see his work.

He nodded slowly and cleared his throat. "Well, at least let me buy you dinner."

She blinked, surprised by the offer. She wasn't opposed to dinner with him, but he'd seemed to be keeping a low profile. Before coming into his shop two days ago, she hadn't seen him around town at the grocery store or bar or anywhere.

Unfortunately, he misread her silence. "Bad idea… sorry."

"No! I'd like that. Um, I just thought you weren't going out much around town."

"I've been keeping a low profile…"

He looked like he was changing his mind, and she really did want to have dinner with him. Maybe get to know him a little better. "Why don't we order in? Eat here?" she suggested.

He nodded, looking relieved. "I'll grab some take-out menus."

"And I'll get back to decorating the tree," she said, her chest light and fluttery as she went back to work.

He'd essentially asked her out. Although, he wasn't sure ordering takeout to the shop as a thank-you was an actual date. Did Jade read it that way?

As he ordered their Chinese food, he watched her working in the window. He couldn't help himself. What she'd done was the best thing anyone had ever done for him. She couldn't possibly understand how much those bulbs meant.

She was wildly talented and creative to come up with the idea, and having his work displayed in the front window like that was something he was proud of. He'd worked hard to make it to where he was in the industry. There were a lot of artists who never got a chance to realize their dream. He'd been doing so well…until getting busted.

And now he was rebuilding his career and his life.

Jade was like an unexpected holiday angel in his time of need.

But did he deserve an angel?

An hour later, the food arrived and he turned off the loud music as they prepared to eat.

"Aw, that was my favorite song," Jade said, singing the chorus lyrics in a deep, gruff, gravelly tone.

He laughed. "Yeah, right." He knew the music must be annoying her.

"No, really, it's growing on me," she said, her gaze locked on his.

He cleared his throat and looked away. "Let's eat. I'm starving."

"I think there's enough food here to feed the entire neighborhood," Jade said, sitting at the small table as he unloaded the Chinese food containers from the paper bags.

"I couldn't decide what dishes to get, so I basically ordered everything." He handed her a paper plate and plastic cutlery. "Dig in," he said.

She did, and once they'd filled their plates, he sat across from her. A silence fell over them while they ate.

It was a little too quiet. He cleared his throat. "This food is amazing." He shook his head. "You never appreciate just how good stuff tastes until you can't have it."

She laughed gently. "Prison food not so hot?"

"Let's just say ramen bought from the commissary is as valuable as gold."

"Remind me never to go to jail," she said with a grin.

Although it was a heavy topic for him, for the first time since getting out, talking about it, thinking about it didn't feel as heavy, not as hard. It was an aspect of his past—a thing he couldn't change. He had to learn to accept his mistake and move on. He suspected Jade was making the conversation a lot easier. She had a natural way of making him feel at ease, unjudged. She wasn't afraid to acknowledge it, but it wasn't a big, dark cloud over his head when she did.

His gratitude for her was growing, and his feelings went even beyond that.

He'd opened the door, but could she really ask? Maybe he *wanted* to talk about it. Maybe it might help. She cleared her throat.

"Can I ask what happened?"

He shrugged. "It's no secret. It was all over the news. I robbed another tattoo shop."

She nodded. She'd read about the robbery. She knew the details, that he'd been working for a shop in Vegas and they'd asked him to get a job at the other shop so they could rob it from the inside. But she was interested to hear what had *really* happened. From him. "Things are never exactly what the media presents them to be."

He sighed. "I moved to Vegas after graduation. I always knew I wanted to be a tattoo artist. I was working my way up by doing odd jobs around a small studio—cleaning, greeting clients—and in exchange being mentored by some really amazingly talented artists. Eventually, I needed to start making cash and I'd put in my time apprenticing, so I applied at the Dark Rebels studio." His voice hardened at the mention of the shop. "I started dating the owner's sister. Fell head over heels for her, actually. Turns out it had just been an act on her part. She told me that there was a family heirloom that had been stolen from their shop—an antique tattooing gun—and they had an idea of how to get it back. I believed what they planned to steal belonged to them."

"So, you did it."

"At the time, I thought I was doing the right thing. In hindsight, I think I was still just trying to win over Kelly. Show her how committed I was, or something equally messed up." He shook his head. "Anyway, it was Christmas Eve when they pulled the job. I let them in, and instead of just grabbing the tattoo gun, they cleaned the place out of cash, tattooing supplies… They'd barely made it two blocks away before I came to my senses and called the cops."

"You turned them in?"

"No, I turned myself in, but the cops had been watching them for a while. They knew about other illegal activities going on behind the scenes at the shop, and now I was tied to all of that."

"You did the right thing." It would have been so easy for him to simply allow them to get away, leave and never look back.

"It was the only thing I could do. I would never have been able to live with myself otherwise."

"How long did you serve?"

"I was sentenced to eighteen months, but I was out in eight. Overcrowding in prisons, it was my first offense, I turned myself in and I had behaved myself behind bars."

"That had to be hard."

"The hard part wasn't jail. It was knowing that I'd thrown away my future. In one stupid bad decision, I cost myself my career…my family."

She touched his hand, and a bolt of electricity sparked between them. "I'm sure your family just needs time."

"I don't know... I've been back three months. Gillian's away on her backpacking trip, and I know Molly wants to reach out, but she's being loyal to my parents and I can't fault her for that."

"Have you gone to see them?" she asked gently. Maybe he needed to be the one to make the first move.

He shook his head, staring at his food. "I've walked toward the diner and then chickened out several times... a lot of times."

His openness and vulnerability meant a lot to her. This probably wasn't a conversation he'd have with just anyone. She felt an unexpected connection to him. More than she'd felt with anyone in a long time. She took a deep breath. "I lost my dad a few years ago. Believe me, I'd give anything to have five more minutes with him. Your family can't stay upset forever. It's the holidays. A season for redemption, forgiveness..."

"Yeah, maybe. I don't know." He turned his attention to the window. "What I do know is that the window looks wonderful. Thank you."

"You're welcome," she said, a warm sensation flowing through her at the praise.

"In fact, you're kinda wonderful, too, Jade."

His gaze burned into hers and she swallowed hard. Her heart was pounding like the beat of the heavy metal Christmas music. He was so attractive. She liked him. A lot. He was nothing like she'd expected when she'd walked through the shop doors a few days before, and he was someone she was desperate to get to know better, spend more time with.

"The feeling's mutual," she said.

He dropped his head as though he didn't believe it. Couldn't believe it. Suddenly, it was her mission to make him believe it. She reached across the table and touched his hand.

His gaze shot up with a fiery intensity that almost scared her, but she didn't pull away. "One mistake doesn't define who you are," she said softly but firmly.

Standing slightly, leaning over the table, he reached for her, his hands cupping her face. She nodded once to answer the silent question in his expression, and then his mouth was crushing hers.

Ho ho hotness.

She wrapped her arms around his neck and deepened the kiss, savoring the taste of his lips, the smell of his aftershave filling her senses with an urgent desire.

The damn table prevented their bodies from touching, which was probably a good thing. If she pressed her body to his, she may not stop at just a kiss.

How long had it been for him? There was definitely a hunger on his end, but she believed it was because he was kissing *her* and not just anyone.

He pulled away abruptly and a look of panic entered his expression. "Shit, sorry."

"For what? The best kiss of my life?"

He relaxed just a little but still looked regretful. "I shouldn't have done that, but you're just so easy to be with, and I'm insanely attracted to you at the same time."

"Again, the feeling is mutual." She kissed him once more. "There's no reason to apologize."

He looked longingly at her lips but held back. "Gossip spreads quick around here, and I don't want people thinking you're mixed up with a guy like me."

"A guy like you? You mean someone successful and hardworking and attractive?"

"Jade…"

She kissed him again and his resolve broke. He moved around the table and took her into his arms. The embrace was long and passionate, full of desire and vulnerability. Her body sank into his and she could feel the reaction the kiss was evoking.

The chiming of the bell above the front door had them both reeling backward, nearly knocking over the table of food.

"Shit," he mumbled.

She wiped her mouth quickly and forced a smile, desperate to act natural, despite the fact that she was on fire. "Hello, Mrs. Silverman." Of all people to catch them in that moment, it had to be the biggest gossip in Wild River. The head of the business association committee, she knew virtually everyone and had no problem spreading local "news" around town.

"Hi," the older woman said slyly, eyeing the two of them with unconcealed pleasure. They'd given her the juiciest story of the week. "I just stopped by to drop off the official entry form into the window display contest."

Griffin cleared his throat. "Oh, right… Thank you." He took it and stared at it intently. "I'll fill it out and drop it off?" he asked when she made no motion to leave.

"You do that, dear," she said, glancing back and forth between them with a grin. "Bundle up if you go out. It's a lot colder outside than it is in here." She winked and pushed through the door.

Mrs. Silverman paused outside the window display, then waved as she headed down the street.

Griffin looked pained. "Tell me she's not the gossip she used to be?"

"By now, half the block knows," Jade said. Then, turning to him, she wrapped her arms around his neck. "And I don't care one little bit."

His look of gratitude was tainted with uncertainty and Jade kissed him again. She planned to keep kissing him until he stopped caring what the rest of the town thought.

Four

Walking into his jail cell for the first time, with its cold, stark concrete walls and the faint smell of a decaying future, a heavy sense of foreboding weighing on him, hadn't felt as hard as walking toward his family's diner the next day.

Maybe because going to jail had almost been a relief. It was the first step in getting back on track.

This could totally blow up in his face.

But the day before with Jade had changed something in him. Sure, he was ashamed of his past actions. He was regretful and desperate to prove that he wasn't the sum of his mistakes, but she'd also helped him realize that he couldn't undo the past and that the people who claimed to care about him should be open to hearing his apology and moving past it with him…not continuing to shut him out or push him away.

Everyone deserved a second chance, Jade had said. And while he was struggling to believe that, he wanted to believe it, and that was a step, at least.

Kissing her in his shop had solidified the attraction he felt for her, and there'd been no denying she felt the same way. He wouldn't rush into things, but the day before had been one of the less heavy days he'd had in a long time and he wasn't going to let something that special go.

He pushed through the door and scanned the room. It was midafternoon, so it wouldn't be busy. Only a few booths were occupied, and a man sat at the counter drinking coffee and reading his cell phone.

Christmas music played and he recognized the old holiday soundtrack. The songs they played in the diner every year since he was a kid. All the popular, familiar classics brought feelings of warmth and nostalgia that nearly knocked the wind from his lungs. It might be too much to hope that he'd have the chance to spend Christmas with them. Baby steps.

Should he sit at a table? Or wait at the counter?

The kitchen was reserved for family members, and in the last conversation he'd had with his parents, they'd made it very clear that that title no longer belonged to him. The hurt and disappointment in their voices when he'd made that one phone call after his arrest had made him wish he hadn't reached out. But it would have been cowardly and unfair for his family to find out about it through news sources like the rest of the world.

Before he could decide where to sit, the door leading from the kitchen swung open and his sister Molly appeared, carrying two plates of the daily special. It was Wednesday, so he didn't even need to check the board to know it was spaghetti with homemade meatballs and garlic bread. The smell of the familiar family recipe had his stomach rumbling, but the sight of his sister put all thoughts of food on hold.

He hadn't seen or spoken to her since he'd gone in.

He'd missed both his sisters but especially Molly. He missed talking to her. Missed her corny jokes. Missed the connection they'd once had.

He knew she'd called him a couple of times over the last three months and hung up. She hadn't blocked the diner's number. He'd waited each time, wanting to say something, but afraid he'd say the wrong thing.

Season of redemption... He was ready to do whatever it took to redeem himself.

Would his family be ready to forgive?

"Hi," he said, opting for a stool at the counter before his wobbly knees decided to give out.

"Hi," she said, and the pain in her tone made all his regret come surging back.

He watched as she delivered the food and then headed toward him. She glanced into the kitchen. "Hungry?" she asked.

Starving, but too nauseous to eat. "Just coffee?"

She nodded and he noticed her hand shake as she poured the cup.

"How've you been?" he asked. Her back was to him as she ripped open two packets of sugar and dumped them in.

"Fine. Nothing changes around here," she said casually as she added the creamer and stirred it. She still hadn't turned back to look at him. She was procrastinating.

He needed the time, too.

Unfortunately, when she did turn, it was just in time for them both to see their mom enter the diner. He'd never seen a person's expression change so quickly— from surprise to hope to pain and then anger—as when his mother's gaze landed on him.

"Hey, Mom," Molly said, still holding the coffee cup.

His mother didn't take her eyes off him. "You're not welcome here," she said bluntly.

"Mom…"

"Don't call me that. The son I raised disappeared two years ago."

He shivered at the chill in her tone. She was the sweetest, kindest, most welcoming woman he knew, so her words hit even harder. "I made a mistake…"

"You did time in jail. You shamed our family and now you're back in town, running a tattoo shop." She shook her head. "You should have stayed in Vegas."

"I didn't want that lifestyle anymore. I'm trying to put my life back together, and I want to make it up to you." She was upset. He didn't fault her at all for that, but he wasn't prepared to give up. He loved them. He'd spend forever making it up to them if she'd let him.

Unfortunately, she stared at him as though he were a stranger. "You're not part of this family anymore. And I heard about Jade Frazier." She pointed a finger at him. "She's a good person, soft heart and gentle soul. She'll try to save you. Be man enough to refuse that help," she said, walking away from him and heading into the kitchen.

Molly suppressed a sob as she disappeared into the kitchen after their mom.

Griffin's chest ached so hard he thought it might explode. Getting up from the stool, he stalked out of the diner.

He never should have stopped by. Not knowing whether there was hope of reconciling with his family had been hard, but knowing there wasn't completely crushed his spirit.

* * *

Later that night, Jade shivered as she pushed through the door of The Drunk Tank, where she was meeting Griffin. Since Mrs. Silverman had told the town about their kiss, there was no point in hiding that they were getting to know one another. She was in a fantastic mood and couldn't wait to see him. She'd submitted her photos of the window display to her professor and a celebratory drink was in order.

She scanned the crowded pub for Griffin and saw him in a back booth. The dim lighting made it a more comfy, cozy place to sit. She smiled as she headed toward him. "This seat taken?" she joked as she removed her coat and hung it on the hook.

His expression was dark when he lifted his gaze to hers, and a chill ran through her. She noticed several empty beer bottles on the table. He'd started without her and, reading his mood, she suspected *he* wasn't celebrating.

"Everything okay?" she asked cautiously as she slid in across from him.

"Fine," he grumbled.

"This is your 'fine' face? We're still getting to know one another, so I'm not sure." She was desperate to lighten the mood. It was as though a storm cloud was brewing above his head, threatening to break any second.

He didn't look at her as he said, "Yeah, hey, I stuck around because I didn't want you to think I'd stood you up." He cleared his throat. "But I have to go."

She frowned as he slid out of the booth.

"Go? Already? I thought we were having drinks?"

"I don't think that's a good idea."

"Since when?" The day before they'd made out. A lot. That morning, he'd agreed to meet her for drinks. What had changed since then?

He lowered his head and shoved his hands deep into his pockets. "I'm not the guy for you, Jade."

"According to who?" She should have a say in that, shouldn't she? Obviously, he was still nervous about the two of them being together. What people would think. What they'd say. She didn't care about any of that.

"Things are just complicated right now, and I don't think you and I are a good idea."

"You're dumping me before we even have an actual date?" He had to relax. Within a week, the town would have moved on to new gossip. In time, no one would care.

"I'm sorry, Jade." He did look sorry, but also unfortunately resolute in his decision. "Have a nice holiday," he said, and walked away.

Jade just sat there, mouth agape, watching him leave. Confused and conflicted, she released a deep sigh as she slumped against the booth.

What the hell had just happened?

Five

December 23...

The large group gathered outside his shop had Griffin resisting the urge to turn and walk in the other direction. They didn't look like they were lined up for tattoos.

From a distance he recognized Mrs. Silverman and several other members of the business association. He forced a polite smile as he stopped next to them. "Good morning."

"Congratulations!" Mrs. Silverman said. "On behalf of the business association of Wild River, we'd like to present you with this award for first place in the window display contest." She extended the gold-plated plaque toward him, and an unexpected sense of pride welled up in him at seeing his shop's name engraved on it. A small validation of sorts.

"I won?"

"Hands down," another woman on the committee said. "This is fantastic! So unique."

He couldn't take the credit. "It was Jade Frazier's design. She did all of it. I had nothing to do with it."

"Well, that girl is talented. I expect you might lose your decorator to some other businesses around here next year, if you're not careful," the other woman said with a wink.

Mrs. Silverman shot him a mischievous grin. "I don't think he'll have to worry about that."

He swallowed hard. Unfortunately, he doubted Jade would be interested in helping him next year after the way he'd abruptly ended things the week before.

The last seven days had been torture. He'd wanted to reach out to apologize or at least explain what he hadn't been able to that evening at The Drunk Tank, but he wasn't sure what he could say. Jade had said it didn't matter what everyone else thought of the two of them together. Maybe it wasn't important to her now, but his mother was right.

He wasn't the guy for her. She deserved so much better.

Unfortunately, that had been easier to believe up until now, when he was staring at the first place plaque with the casual, good-natured group of business owners congratulating him. He'd won, and in a small way, he felt as though the community was accepting him back. He still had a long way to go to fully earn the community's trust, but it was a start.

And he owed this first gesture of acceptance to Jade.

Sitting in a booth at Carla's Diner, she hit the refresh button over and over on her email. The term grades would be posted any minute. Jade guzzled her coffee, then tried to counteract the caffeinated buzzing throughout her body by taking a deep breath.

The store window was incredible. She was so proud

of how it had turned out. Unfortunately, her chest ached whenever she walked past it. She was desperate to reach out to Griffin, but he'd been pretty clear that he wasn't interested in pursuing things. He hadn't reached out to her either. She knew the attraction between them was real, that they'd formed a special connection, but what could she do?

He wasn't ready yet and she couldn't force him into a relationship.

She hoped maybe…in time.

She hit the refresh button again and the term grades loaded on the screen. She scanned quickly, and her heart rose for the first time in a week.

She got an A! She'd done it!

"Yay!" It was a small victory after getting dumped just before the holidays, but she'd take it. Finally, the validation she'd needed to know she was on the right track with this profession. It was something she truly enjoyed and was good at.

"Good news?" Molly asked, stopping next to her booth and refilling her coffee cup.

She nodded. "Yeah. Term grades came back. I passed my interior designer class," she said with a smile. She wasn't going to brag about the A, tempting though it was.

Molly's smile was sad as she nodded. "That's amazing and well deserved—congrats. I saw the display in my bro—in the tattoo shop window," she said, lowering her voice. "It is really wonderful. He definitely deserved that win."

"He won the business association window display contest?" Wow. She hadn't heard yet. Too bad they couldn't be together to celebrate their good news.

Maybe she could stop by…congratulate him? Nope. She needed to let him come to her if and when he was ever ready. She cleared her throat. "Have you talked to him?" she asked Molly gently.

Molly glanced toward the kitchen, where Carla was working. "He stopped by a week ago."

He had? Her gut turned. "And…" She didn't mean to pry, but she suspected that maybe that was where his bad mood had stemmed from that evening at The Drunk Tank.

"Mom basically kicked him out," Molly whispered, busying herself with the salt and pepper shakers, her red braid falling across her shoulder.

"Of the diner?"

"Of our lives," Molly said sadly.

Jade's chest ached for him and she felt more than a little responsible. She'd encouraged him to try to reconnect with his family. He'd thought they weren't ready to forgive him yet and he'd been right. She shouldn't have interfered. "I'm sorry, Molly." She hesitated, opened her mouth to say something, then slammed her lips back together.

Nope. No more interfering. She'd done enough.

Damn it! She couldn't help herself. Griffin was a great guy and this family was hurting. They obviously wanted to reconcile…and didn't know how. "You know, just because your mom is still unwilling to forgive and move forward doesn't mean you and Gillian can't."

Molly toyed with the string on her apron as she shook her head. "Our family doesn't work that way. Siding with Griffin would be a slap in the face." She gestured around her. "This is my life."

Jade nodded. "I understand."

Molly walked away and Jade sighed. She closed her laptop and tucked it into her case. She'd lost her appetite.

"Leaving, Jade? You haven't eaten yet." Carla's voice, as she delivered that day's special to a nearby booth, made Jade pause.

She turned with a polite smile. "I'm not hungry today."

Carla eyed her. "Everything okay, dear?"

Obviously, the woman had heard the gossip about Jade's kiss with her son. Everyone had by now. "Fine," she said simply. It wasn't fine, but there was no sense getting into something that was no longer happening. She climbed out of the booth and headed for the door. Resisting the urge to turn back took all her effort.

Just leave. Their family dynamics are none of your business.

She turned back. "You know, everything's not really okay." She took a deep breath and pushed on before she could lose her nerve. "This place has always welcomed people with no place to go. The Christmas after our dad died, that was Maddie and I. We were sad and facing a holiday season without him, and we came here for Christmas dinner. Everyone, especially you, Carla, welcomed us with open arms, open hearts... We've never forgotten your kindness toward us. Your kindness toward everyone." She paused. "Can't you find it within your heart to offer that same love to your son?"

Carla cringed, and Jade could see tears burning the backs of the woman's eyes. She glanced around the diner, avoiding Jade's gaze. "This is different."

"And absolutely none of my business, I know. But

all I'm going to say is, Griffin made a mistake. Don't make one yourself." She touched Carla's hand gently, and then turned and left the diner.

Six

Apparently, tattoos were the new Christmas gift idea.

His shop hadn't stopped with walk-ins all day. It being Christmas Eve, Griffin hadn't expected to see anyone at all, but his waiting room was full.

Winning the window display contest had obviously been a bigger deal than he'd thought.

Men, women, some old and some barely old enough to sign the waiver for themselves, flocked in, and six hours after opening, Griffin was exhausted and calling it a day.

"First thing the day after Christmas, I'll be here and ready to give you that sugar skull, Mrs. Kingsly. I'm just afraid I won't do it justice after all the others I completed today," he told the last customer waiting.

The woman looked grateful. "I appreciate that. So, ten a.m. on the twenty-sixth?"

"Perfect." He walked her to the door and, after shutting it behind her, flipped the sign to Closed. He was happy about his productive day, but he couldn't dull the ache in his chest that it was Christmas Eve, and he couldn't get his mind off Jade. How great would it have been to spend the holidays with her?

Still, his mother was right. He didn't deserve her. She'd not only decorated his window and won him the contest, but she'd also inadvertently shown the town that it was okay to accept him as one of them again.

A knock on the door had him sighing. *Damn, people. I'm closed. Read the sign.*

He turned and, seeing his mother outside the door, his stomach lurched. She offered a quick, uneasy wave through the glass and he opened the door. "Hi…" How could one single syllable hold so much emotion? He thought the word might actually strangle him.

"Can I come in?" she asked, looking nervous—as though she was still contemplating whether or not to be there.

He didn't want her to leave, so he stepped back quickly to let her enter.

A long moment of awkward silence followed as she took in the shop, the tattoo designs on the wall, the chairs…anything to avoid his eyes.

He waited. He had no idea why she was here, but he'd let her say what she came to say. Good or bad, at least she was here. Getting to see her on Christmas Eve, no matter what the reason, was an unexpected gift.

She took a deep breath and stared at her hands. "The shop looks great."

Her praise meant everything, and he nearly choked on the lump rising in his throat. "Thank you."

She opened her oversize purse and took out an old poster. She handed it to him. "It doesn't really match the window decor, but the contest was over, so… I wanted to drop this off… Just in case you wanted to have it."

He unrolled the old familiar poster he'd given her for Christmas the year he'd turned nineteen and gotten his first tattoo, to ease the sting.

The image of a buff Santa Claus with the word *Mama* in a heart tattoo on his chest made him laugh. "This was your gift. Your poster."

She nodded. "I just found it among the decorations this year."

And she hadn't immediately destroyed it or thrown it away. That meant a lot. "Thank you for bringing it," he said. "I'll definitely use it next year." It might be the only decor in his shop the following year. A thought that depressed him on so many levels.

His mother nodded and cleared her throat. "Jade stopped by the diner yesterday," she said slowly.

His chest tightened at the mention of her name. He wanted to do the right thing, and now he wasn't even sure he knew what that was.

"She had a few things to say." His mother paused. "And she was right about it all. You going to jail broke my heart, as I know we raised you better than that. You were so smart and talented, and I thought you'd gone and thrown your life away. I felt helpless and that had to be the hardest part of all—knowing I couldn't fix things for you. It felt as though I'd lost you," she said, looking pained.

He nodded. "I know, Mom. I'm sorry."

"But I didn't lose you. You made a mistake, did your time, and now I realize that one choice doesn't define who you are. You're still the smart, talented, caring son I know. You were also brave enough to come back here and try to make amends, and I'd be a fool to shut you out when all I want is to be a family again, have you home again." Tears burned in her tired-looking eyes even as a hopeful look lit up her expression.

He swallowed hard, and dared to step forward and open his arms.

She hesitated, then stepped into them, clinging to him tight. "I'm so happy you're home, son," she said.

He didn't trust his voice, so he kissed the top of her head.

"And the thing I said about Jade." She pulled back to look at him. "Forget every word. That girl is special, so don't do anything to mess that up."

He sighed. The advice was coming a little too late.

Seven

Christmas Eve and all alone.

Jade scanned the crowd inside The Drunk Tank for the annual Christmas Eve party. Had everyone in town coupled up overnight? She stared wistfully across her candy-cane martini at her sister and Mike cuddled up in the booth across from her, dressed in matching ugly Christmas sweaters. For the first time in her life, she understood completely why the Grinch decided to cancel Christmas.

For a brief few days, she'd been enjoying the season, launching her new career, falling in love unexpectedly…

She scanned the bar, but there was no one she wanted to talk to, dance with or really be around, and her mood would only ruin Maddie's night. If she knew Jade wasn't having a good time, her sister's protective instincts would kick in and she'd spend the night trying to make Jade feel better.

That wouldn't be fair. So, she faked a yawn and stretched. "I'm exhausted. I think I'll call it a night."

Maddie tore her eyes away from Mike and checked her watch. "It's only ten thirty."

"This school semester really took it out of me, but you stay and enjoy, and I'll see you under the tree at six a.m. for gifts," she said, forcing a smile and sliding out of the booth. Unfortunately, she wasn't really looking forward to the early-morning Christmas Day tradition with her sister. Mike would be there, which would be fine if Jade wouldn't once again feel like a third wheel. She and Maddie hadn't discussed it yet, but she knew the time was coming when Maddie would be moving in with Mike. They'd been seeing one another for a while, things were serious, and eventually it would happen. Jade would be alone. They were adults now, and that was how life went.

Mike quickly kissed Maddie and started to climb out of the booth. "I'll walk you home."

Jade pointed at him. "You will not. You will stay with my sister."

Mike hesitated.

"You sure you'll be okay, Jade?" Maddie asked.

"Absolutely. Have fun." She zipped her winter coat as she crossed the wooden floor toward the door. She pushed through and stepped out into the frigid night air. Large fluffy snowflakes fell to the ground on the quiet street, and she sighed as her boots left a solitary trail down the snowy sidewalk.

He'd screwed things up. But these days he wasn't so afraid to admit it and try to fix it before it was too late. Climbing the steps to Jade's apartment, Griffin held his breath and knocked. A long moment passed, and no sound came from inside. He knocked again and waited.

Nothing.

It was Christmas Eve. Of course she wasn't home. She had family and friends to celebrate with. She wasn't home pining over him.

Unfortunately, there was no way he could let this night end without finding her and telling her how he felt. Apologize for pushing her away, thank her for everything she'd done for him and tell her he was falling in love with her.

Descending the stairs two at a time, he headed toward Main Street. Most stores were closed until after Christmas and the street was quiet, illuminated only by streetlights. The sound of holiday music grew louder the closer he got to The Drunk Tank. The bar was the only place still open, hosting its annual Christmas Eve party, so it made sense that she might be there. He pushed through the door and rubbed his hands together for heat as he entered and scanned the bar.

Couples were everywhere, dancing, singing holiday tunes, drinking holiday-themed cocktails. A full, festive mood enveloped him. He'd love to be here with Jade. Celebrating a different kind of Christmas—one full of hope and the promise of a better life, a better future. If she was here, maybe it wasn't too late.

In a booth toward the back he spotted her, and his heart pounded as he made his way toward her. His gut turned seeing her cuddled into another guy… Mike? The man he'd tattooed a few weeks ago?

Then relief washed over him seeing that it wasn't her. But a striking resemblance. Her sister, Maddie?

Mike glanced up and waved him over.

"Hey, man…how's the tattoo healing?" he asked, still scanning the bar. If her sister was here, maybe Jade was, too. A candy-cane martini sat on the table across from where the couple was sitting.

"Great. No issues at all. Here alone? Want to join us?" Mike asked.

"Um...is Jade here?"

Maddie shot him an unimpressed look. "What exactly are your intentions with my sister?"

He deserved the overprotective sister drilling. "I messed up and I wanted to apologize." He looked around. "She here?"

"She left about half an hour ago. Headed home," Maddie said, seeming reluctant to let him off the hook so easy, but caving just a little.

"I was just there... No answer."

Maddie's face now took on a look of concern as she reached for her cell phone. She dialed and they all waited... No answer. "Damn, voice mail."

"Maybe she's asleep already," Mike said. "She did say she was tired."

"I should go." Maddie reached for her coat and Mike nodded.

But Griffin held out a hand. "Why don't you stay in case she decides to come back, and I'll head out to see if she's still walking? It's a nice night. Maybe she just needed some air."

Maddie hesitated, then nodded, still looking concerned. "Okay, but text us if you find her, and I'll try calling again." She scribbled her cell number on a napkin and handed it to Griffin.

"Will do," he said, tucking it into his pocket. He walked away from the table and headed out of the bar.

Outside, he looked up and down the street, then

headed in the opposite direction of her apartment. He hadn't seen her on the street on his walk to the bar.

He walked along Main Street, and as he went, he quickly surveyed his competition for the window display contest. There were some seriously impressive designs. Flippin' Pages, the local bookstore, had stacked books in the shape of a Christmas tree. The Chocolate Shoppe had used hollow chocolate figurines to create a scene with Santa and his reindeer... Great stuff.

None as amazing as Jade's, though.

He continued walking, and when his own shop came into view, his heart pounded. There she was. Standing outside looking at the display. Dressed in the faux fur coat she'd been wearing the first day she'd walked into his shop, her heeled leather boots and a festive red hat, she took his breath away.

He smiled as he approached. "An incredibly talented woman designed that one," he said.

She turned, and a slight look of hope reflected in her green eyes as she shrugged. "Wanted to take another look before you dismantled it."

"I was actually thinking of leaving it up year-round," he said.

"That's an idea."

"But then I thought if I did that, there'd be no reason for you to design a new one next year."

"Next year's won't be free," she said with a small smile.

Damn, he wanted to reach out and kiss her, but first things first. "Jade, I'm sorry. I guess I panicked a little."

"I understand. You're not quite ready..."

"No. I thought I wasn't good enough for you. But, selfishly, I'm also not ready to give up the best thing that's ever happened to me." He moved toward her and took her hands in his. "I came back here looking for family. But family doesn't have to be blood. You made this homecoming a lot easier…"

She stared up at him and he kissed the snowflakes on her eyelashes.

"I'm sorry I interfered with your own family, though. I shouldn't have convinced you to see them when things were still too raw."

"You were trying to help. And you did," he said, staring gratefully into her eyes. He owed so much to her. He didn't even know where to begin in thanking her. "My mom came to see me at the shop." He still couldn't believe it. It was going to be a long road to healing, but at least they'd be on that path together.

"She did?"

"She did…and while we have a way to go, I think we can get there," he said.

Jade let out a happy sigh full of relief. "That's really great, Griffin."

"She also said that I better not mess this up with you and I'm desperate not to," he said, and paused. "Because I'm falling for you, Jade."

Her smile was wide and so incredibly beautiful as she stared up at him. "I'm falling for you, too."

"Is that your 'happy' face, because we haven't been together long enough—"

She cut off his words with a kiss. A deep, passionate kiss that beat any other kiss he'd ever had. He held her close and savored the moment, never wanting to let go of the best holiday gift he could ever have hoped for.

"So, you forgive me for being an idiot?" he asked softly as he pulled back.

"'Tis the season," she said with a wink.

He held her tight as the town square clock chimed with the sounds of midnight, signaling the beginning of Christmas Day and the beginning of his new life in his hometown of Wild River, Alaska.

* * * * *

Get 4 FREE REWARDS!

We'll send you 2 FREE Books plus 2 FREE Mystery Gifts.

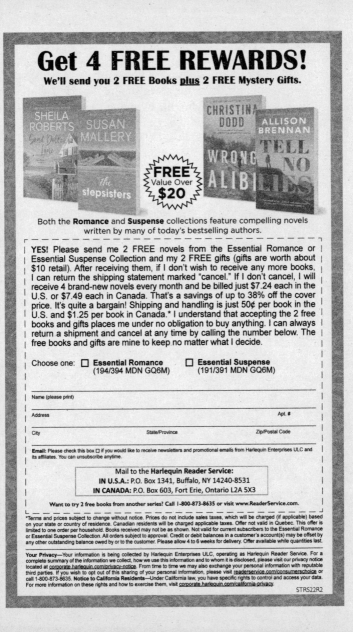

FREE Value Over **$20**

Both the **Romance** and **Suspense** collections feature compelling novels written by many of today's bestselling authors.

YES! Please send me 2 FREE novels from the Essential Romance or Essential Suspense Collection and my 2 FREE gifts (gifts are worth about $10 retail). After receiving them, if I don't wish to receive any more books, I can return the shipping statement marked "cancel." If I don't cancel, I will receive 4 brand-new novels every month and be billed just $7.24 each in the U.S. or $7.49 each in Canada. That's a savings of up to 38% off the cover price. It's quite a bargain! Shipping and handling is just 50¢ per book in the U.S. and $1.25 per book in Canada.* I understand that accepting the 2 free books and gifts places me under no obligation to buy anything. I can always return a shipment and cancel at any time by calling the number below. The free books and gifts are mine to keep no matter what I decide.

Choose one: ☐ **Essential Romance** (194/394 MDN GQ6M) ☐ **Essential Suspense** (191/391 MDN GQ6M)

Name (please print)

Address   Apt. #

City   State/Province   Zip/Postal Code

Email: Please check this box ☐ if you would like to receive newsletters and promotional emails from Harlequin Enterprises ULC and its affiliates. You can unsubscribe anytime.

Mail to the **Harlequin Reader Service:**
IN U.S.A.: P.O. Box 1341, Buffalo, NY 14240-8531
IN CANADA: P.O. Box 603, Fort Erie, Ontario L2A 5X3

Want to try 2 free books from another series! Call 1-800-873-8635 or visit www.ReaderService.com.